WORKING STIFFS

Blue Cubicle Press, LLC

Working Stiffs

Published by
Blue Cubicle Press, LLC
Post Office Box 250382
Plano, Texas 75025-0382

ISBN 0-9745900-4-5
EAN 978-0-9745900-4-2
LIBRARY OF CONGRESS CONTROL NUMBER 2006920986

Printed in the United States of America

First Edition
291 2006 500

Credits:
   "My Father's Secret" appeared in the magazine, *Hand Held Crime*, June 2002, Issue #30
   "The Fall Guy" is based on the short story, "Fender Bender," which appeared in the
      anthology, *Small Crimes*, published in 2004 by Betancourt & Company.

Table of Contents

Old Flames Burn the Brightest

Colin took the book from the woman singing his praises. Her compliments echoed what so many other people had said about him. Unlike his peers, his novels weren't whodunits where the ingenious professional or amateur sleuth brought the criminal to justice. No, he went in the other direction. His novels chronicled the exploits of the criminal from their point of view. Everyone liked to quote the *Daily Telegraph*'s review: "Colin Hill is the finest criminal mind in Britain today." These were fine words from people who'd never committed a serious crime. He listened, smiled, and nodded to the woman while he autographed the book.

His wrist ached as he handed the book back to the excited fan. He scanned the lunchtime line of autograph hunters and sighed inwardly. He still had another month of these events before he could return to the comfort of his home. It was easy to get jaded about this side of the book biz, but he hadn't yet. He enjoyed more critical acclaim than financial. He'd earned enough to dump the day job, but was a long way off from retiring to Jamaica. Hitting the bricks to sell his books came with the territory. It wasn't his readers that got him down—it was the traveling. Julie always put him straight when he complained too much over the phone from some hotel room.

"You're living your dream. Don't knock it."

And she was right. She'd been with him every step of his writing career, from the short stories written in the wee hours to his first novel acceptance. Four weeks more of this wasn't so bad. At least he'd be home before their anniversary. He took the book from the next person in line.

The rain picked up outside as he continued to sign away. When everyone had their books signed, Colin signed the bookshop's stock. A shadow fell over him, but he didn't look up.

"I hope I'm not too late."

Colin recognized the voice immediately. A tidal wave of memories swept him away, and the pen slipped from his grasp.

"Denise."

He looked up. Ten years hadn't touched her. She was still breathtaking. Her loosely curled red hair tumbled down her shoulders, and her form-fitting blouse and knee-length skirt revealed her elegant figure. He couldn't stop a blush from reddening his cheeks and sweat from beading at his hairline.

"Could you sign one to me?" She held out a book.

"Of course." He worked hard to keep the tremor out of his hands as he took the hardback.

Colin picked up his pen to sign. His fingers felt fat and uncoordinated. He took a moment before writing, then blanked. Instinct urged him to write, "To the woman I love," but he blocked the urge. That had been how he felt about her a decade ago, and he'd never told her, much to his eternal regret. If he had, things would have been different. There certainly wouldn't have been Julie or his writing career—two parts of his life he held dear. Denise was someone who required total devotion. Even breathing had to come secondary to Denise's needs.

But that was then, certainly not now.

He gripped his pen and wrote with a flourish, "Good seeing an old friend, Colin." Handing the book back to her, he asked, "Are you busy?"

"No, I was on my way home after this."

"Do you want get a late lunch and catch up?"

She beamed. "Yeah, why not?"

They found a pub with a good selection of food and settled into a table with their meals and drinks.

"I can't believe you're a writer," she said. "I don't ever remember you expressing any interest when we worked together."

He shrugged. "It wasn't of interest at the time. The dream was there but not the drive to make it a reality."

"What changed that?"

"Circumstances. Redundancy, actually. Since I had no job, I had plenty of time to explore the notion."

"When I saw your name on the books a few years ago, I considered writing to you."

"Why didn't you?"

"I didn't think you'd remember me."

"How could I forget you, Denise?"

She smiled and placed a hand on his. The gesture was hardly tantamount to an affair. The show of affection was innocent enough, but a flush of guilt and embarrassment tore through him. He was married. He may have wanted Denise at one time, but that ship had sailed. Denise would never be his. But if he was being honest, he still desired her. There'd always been that question mark surrounding her. What if they had explored the option of a relationship? How would it have gone? Guilt swept over him again. He shouldn't be having these thoughts. Julie trusted him. Julie loved him. And he loved her back.

Their conversation settled into the obligatory autobiographies. He told her about his writing, Julie, where he lived, blah, blah, blah. Where his life had changed for the better, Denise's hadn't faired so well. Married three times. No kids. A string of meaningless office jobs that earned her a modest salary and the package holiday to somewhere Spanish every now and then. When he quizzed her on the current Mr. Denise, he got the feeling things weren't going so well with husband number three, regardless of what she said. She looked down and away when she spoke of him and kept the report concise and vague. A hint of affection for this man never entered her words. He guessed it was a loveless marriage—not uncommon in this day and age.

He found Denise's life sad. Her vivacious nature should have inspired a life just as vivacious. Anything less seemed folly.

They ate when talk fell into a lull and revived it with drink after drink. They were buzzing with laughter before he noticed the effect of the alcohol. He checked his watch. It was almost six.

"I need to get to Newbury tonight."

"Are you driving?"

"Yes."

"Well, you aren't going too far in your condition. You're gonna have to wait awhile."

She was right. He reckoned he'd have to blow off his hotel in Newbury and find one here in Reading. Unfortunately, he had a book group he was supposed to talk to in Newbury tonight. Well, he could always take a train.

"I'll come along," Denise said when he explained his plans.

"What about your husband?"

"He won't mind."

Or won't care, Colin thought.

They took the train to Newbury and caught a cab to the library. Using public transport made him a few minutes late for the event, but he blamed his schedule and not Denise for the delay. The book group bought the lie, and the talk went well, judging from the applause.

Afterwards, they traveled back to Reading and parted ways after a quick dinner. He found a hotel for the night, leaving his car where he'd parked it that morning. The hotel room was sterile and uninviting like all hotel rooms. He called Julie on his mobile and chatted to her about his day. He omitted Denise from the report. Nothing physical had transpired, but mentally it had. He'd fantasized about having sex with Denise. He put the fantasies down to a whim and a one-time whim at that.

Julie talked about her day, but he gave her scant attention. Instead, he examined one of his bookmarks with Denise's phone number scrawled across it. Regardless where his flight of fancy took him, he doubted he'd ever hear from Denise again.

He was wrong.

Three days later, she called him. His book tour had moved north to Northamptonshire and Leicestershire. He'd attended a book party held after hours in a bookstore that ran many such events and was making his farewells when his phone rang.

"Colin, it's me." Tears and desperation clogged her voice.

"Denise? Is that you?"

"Yes."

"What's wrong?"

"He's hurt me again."

"Who's hurt you?"

"Keith, my husband."

Spousal abuse had sickened him since he'd researched the subject for one of his novels. He'd spent months talking to victims— children as well as wives. He had no sympathy for a man who used his fist instead of reason to settle his problems. He saw it as the ultimate betrayal of a relationship and said as much in an afterword to the novel. Denise's earlier reluctance to discuss her relationship with Keith made sense.

"Go to the police."

"I can't. He'll hurt me again."

"Not if the police intervene."

"It didn't work last time."

Colin imagined the scenario. Keith would break down when he saw the enormity of his crime, then plead for a second chance and promise never to hurt her again. The promise would last until the next time he brutalized her.

"Where are you?" he asked.

"In my car."

"Stay with a friend."

"I don't have any. My friends are Keith's."

"Go to a hotel. Don't go back."

"Can't I stay with you? Come and get me, Colin."

"I'm nowhere near you."

"Please. You're the only one I can call."

"I can't help you. I'll be in Scotland by the end of the week."

"Please, Colin."

The 'please' got to him. Denise filled that single word with all the fear and dread she could muster and stretched it into a page of heartfelt prose. He couldn't turn her away.

"I'll be in Coventry tomorrow. Meet me there. I'll pick you up from the railway station. Call me when you arrive."

"You mean it?"

"I wouldn't say it if I didn't."

She broke into tears, and he comforted her. It was several minutes before she got herself under control.

"Now, check into a hotel, and I'll see you tomorrow."

Denise reached Coventry by early afternoon. She bounded out of the station and rushed over to Colin's car. She slipped into the passenger's seat, smothered him in a hug, and kissed him passionately on the mouth. He didn't return her affection. She sensed his stiffness and pulled away.

"What's wrong?"

"I thought you said he hurt you." He'd expected bruises, cuts, damage. There was none.

"Keith's smart. He doesn't like anyone to see his handiwork." She unbuttoned the bottom buttons of her blouse and exposed her midriff. Knuckle shaped bruises mottled her flat stomach. "I'll show you my arms and thighs later, so you can see the whole picture."

"My God."

A car wanting Colin's parking spot honked, and he rejoined the traffic. He didn't have a signing until the evening, so he drove to his hotel. Once there, he checked her into a room as close to his as possible. She flashed him a queer look. He read her face. Here was a chance to finish unfinished business. He knew this because he had thought these things too, but it wasn't to be. He was happy with his life and the choices he'd made. Those roads would stay untraveled.

"Come in," she said, opening the door to her room.

He followed her in and leaned against the window overlooking the car park. "Until you decide what to do, you should stay with me on the tour."

Denise frowned.

"What's wrong?"

"I don't have any money. I have a joint account with Keith. He'll cut me off when he realizes I'm gone. I won't have the money for rooms."

"Don't worry about it. I'll pay, and when you've got yourself sorted out, you can pay me back." He wanted to make it very clear what type of relationship they were entering into. "I still think you should go to the police."

"I told you that I can't."

"At least contact a battered women's shelter. I know some people."

"Don't try and palm me off on a shelter. If you don't want to help me, then don't."

"Hey, I'm trying to help you here. The shelters have advisors who can help you cope and offer you solutions."

"Oh. Sorry."

"Forget it. You're distraught." She looked like she needed a hug and someone to tell her it would be okay, but he resisted being that someone. She was vulnerable right now—and so was he. "You should at least begin divorce proceedings."

She shook her head. "Keith won't hear of it. He's a devout Catholic."

"Shame he doesn't act like one."

She dropped her head.

"Sorry. That was the wrong thing to say."

"No, you're right. He's a bastard, Catholic or not."

"So what do you want to do about it?"

"Kill him."

Silence filled the room.

"Are you serious?"

"Yes."

"You think that's a solution?"

"Depends on your circumstances."

"Denise, you shouldn't be telling any of this to me."

"You're wrong. You're the perfect person to tell."

"How's that?"

"You're a crime writer. There's a quote on the back of your book about you having a brilliant criminal mind."

"That's fiction. Killing someone in real life is totally different."

"No, it's not." She crossed the room and stood in his personal space. He felt her breath against his face when she spoke. "Your books are how-to manuals. If we follow the guidelines to the letter and don't break the rules, it'll work."

"We?"

"Yes. I can't kill him without your help."

"I'm not going to kill anyone for you. Are you crazy?"

He slipped by her and made for the door. Denise raced by him and blocked his escape. She pressed a hand against his chest. Her touch ignited him, rekindling old desires.

"You have to help me, Colin. You don't want to see me get hurt. I thought about it on the train ride up here. It's the only way. You must see that, surely?"

"I'll help you any way I can, but not that way." He couldn't bring himself to say murder.

"Then I might as well go back to him and let him do this." Denise ripped open her blouse, pulled up her bra and pressed his hand against her breast. "Do you feel that?"

He did. He felt the softest of skin. Skin he'd always desired. He felt her heart beating out of control. It mimicked his. But he also felt what she wanted him to feel—an inch-long scar on the underside of her right breast.

"Keith did that with a knife to teach me a lesson. If I break one of his rules again, he won't stop there. He'll make sure he pushes it all the way through."

She embraced him. Her body pressed against his, crushing his hand against her scarred breast. Her warmth penetrated his clothing.

"I know you care for me. I've always known it. You can't stand by and let this continue. Help me do this."

"No."

"If you won't, I'll do it anyway."

"You'll get caught."

"Then help me."

He said nothing. Here was a fork in the road. If he took it, the journey would be treacherous.

"Will you help me kill him?" she asked.

Cars raced by on the motorway. Colin watched them slice through the darkness. The motorway services restaurant was quiet by comparison. No one wanted dinner at this time of night—people just wanted to get where they were going. He was no exception. The book tour was over. He wanted to see Julie and sleep in his own bed. Denise had shared his hotel beds for the last two weeks. The sex had been all that he'd dreamed it would be. Passionate. Exciting. Adventurous. Acrobatic. Parts of him ached which shouldn't ache. But where should he go from here? Who did he want—Julie or Denise? He could call it a day with Julie, but they'd traveled a lot of miles, and he still loved her. Ending it with Denise seemed like the better solution, but Denise was dangerous. She had dirt on him that she could fling if he broke things off. He looked at the speeding cars again. They knew where they were heading. He wasn't sure he knew—not that he minded—he was enjoying the ride. He smiled and picked at his tepid meal.

Denise slipped into the seat opposite him. She pushed her tray of uneaten food to one side. "I called him."

"How'd he sound?"

"How do you think?" She grinned. "Angry. Upset. Murderous."

"Did he agree to meet you?"

"Yes."

"This time tomorrow, you'll be a free woman."

"I know. I can't wait. I wish it was happening tonight."

"Don't wish for things to happen too quickly. You'll hurry and forget something. If we're going to kill Keith, it has to be planned and meticulous. Methodical is our watchword."

"Yes, you're right. You're the expert at these things. I'll be patient."

"Good, there's still plenty for us to do. Tomorrow will be a big day."

Having long since been abandoned, the Fox and Hound pub looked suitably bleak. It stood alone atop some nameless Berkshire hill shrouded by trees. No wonder it had failed to stay open. It was the perfect place for Keith to meet his doom. Denise said they'd first met there, and it had become *their* place. Heavy-handed Keith wouldn't think twice about reconciling there. He'd be comfortable, malleable, killable. He wouldn't see his undoing until it was too late. It would be as humane as murder could get, even though humane was something Keith didn't deserve. Colin drove and parked off the road a mile beyond the pub.

As he walked back to the Fox and Hound, he ran over the plan in his head. He'd accounted for everything. He plotted the killing out the same way he plotted out one of his books. He'd even back checked it to ensure it worked without fault. He just hoped Denise was doing the same. He checked his watch. She wasn't due for another hour.

Reaching the pub's car park, he snapped on a pair of surgical gloves. He tried the porch-covered front entrance. Locked. He expected as much. He removed his skeleton keys. A fan had sent them to him a few years back with instructions on how to use them. Obviously, the fan possessed a past. Now, Colin always carried them. They were a lucky charm and useful tool when he locked himself out his car or hotel room. He made short work of the lock and stepped inside, leaving the door open behind him.

The pub reflected Keith and Denise's marriage—derelict, hollow, and cold. All the fixtures, except the bar, had been removed. A couple of broken-down tables and chairs remained. Paint peeled. Mould grew on peeling wallpaper. Damp permeated the air from rotting wooden beams.

Colin stage-managed his scene. He inserted and removed props, while relocating others. Everything was perfect. All he needed were his players. He retreated into the shadows and waited for them to arrive.

Denise drew up right on time. She ventured inside the pub, but only came as far as the rotted welcome mat. She called out Colin's name. Her voice trembled.

"I'm here," he answered and emerged from his hiding place.

A smile warmed her face, although she shivered under her coat.

"You look cold," he remarked and wondered if fear caused her shivers. He could understand it.

She nodded.

"I'll light the fire."

He loaded the hearth with newspapers that were lying around, broke a barstool and placed it on top. He squirted lighter fluid over the wood and newspapers and lit it. The fire caught on the first attempt.

"You came prepared," she said.

"It pays to. Besides, I'll need an accelerant to cover my tracks."

"So you're really going to kill Keith?"

"Of course." Colin held his gloved hands over the flames. He hadn't realized how cold his hands were until the heat soaked into them.

She came close. He stood and stepped back for her to get to the fire.

"How are you going to do it?"

"Club him. Make it look like one of these beams came down on top of him. Then I'll scatter a few whisky bottles around and torch the place. Makes for a nice cover story. Unhappy husband drinks too much over loss of wife, comes back to place of first date, has accident, and place burns down. Tragic but accidental."

"You've got it all worked out, haven't you?" Flames lit up her face, contorting her smile into a leer.

"I believe so."

"But you forgot one thing."

The voice came from the rear of the pub. A broad-shouldered man, a few years older than Colin, emerged from the doorway leading from the bar. He exuded natural strength. Colin knew he was no match for this man.

"Keith?" Colin asked.

The man grinned and nodded. He came around the bar to block Colin's escape through the front door.

Denise removed a tape recorder from her coat pocket and snapped it off. "We have a lot of evidence on you, Colin."

"Evidence of what?"

"Planning a murder."

"You've got nothing."

She shook her head.

"You're just as involved as I am," Colin said.

"No, I'm not. Our paths crossed at a book signing. You became infatuated with me and took me all over the country with you. You wanted me to stay, but I had a husband. I didn't want to divorce, but your crazed love meant you would kill rather than be apart from me. I came here to stop you." She grinned. "Sounds like one of your books, doesn't it?"

It did. It was a nice scam. But it had its drawbacks.

"Nice try, but it won't fly. The police won't be too interested. I doubt they'll prosecute."

"I don't doubt it," Denise said, "but it's not the police you should be worrying about."

"Whom should I be worrying about?"

"The press," Keith answered. "The public will try you, and I doubt they'll side with you. Your reputation, not to mention your career, will be in ruins."

"You'd be surprised at my reputation. I'd survive."

"Can you be so sure?" Denise asked. "Is it worth taking the risk?"

In all honesty, he wasn't sure. Something would stick. Something always did. Colin shrugged.

"What about Julie?" Denise asked. "I doubt Julie would be so understanding."

No, Julie wouldn't be very understanding. He would survive the slings and arrows, but she wouldn't. Each one would wound. Mortally so.

"I'm guessing all this can go away, though."

"You learn fast," Keith remarked.

"Fifty thousand, and our secret will remain our secret," Denise said.

"You overestimate my wealth. I earn a living from writing, not a fortune."

"You can take out a loan. I'm sure you have good credit."

"You seem well-practiced," Colin admitted. "You're not first-time opportunists."

"We make a nice living."

"Why me?"

"I saw one of your books and remembered how you always fancied me. You were ripe for the picking. I'm surprised I never thought of targeting you earlier. As soon as I read that bit at the end of your book about how you hate spousal abuse, I knew I had the perfect bait to hook you with." A malicious leer distorted Denise's face. She wasn't beautiful anymore.

"The bruises were a nice touch. Very convincing. How did you get the scar?"

"From someone who didn't take this news as well as you."

"So how do you want to play it, Colin?" Keith asked and edged a step closer.

There was only one way he could play it. They didn't know it, but their con had settled matters for him. His life no longer had multiple directions. He knew where he was heading now.

"Denise," he said.

"Yes, Colin?"

"I wish things hadn't ended this way, but I'll always remember you."

"That's nice."

"No, not really."

He slammed a fist into Denise's face. She staggered back before her legs gave out and collapsed into the fireplace. Her coat ignited, but the densely woven natural fibers slowed the burn rate. She tried to pull herself out, but everywhere she touched was scorching heat.

Keith cried out and lunged. He went straight to Denise's aid and yanked her free of the fire. She tumbled forward onto her knees as Keith slapped out the flames. Colin snatched up the poker leaning next to the fire.

"Keith," Colin shouted.

Instinctively, he looked up, and Colin sideswiped him across the left temple. He collapsed to the floor next to Denise.

Denise groaned and tried to move, but her burnt and blistered hands failed to support her. The flames on her coat died. Colin felt genuine pity at the sight of her singed red hair, but he didn't have time to mourn. He raked through the fire, knocking the burning wood onto the floor. He scattered newspapers between the flaming logs and emptied the lighter fluid and the whisky bottles all over them. The fire spread.

He knelt by Denise's side and placed the poker in her hand. She stirred.

"I told you I came prepared for any eventually. Even betrayal. I commit the perfect crime every time."

She looked at him, but he couldn't tell if anything registered. No matter. She'd have eternity to ponder her mistakes. She lapsed into unconsciousness.

Colin found the tape recorder and waited for the fire to take a real hold before returning to his car. He didn't want to take any chances. He wasn't called the finest criminal mind in Britain for nothing. He put that down to research. First-hand knowledge was the key. You couldn't write about it unless you'd done it.

As he slipped behind the wheel of his car, his mobile rang. He answered.

"Are you coming home?" Julie asked.

It warmed him to hear his wife's voice. "Yes, I'm just leaving."

"Good. I've missed you."

"I've missed you too. I'll be home in a couple of hours."

"I'll wait up."

He reversed the car out of its hiding place and onto the road. "Hey, I've got a new idea for a book. It came to me during the book tour. Wanna hear?"

My Father's Secret

My old man didn't keep secrets. He just never said anything. Mom was always saying, "Don't ask your father questions. He won't appreciate it." And he wasn't the kind of man you coerced into revealing something he didn't want to reveal. His construction background made him mountainous. He had the kind of handshake that came from cutting rebar with hand shears, and he had a backhand to match.

People were always saying I was like him. True, I had his height and build. They also said we sounded alike, although I never heard the likeness. But, I did lack one attribute that no one denied—his coldness. Thank God.

I got to study my Pop a lot, seeing as we worked together in his hardware store with my two younger brothers. I watched him deal with customers with the same lack of affection that he showed his family. It was amazing how he exuded caution. Customers knew better than to haggle over returns like they would with me, Tommy, or Art.

And I came to realize that I only knew my father through observation. I was twenty-two and knew nothing about him. I didn't know if he'd played high school football, gone to college, or how he'd even met my mom. I wondered how much she really knew about her husband. None of us were allowed into his hermit world—until last year.

It was February, and Minneapolis was struggling to throw off winter when Dad's phone rang in his office. We were forbidden from answering that phone. It was a private line—for his use only.

Dad's instructions were clear. "Don't touch that phone. Don't take a message. If I'm not here, let it ring. And, don't come in when I'm on a call."

We always knew when the phone rang. Dad had bells hooked up throughout the store and warehouse, even in the john, so he could hear it anywhere. Everyone froze when it rang and waited for him to lock himself in his office before answering the call. No one ever said anything during his calls, customers included. I don't know why. It wasn't like we were going to hear anything. But that was the kind of respect Dad commanded.

Dad emerged from his office ten minutes later. "Vincent."

I looked up.

"Here." Dad held the office door open and closed it behind me. "Sit down."

Dad was grim-faced.

"Anything wrong?"

Dad shook his head and sat at his desk.

"I've got to go to California and you're coming too."

I perked up. After every closed-door call came a business trip. My father never divulged any details about the trips other than they were for business. For me to be included was an honor indeed.

"You've grown into a sensible young man and an asset to me." These were hard words for my father to say. Affection, like the dead, was kept six feet under. "It's about time you got involved in another side of our business."

"Thanks, Dad." My mouth was arid, and the words struggled to come out. "When do we leave?"

"Now."

Leaving Sacramento International, I peeled off my coat. California's warmth was a vast difference from the frozen gray of Minneapolis.

Dad led me to our rental car. Except, we hadn't rented a car. Our car was in the short-term parking lot. Dad knew exactly which was ours and unlocked the trunk on a four-year-old Taurus with Nevada plates.

I went to put my bag in. Dad blocked my view into the trunk with his body. "On the back seat," he barked.

More secrets. I frowned. He was giving me nothing, as usual. Nothing was ever a picnic with Dad. It was better to sit back and just enjoy the ride.

I dumped my bag on the back seat and slipped into the passenger seat while Dad fiddled with something in the trunk. The Ford rocked with his efforts. I stared at his form in the vanity mirror on the back of my sunshade. The open trunk shielded his body. I caught flashes of movement in the gap created by the trunk's door hinges. When he was finished, he joined me in the car.

"Where did the car come from?"

"Business contacts." He gunned the engine.

Dad didn't use a map. He knew where he was going, which was more than I could say. We ended up in Midtown, close to the rail lines. I was getting used to the unusual. I wasn't surprised to find we weren't holed up in a Radisson. Dad parked behind a three-story Victorian.

We unloaded the car. I grabbed my bag off the back seat, and Dad retrieved his overnight and duffel from the trunk. He hadn't checked in a duffel at the airport.

"Don't forget the groceries."

I gathered up the box. We'd trawled the aisles of a local Raley's, Dad singling out the damnedest things. He picked up coffee, a coffee pot, caffeine pills, a can opener, canned goods, energy bars, camp chairs, a camp stove, and other assorted oddities. I examined our eclectic buys as I followed him to the back steps.

Dad opened the door, using a key he'd removed from a manila envelope marked, "Keys." We let ourselves in. The place was empty and smelled musty. I went to put the groceries in the kitchen, but Dad stopped me.

"Not there."

"Where then?"

"Upstairs. We won't be out of our room much." Dad picked the mail off the doormat. "This way."

We settled into a third-floor bedroom facing the street with no bathroom and no bed. I dumped the groceries on the floor, glad to be relieved of the weight, and let my bag slip off my shoulder.

Dad put down the mail and descended on the groceries, taking what he wanted. I noticed the letters weren't addressed to him. I'd never heard of Alfred Taylor.

"We've got power, so get some coffee going."

I did as I was told.

While I made coffee, Dad positioned the camp in the front window. He adjusted the Venetian blinds to slits and dropped into one of the chairs. From the duffel, he pulled out two pairs of binoculars. One pair he put on the other chair for me. The last of his preparations was to place a notebook and pen in the chair's side pocket.

"Dad, what are we doing here?"

He didn't reply. Instead, he focused the binoculars on a house outside. Some might have thought my father hadn't heard me over the brewing coffee pot, but I knew better. The whitening of his knuckles was all the acknowledgment I needed. He'd answer when he was ready.

"Coffee, Dad." I took my seat next to my father and placed a mug on the floor, next to his chair.

Dad kept the binoculars trained. "See that battleship-gray, two-story across the street?"

The house directly opposite ours was of the same era as the Victorian we'd taken up residence in, but was in better condition. Mature eucalyptus trees, shedding their bark, marked the corners of the lot.

"Yeah, what about it?"

"I want you to watch it. Don't take your eyes off it."

"What am I watching it for?"

"We're looking for a man."

"Who?"

"I'll tell you when we see him. Now, just watch."

Obviously, our business in Sacramento had nothing to do with a trade show, a client, or the hardware industry in general. "Are we on a stakeout?"

Dad exhaled and a growl crept out with it. "Just shut up and do as I tell you. Use your ears and your eyes and maybe, just maybe, you'll learn something. Okay?"

"Okay."

My question was redundant. Of course we were on a stakeout. I'd seen enough cop films to know, but why were we staking out some stranger's house? Was Dad a cop or a fed? Was that why he kept his life so secret? But my gut told me otherwise. With paralyzing, arthritic fear, I guessed we weren't on the side of the angels. I picked up the binoculars and studied the house across the street.

Twenty minutes ticked by. Nothing happened. People passed. Vehicles passed. But no one stopped at the gray house across the street. I checked my watch. It was twenty after four. If our guy was a regular working stiff, then I reckoned he wasn't going to be home for another hour. I put the binoculars on the windowsill and stood and stretched, moaning as I did so.

"Did I say you could get up?" Dad growled from behind the binoculars.

"No, but nothing's happening and nothing's gonna for an hour or so."

"Sit down."

"Dad, come on."

"Sit the fuck down. You're killing my concentration."

There was no point in arguing. I retook my seat.

"You can have a two minute break every hour."

Just before five, the mailman came. Dad noted the time in the notebook. Six o'clock came and went, but Dad got excited at seven-oh-two.

"This is him."

I stiffened in my seat.

"Look at him. Study him. Be sure you'd recognize him in a crowd."

I snatched my binoculars and trained them on the man heading for the gray house. The sun had gone down but there was good street lighting. He was around forty, soft looking with a paunch and spectacles. He was nothing spectacular, and I couldn't understand why he deserved all the attention.

Dad didn't speak until the man went inside the house. "Right, this is what we've been waiting for. We watch Spectacles. If you want a piss, do it now. I need both our eyes on him. We can't make a move until we know exactly when he comes and goes. Understand?"

I nodded.

Spectacles didn't act like he was expecting a stakeout. He was far too relaxed. He entered his house and put the lights on. One by one, the rooms lit up. He didn't even bother to pull the drapes.

For two hours, we watched him go about his business, watching TV with his feet up, eating dinner, and drinking juice straight from the bottle. At nine-fifteen, he left the house.

"Do we follow?"

Dad shook his head.

"Don't we want to know where he's going?"

"He can fuck alley cats for all I care; I just want to know his habits while he's here."

"Shall I get some food on?"

"No. I need you to keep watch." He handed me the notebook. "I'm going out."

Dad slipped his jacket on.

"Where you going?"

Dad frowned and left.

The door slammed, and I returned to my task. My jaw dropped. Dad was walking south on Spectacles' side of the street. When he came to Spectacles' house, he ducked inside the side alley and disappeared into the backyard. Five minutes later, he rejoined the street and continued walking south. I waited for his return.

Retaking his seat, Dad said, "You can get that food going."

"Why'd you go to his house?"

"Food," Dad insisted.

"Dad, I can't learn by just watching. I need some explanation."

Dad mulled the idea over. "Okay. When the time comes, we can't let him get away. If he bolts, I need to know if he has an escape route. He doesn't. He's boxed in by six-foot fences. Now, food."

Dad didn't want people thinking anyone was living in the Victorian, so I had to make the food in the rear of the house. I heated two cans of pork and beans on the camper stove and brewed more coffee. We ate our food in silence and in the dark, watching an empty house do nothing. Regardless of our cause, glamour wasn't part of the job description.

"Take these," Dad said, tapping my arm.

He gave me four caffeine tablets. I took them with the coffee, hoping to wash away the artificial, canned flavor of my dinner.

"We're gonna have to stay awake all night and all of tomorrow." I frowned.

"But seeing as there's two of us, we can afford to take shifts. As long as you don't fuck up."

Just like Dad. No concession came without a price.

"Remember, if you did this alone, you wouldn't get the luxury of sleep or toilet facilities. You'd eat, piss, and shit where you sat. You're getting off easy."

Lesson over, we settled back into the routine of window gazing. However, I found I wasn't glazing over so much. I kept sharp by not simply staring at the house but examining the environment. I catalogued the image outside the window, reading the outside world the same way I would read a line of text. And with stunning admiration, I came to realize how my Dad could just sit for hours on end.

Time passed as swiftly as molasses on a blanket. As weekday nightlife drew to a close, traffic dried to a trickle. By one-thirty, street activity had been reduced to black and whites on routine patrols.

I checked my watch. It was nearly four and still no sign of Spectacles. Apparently, he was a night owl.

"What if he doesn't come home?" I asked.

"He will."

"But what if he doesn't?"

"He has no reason not to. He didn't leave with anything, so it's unlikely he's done a runner. So, he'll come home, and we'll wait."

"I hope you're right."

Dad examined me up and down. "Take a break. Get some sleep."

"What if he comes?"

Dad's face creased—his closest impression of a smile. "A second ago you were wondering if he wouldn't return."

"Yeah, well . . ."

"If you're going to be any good at this game, you've got to learn patience and how to roll with the punches. If he comes, I'll call ya."

"Okay." I bunked down on the floor, thinking I was too full of caffeine to sleep, but I was dead to the world within minutes.

Dad woke me at seven-fifteen. It seemed as if I'd been asleep for minutes rather than hours, and I felt the worse for it. I collapsed into my seat.

"He's back," he said.

Spectacles let himself into his house. He didn't bother with breakfast. He went straight to bed.

"I hope this is the start of a pattern," Dad said.

And it was. For the next three days, Spectacles was as regular as oat bran. He left at nine in the evening and returned around seven a.m. He slept in, went for a late breakfast, and ran errands. We did indeed have ourselves a pattern.

Spectacles had just left for his fourth night when Dad said, "We're doing this thing in the morning."

"What thing?"

"Get our shit together and pack up the car. When it's done, get your head down. We've got an early start. You'll know all you need to know in the morning."

I didn't argue and did as I was told. I packed our junk in the car. The duffel was the last thing left, and I got as far as grabbing the handles when Dad's pipe-wrench grip crushed my wrist.

"Leave it," he growled. "This one stays."

I left it.

We slept. It was the first time in days. So far, I'd snatched the odd hour here and there, relying on caffeine and adrenaline to keep me going. My heart had been redlining since the second day, and a caffeine headache slammed me every three or four hours. I felt as though someone had crapped in my head and forgotten to flush.

But not Dad. I don't know how he did it. Like me, he could have won Sacramento's Mr. Hobo pageant, but his focus was still razor-keen. Just looking at him drained me.

Dad woke me with a tap and a "Hey!"

He wasn't tapping me with his hand but the butt of an automatic. I recoiled from the weapon, sleep confusing the situation.

"Take it." Dad thrust the pistol at me.

I took it, sliding my index finger over the trigger. Dad released his hold, and I took the weight of the gun unassisted.

"You've fired a .45 before, haven't you?"

A few years back, my brothers and I had spent a year in the reserves at Dad's request, where we'd been taught how to use firearms. He said it was our duty—but our duty to whom?

"I've fired a Colt before," I replied.

Which was true, but nothing like the Colt I held. Our drill sergeants would not have been impressed with the piece of hardware I was examining. The .45 was old and worn. The oil-black grip showed bare metal and was covered in scuffs and scratches. It looked like it had been used as a makeshift hammer.

"Don't worry about its condition. It's been cleaned and checked out."

"What do I need a gun for, Dad?"

"Come here."

I stood next to my father at the window.

"We're going to park in front of Spectacles' house and wait for him. When he goes for his keys, we'll shoot him."

"Shoot him?"

"Put at least four or five shots in him. Don't rely on one. Put the shots in the back of his head. If you think you'll miss—put 'em in his back."

"Dad!"

"Ditch the guns there. We don't keep mementos."

"Mementos? Christ, Dad, you're talking about murder."

Dad's hand shot out and snatched my throat. His momentum slammed me against the wall, and he stuck his automatic against my temple.

"We're not talking about murder. We're talking about a professional hit. I'm a shooter—that's what I do. I kill who I've been told to kill. You can be a shooter too—if you've got the guts for it. If you don't, I'll put a bullet in you now." Dad snapped off the safety. "So, what's it to be?"

I'd already given him his answer. He looked down and smiled. My

Colt was jammed in his guts. His gun slipped to his side, and his throttling grasp changed into a pat on the cheek.

"You'll do. You're ready. Let's go."

If I followed, I would be crossing a line, one from which I couldn't return. I went without trepidation. Why, I don't know, but I did, without a second thought. I was going to kill a man I didn't know. And I wasn't bothered.

We waited in the car for Spectacles, outside his home. We had the windows open. It was a pleasure to breathe air instead of the stench of our own breath, sweat, and gas.

Ten to seven. He'd be along any minute.

"Why aren't we wearing gloves?"

"No need. We don't have rap sheets. The cops only have DMV records to fall back on, then they've only got a thumbprint, and we're out of state. Essentially, we're foreigners."

"What about the guns?"

"Don't sweat it. These guns have had so many owners that the poor bastards who legally owned them won't remember when they were stolen."

I didn't have to ask who our employer was. These weren't the tactics of law enforcement agencies. Organized crime operated this way.

"He's here."

Spectacles walked straight toward us. He didn't notice us and reached inside his pants for his keys.

"We go when he's got his back to us. Don't chase him. We do this on the porch."

I couldn't speak. My brain blistered with adrenaline. I was tense, and my finger tightened on the trigger. My gaze followed Spectacles up the path to his front door.

"Go."

We slipped out of the car. Stray vehicles sped by. The sidewalks were clear. We strode with conviction, power, and pace. We knew our job, and we were going to do it.

Spectacles stuck his key in the lock. We were ten feet behind, at the base of the porch. We didn't give him a warning. We just opened fire.

My Dad and I, for once not father and son or boss and employee, but partners, pumped bullet after bullet into Spectacles. I didn't falter. I went for the head, like my father. Spectacles' skull disintegrated. Globs of brain and bone splattered the front door.

Ten shots had made oatmeal of his head, and we dropped the automatics before Spectacles hit the ground. Our job was done.

We raced back to the car. A dumbstruck woman walking her dog was rooted to the spot. She stared directly at us, but I saw a blank sheet behind her eyes. She wouldn't remember a thing when the cops got to her. Dad gunned the engine and floored it.

We went straight to the airport and left the car exactly where we'd found it. Dad told me we didn't have to worry about the car or our camp gear. The car and contents would be disposed of, and the Victorian would be sanitized. He would pay me out of his share. None of that information was important. What counted was what he said last.

"You did good, Vincent, real good. I'm proud of you."

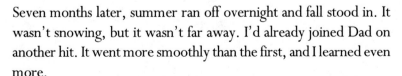

Seven months later, summer ran off overnight and fall stood in. It wasn't snowing, but it wasn't far away. I'd already joined Dad on another hit. It went more smoothly than the first, and I learned even more.

Dad's phone had been ringing a lot lately. But he hadn't gone on any business trips, and neither had I. He took the calls in his usual manner and I, like everyone else, was locked out. I knew there was a problem, and I wasn't happy to sit back.

Thursday afternoons Dad always went to the bank, so I followed. He took care of business inside while I parked in a red zone across the street and waited. Normally, he returned to the store, but this time, he didn't. He took the highway out of town. Twenty miles out, he pulled into a rest stop.

I don't know if he knew I was shadowing him but it seemed like it. I followed him into the rest stop and parked as far back as I could. I watched him. He did nothing. He sat and gazed at a bleak sky rolling by. I got out.

The F-150's passenger window was open, and I leaned through. "Dad?"

He turned, and I pumped three rounds into his face, blowing out the driver's side window. I left the .357 on the bench seat next to him and raced back to my car.

Dad had slipped up in Vegas the year before. The Feds had made indictments. They had a blood trail, and eventually it would lead back to him. The trail had to stop.

I knew this from the call. I'd answered Dad's phone. He'd been out, and the damn thing had rung for ten minutes straight. They'd thought I was him. Maybe our voices did sound alike. When they'd realized who I was, they offered me a promotion, and I accepted.

Now, when the phone rings in the store, it's me they wait for. No one answers Vincent's phone.

A Break in the Old Routine

The woman sitting across the aisle from Sam was staring at him. He knew this because he'd been watching her surreptitiously for a couple of minutes now. He kept his gaze just to the left or right of her head or watched her in the reflection of the BART train's windows. Her stare put him on edge at first. He never expected his voyeuristic flight of fancy to be returned, but eventually, he warmed to her stare. He looked away from her to study the BART map so that she could examine him without fear of awkward eye contact.

Oddly, he'd not noticed her at first. He had no idea when she'd gotten on the train. He was slipping. This woman was worth looking at. She was no bubblegum blonde, exposing lashings of bare flesh. No, this woman was striking. Strong cheekbones tapered down to a pointed chin. Tresses of raven black hair tumbled over her shoulders. Her brown eyes were so dark they were almost black. He guessed she possessed Italian or Spanish origins. She was a similar age to him, nudging forty, but she was one of those few women who exhibited ageless beauty.

This woman made quite an impression, considering Sam could only see her from the shoulders up. Rows of seats and other passengers obscured his view. Even without seeing, he knew, just knew, the rest of her would be just as stunning. He hoped she got off the train before he did. It would be a tragedy not to confirm his theory.

Sam looked her way again. She was still staring. They made eye contact for the briefest of seconds. He could have acknowledged the moment by smiling, but took the coward's way out instead and looked away.

The train passed from station to station, and her gaze never left him. Sam failed to prevent a blush from slipping out. His fascination for this woman cooled. He wondered if this was some sort of revenge tactic. Maybe she'd seen him watching her and didn't like it.

He got the message. Sorry. He meant no harm by it. It wouldn't happen again.

When the train slowed for the Embarcadero station, Sam rose to his feet and slipped his laptop case over his shoulder. The woman stood too. He should have known she would be going his way. Fate was mean like that sometimes.

She stood next to him. He knew he shouldn't check out the rest of her, but he couldn't resist. He cast an admiring eye over her figure. She wore a black topcoat over a fitted business suit that showed off a waspish figure. A white silk blouse clung to her full breasts. She'd left the top two buttons undone, exposing that vulnerable part of her throat where it hollowed. Her high heels gave her a couple of inches on Sam. Without warning, the word "goddess" popped into his head.

The train drew to a halt, and a dozen people poured onto the platform from their car alone. Sam stepped off without casting a backward glance. He rode the escalator knowing she was only a person or two behind him. He pulled his ticket from his wallet as he headed toward the ticket barriers. In a few moments, he'd be free of her, on San Francisco's streets never to be seen again. Inserting his ticket into the barrier, his hand trembled ever so slightly.

"Excuse me," the woman said from behind him.

He didn't have to turn around to know she was calling out to him. *Ignore her, ignore her*, Sam thought. The ticket barrier snatched his ticket from his grasp.

"Excuse me," she said again and placed a gentle hand on his shoulder.

He turned to her. She smiled.

"Yes?" he asked.

"Could I have a word?"

The man behind Sam moaned about being held up.

"I'll just step through," Sam said.

"Thanks," she said.

He stepped through and waited for her. He shouldn't have. He could have avoided the dressing down by walking away, but he waited. *Stupid*, he thought.

She slipped her ticket into her pocket and strode toward him, smiling and exposing perfect teeth. She came close, too close for strangers, and placed a hand on his forearm. "I just wanted to apologize to you."

"To me?" His dumbfounded expression was more genuine than she could ever know.

"Yes, I was staring at you. Rude, really. It's a habit with me. I just hope I didn't make you feel uncomfortable."

"No, no," he assured her. "I noticed, but when an attractive woman checks you out, you aren't going to complain too much."

She laughed and squeezed his forearm. "Attractive—is that how you see me?"

Sam blushed.

"I'm sorry. I have embarrassed you. I'm doing this all wrong."

"Doing what all wrong?"

She fumbled for the right words before giving in and said, "Trying to pick you up."

"Excuse me?"

"I don't want you to get the wrong idea. I don't go around picking up guys on BART, but it's hard to find the right guy these days. I've done the dating agency thing and the co-worker thing, and nothing good ever came of them. I saw you, thought you were cute, and thought, what the hell? I'm not usually this adventurous, but . . ."

"But what?"

"If I wasn't mistaken, you were looking at me too."

Sam's body temperature soared by a hundred degrees. "Yeah, well, like I said, you are attractive."

"Great! You're cute. I'm cute. Let's go get some coffee."

Coffee sounded good, better than good in fact, but it was out of the question. He was in San Francisco to pitch to CalBank. His ad agency was in line to land the bank's advertising budget for the next two years.

He'd chosen to BART in rather than sit in traffic with his partners because he liked the peace and quiet of the transit system. If he was really being honest, he used BART out of superstition. Mass transit had won him his first major account. His car had broken down, so out of desperation, he'd ridden the bus to the client with his display boards taking up two bench seats, much to his fellow bus travelers' disgust. He won the account and from then on, he traveled by public transportation to meet with his clients. He considered it his good luck charm. The last thing he needed was his routine being disturbed. He needed to be relaxed when he pitched to CalBank so that his cool manner would win them over like it had with so many other clients.

"I appreciate the offer, but I can't. I have an appointment."

"Please don't say that. I've gone all out here. Don't blow me off. Please. There's a Tully's just a couple of blocks from here."

His meeting was two hours away, but he still should say no. Playful voyeurism was one thing, making contact was another. But those eyes, that sensual mouth, and her vulnerable throat were so hard to resist.

"Please," she pressed.

"Okay, yes."

They rode the escalator to street level. She pointed at a Tully's in the ground floor of an office building and led the way.

"I'm Fran, by the way." She held out a hand.

No, last name, he thought and shook her hand. Surprisingly, for all her coolness, her palm was moist. *Nervous*, he thought. "Sam."

"You work in the city, Sam?" she asked.

"No, meeting with a client."

A woman on her cell phone shouldered the door open as she left the Tully's. Sam caught the door, and they went inside. The place was busy, and Fran snagged a table in the window. He ordered a mocha for himself and a hot chocolate for her with a twenty she'd given him. He set down their drinks and sat beside her.

"What's so important about your bag?" Fran asked.

The question knocked him off guard. "What do you mean?"

"From the way you're clutching it, you look as though you've got the secret to the DaVinci Code in there."

Sam checked himself. She was right. He was hugging his laptop case to his chest even though the shoulder strap kept it from falling. It was a totally unconscious action. Embarrassed, he released his drowning-man grip on the case.

"It's my laptop. It's got my presentation on it. I work in advertising, and I'm pitching to a new client today."

"Oh, is that all?"

"No, it's not all." He hadn't intended to sound sharp, but he couldn't help it. On his computer was a work of art. Some might not see it that way, but advertising was an art form, and he was a great artist. His ad team might be joining him, but they were window dressing. CalBank hadn't asked for the agency to pitch to them. They'd asked for him. It was the reason he lugged the laptop around with him rather than entrust it to his colleagues. If they were late, it didn't matter. It was all about him and his creation. He wasn't about to let it out of his sight. It might seem selfish, but that was his rule.

"Sorry, I didn't mean it to sound the way it did," she conceded.

"That's okay. I'm a little obsessive about my work. So what do you do?"

She didn't answer.

"Fran?"

She was oblivious of him. Had he lost her already with his snippy remark?

"Earth to Fran? Come in, Fran."

He realized she hadn't drifted off because his company bored her. She was frozen in fear. He touched her on the shoulder. She was shaking.

"Fran, what's wrong?"

"Do you see that man over there?" She nodded in his direction, but the movement was almost imperceptible.

Sam scanned the faces walking along Davis and California. "Which man?"

"Black hair, leather jacket, jeans, leaning against the trashcan across the street."

It took Sam a moment to pick the guy out. He was a little older than him. Late forties, possibly. He looked pissed, and he was staring directly at Sam. *Marvelous*, he thought.

"Who is he?"

"Garrett Burke. We used to work together for the Port of Oakland. He seemed nice, so we dated for a little bit. Things started off well enough, but I realized he wasn't for me. When I broke things off, he got nasty, made threats, even at work. I was going to leave, but the Port fired him. That just made things worse. Since then, he's been following me."

Sam pulled out his cell phone. "I'm calling the cops."

Fran put a hand over his phone. "No, don't. It'll just make things worse."

"You can't keep having this freak follow you."

"I know, but I've been to the police already. They won't do anything because he hasn't done anything."

"Except terrorize you."

"Yeah, but that isn't a crime, unless he lays a hand on me."

This sickened Sam. He understood that justice had to be balanced and everyone was innocent until proven guilty, but hell, sometimes justice needed to pull the blindfold off and kick some butt.

"That's why I'm in the city. My lawyer is working on a restraining order, but that takes time. I'm finalizing details."

"Then call your lawyer. Do you need a phone?"

"I've got one." She pulled a phone out of her bag and called her lawyer. She explained the situation and listened attentively, not arguing, saying yes and no to questions Sam couldn't hear.

"He says we should find a hotel. Do you know one close by?"

Sam thought for a second. "The Ramada Plaza on Market."

Sam checked his watch. Just under two hours before showtime. There was still more than enough time to get Fran to the hotel and make it to CalBank's office to decompress.

He looked over at Burke again, but he was gone. It took a moment, but Sam spotted him heading toward the coffee shop. Burke reached inside his jacket pocket, and Sam saw a flash of a gun barrel against the sunlight.

"We need to go," Sam said, helping Fran from her seat. "He's coming this way."

The news didn't seem to make it through to her. There wasn't time to explain. Sam snatched the phone from her. "He's coming. We'll call back," he said into the phone, then snapped it shut. He hustled Fran out of Tully's side door, just as Burke entered through the other.

"We've gotta move. He's right behind us."

He had her at a near jogging pace on Davis Street, but her high heels were slowing them down. Sam cast a glance back at the Tully's. Burke had shoved his way through the crowded coffee shop and was on the street. To Sam's relief, he hadn't broken into a run. He just lived up to his reputation and stalked, keeping a steady distance between them.

"What did your lawyer say?" Sam asked.

"He said to get a room and stay there until he can meet up with us. He's going to try and get a restraining order now. Oh, God, he's right behind us."

"Don't look back. Don't give him the satisfaction. Just keep walking."

He wanted to mention the gun, but Fran was a mess. That assured demeanor he'd witnessed on BART was gone now. He wasn't much better, but he still had a grip. He was in this for the long haul now. What was stopping this psycho from stalking him to CalBank? Nothing. He had to do the thinking for both of them. The Ramada Plaza was a mile away—only a few minutes walk. That didn't give them much opportunity to lose Burke.

A cab approached them on Davis. Sam waited until the last moment to hail it. He hoped he hadn't waited too long. Once Burke saw they were aiming for a fast getaway, he'd make his move. Luckily, the cab stopped with a screech of tires.

Sam bundled Fran inside the cab and clambered in behind her. "The Ramada Plaza Hotel," he called out to the driver.

He turned to see Burke, his face flushed red with fury, racing toward them with his hand wrapped around the gun jammed firmly in his pocket, but it was too late. He lunged for the door handle, but missed when the cab roared away.

He and Fran both watched Burke shrink as the cab gathered speed. The color returned to Fran's face. She smiled at him. "Thanks."

"It's okay."

"No, it's not okay. I shouldn't have put you in that position. Thank you."

Sam let the compliment stick but didn't know what to do with it. He noticed the cabbie staring at them with a curious expression. *Don't ask*, pal, Sam thought, *don't ask*.

Their journey ended when the cab driver drew up in front of the hotel. Sam handed him a ten and didn't wait for change. A doorman held open the door, and Sam guided Fran in. A desk clerk welcomed them to the hotel, and Fran asked for a room.

While Fran checked in, Sam watched the entrance. Burke didn't burst through.

The desk clerk recapped. "That's a room for one night, double occupancy."

Double occupancy—what was that all about? Sam shot Fran a glance. With the slightest of movements, she shook her head. This wasn't the time or place to air their laundry.

"Luggage?" the desk clerk asked.

"It's coming along later," Sam answered.

The desk clerk looked at them with disbelief plastered across his face. Sam didn't blame him.

"I'm expecting someone to meet us here, a Mr. Charles Lieber," Fran said. "Could you call us when he arrives?"

"Of course," the desk clerk said and handed Fran her keycard. As they walked toward the elevator, he added, "Enjoy your stay Mr. and Mrs. Delco," leaning hard on the 'Mrs.'

"Just keep walking," Sam said.

Fran's hand shook so much she couldn't get the cardkey into the slot, so Sam opened the door to the room. The room's air conditioning kept it several degrees cooler than comfortable, but Fran shrugged off her coat. She slumped onto the corner of the bed and broke into sobs. Sam fell to his knees to console her and hugged her close. He smelled an attractive mix of her perfume and her shampoo.

"It's over now." He eased her away from him. "When's your lawyer arriving?"

"Shouldn't be long. Within the hour, he said."

"Good." Sam checked his watch. Although it seemed like a lifetime, less than thirty minutes had transpired since Fran had asked him out for coffee. He still had plenty of time to regain his cool for his meeting. Rising to his feet, he said, "I should be going."

"Please stay."

"You're perfectly safe. He can't hurt you now."

"I know, but I feel safe with you around."

He shouldn't stay. It wasn't his fight. He'd done his civic duty for the day, and it was time to go. But what kind of person would he be to leave now?

"Lieber will be here within the hour?" he asked.

"Yes, but I'll check." She used her phone to call. She spoke briefly to Lieber and confirmed that they'd made it to the hotel. "Yes, he'll be here by nine."

"Okay, I'll stay."

"Thank you, Sam." She wrapped her arms around him. "I really appreciate it."

She held the embrace for a moment longer than necessary. It was understandable. She'd had a rough morning after a rough couple of weeks. Sam wriggled himself free without embarrassing her.

He considered calling his partners, but dismissed the idea. He didn't want them knowing about Fran. Silly really. He hadn't committed a carnal crime, but carnal thoughts had gotten him into this. Hero or not, no one was to know about this. He tugged off the laptop case, dropped it on the bed, and sank into the armchair by the window.

Fran sat back down on the bed. She leaned back, supporting herself with her hands behind her, and parted her legs a few inches. It was nothing tawdry and seemed a totally unconscious move. Sam tried to not to look, but his gaze fell on her exposed legs and the shadows cast by her skirt. She kicked off her shoes. She had pretty feet. Her toenails were painted the same shade of scarlet as her fingernails.

Was she coming on to him? No, she was relaxing, Sam told himself. He was imagining things. There was no denying he was attracted to her. Well, he could window shop all he liked, as long as he didn't go inside to try anything on for size.

Fran glanced over at the clock on the nightstand. "It's going to be a long forty minutes before my lawyer gets here if we sit here in silence."

Sam groaned inside. If she made a play, the deal was off. She could wait for Lieber all by herself. He had his presentation to worry about.

"Talk to me, Sam."

"What do you want to know?"

"Anything. Everything. Just take my mind off that psycho out there."

"Have you eaten?"

"No, not really."

"Then order something from room service. It'll take your mind off him."

"Good idea. Room service would be nice."

She leaned over the dresser next to him and flicked through the leatherette binder with the menu inside. Her silk blouse tented. This afforded Sam a partial view of her breasts straining at her bra.

Keep your eyes on the road, Sam, he told himself.

Fran picked up the phone and ordered a plate of fruit and a pot of coffee. The food came swiftly enough. When it arrived, Fran slipped into the bathroom to wash up. Sam tipped the waiter and placed the tray on the table. The kitchen had provided a nice assortment of fruit, including cantaloupe, pineapple slices, and berries. Returning to the room, Fran took a paring knife and removed the skin from the cantaloupe. Juice ran down her hand and wrist. She jerked her hand to her mouth to stop the juice from flowing down her arm.

Sam stood. "I really should be going. Your lawyer's going to be here in a few minutes, and I need to be elsewhere."

"Oh please, stay. Lieber might need you as a witness or something. He might need a statement."

"Okay."

"Good. Now try some of this. The fruit is a lot a better than I'd expected."

After Sam had helped himself to a few pieces of the fruit, the phone by the bed rang. Fran answered it. Lieber had arrived. She told the desk clerk to send him up.

Good, Sam thought. This would all be over in a few minutes.

When Lieber knocked on the door, Fran opened it. Lieber was a narrow pole of a man with a nervous look on his face. Concern for his client, Sam surmised, until the gun appeared—not in Lieber's hand, but in Burke's. He emerged from a blind spot in the hall and shoved Lieber into the room, sending him crashing to the floor. Sam knew he should have chosen a hotel further away. It wouldn't have been hard for Burke to keep pace with the cab, even on foot. He'd lain in wait for them to come out, but had struck it lucky when Lieber came in asking for Fran. Burke kicked the door shut.

"Isn't this cozy?" he snarled.

"Garrett, I can explain," Fran stammered.

Burke backhanded Fran. The bed caught her fall. "Keep your lies to yourself."

"You've entered felony territory now," Lieber advised. "Leave now and we can forget about this."

Burke shoved an angry looking revolver in Lieber's face. "Does this look like I care?"

Lieber shook his head.

"Didn't think so." Burke focused his attention on Sam. "And who's this? Your next boyfriend?"

"No, it's not like that," Fran answered.

"It's not?"

Burke's gaze bore holes into her. Sam, still standing by the fruit, noticed the paring knife on the tray. He edged a step toward it.

"What's your name, friend?" Burke asked.

"Sam."

"What'd she tell you about me?"

How did he answer a hair-trigger question like that? A sugarcoated response would provoke just as bad a reaction as a brutally honest one. Well, if he wasn't going to leave this any other way than in a body bag, there was only one way to answer the question.

"She said you were a never-was boyfriend turned stalker."

Anger turned Burke's face puce. His grip tightened on the revolver, and he cocked the hammer back. "Is that right?"

Sam didn't answer.

"No. No, that's not what I said," Fran blurted. "What are you trying to do, Sam—kill us?"

"Shut up," Burke bellowed. He jammed the gun in her face.

Lieber remained on his back with arms and legs in the air in a dog-like submissive position.

With all attention off him, Sam palmed the paring knife.

"Take it easy," Sam said.

Burke swung his gun and his attention to Sam. "You're in charge, are you?"

"No, you are. You're the one with the gun."

"That's right, I am. I suggest you don't forget that." He released his grip on Fran and crossed the room to Sam. "Why are you involved, Sam?"

Sam said nothing.

"Did she show you a peek of her tits, and you thought you'd dust off the shining armor? Is that it?"

"Something like that, I guess."

"Here's something you don't know. That's how I met Fran. She gets her rocks off by playing the damsel in distress. Her shyster does a nice little trade screwing guys like me over—and you'll be next. Isn't that right, Lieber? How many times have you been in court on her behalf?"

"Don't listen to him, Sam," Lieber said.

"The thing of it is, I wasn't stalking her. I was trying to get evidence on her. I wanted to stop her fun and games."

Sam wasn't listening. He didn't care. He just wanted to get out of this room alive. He needed an opening to turn the tables on Burke and the opening presented itself.

Fran leapt to her feet. "Shut up. Shut up. Shut up!"

She lunged at Burke. He swung the gun at Fran. She slammed into him as the gun went off, its bark muffled against her body. Everyone froze in shock until Fran slid down Burke's front, leaving a bloody streak down his clothes.

"Oh, God," Lieber cried. "What have you done?" He rushed to Fran's side and tried to staunch the blood spreading across her stomach with a handkerchief. "Fran, Fran, are you okay? Talk to me."

Fran gurgled.

"I didn't mean it," Burke stammered. "It was an accident." He knelt at Fran's side and stroked her hair like she was a beloved pet.

"Sam, go get help," Lieber barked.

"I'll call 911."

"No, I'll do that." Lieber snatched the phone off the nightstand and punched in a number. "Get someone from the front desk. They must have a medic on staff."

"I'm so sorry, Frannie," Burke said, sobbing, the gun at his side now.

Sam dropped the paring knife and bolted for the elevators. He hammered away at the call button, but it was taking an eternity for the elevator to arrive. He couldn't wait. Fran could die. He took the stairs, hurling himself down them two and three at a time. Bursting into the lobby, he raced over to the snotty desk clerk who expressed nothing but shock as Sam hurtled toward him.

"A woman's been shot. Do you have a paramedic on staff?"

"What?"

"The woman I came in with. She's been shot."

None of this seemed to be sinking in. The desk clerk looked as if he'd just been slapped. Sam tried again.

"She's dying in your hotel."

That got through. "I'll get someone right away. Room five-fifteen, right?"

Sam nodded then raced back up the stairs to the room. The door was ajar when he charged through it, slamming it back against its hinges. "It's okay. Someone's on the way."

But Sam was talking to himself. Lieber, Burke, and Fran were all gone. There wasn't a trace to prove they'd ever been there. There wasn't even a drop of blood on the carpet.

What just happened? Surely Burke hadn't persuaded Lieber to make off with Fran before the cops came. That only could have happened if Burke had held Lieber at gunpoint. But Burke had fallen apart. Maybe he'd pulled himself together and regained his murderous intent. Then all of Sam's thoughts came to an abrupt end, and he felt much colder than the air-conditioning dictated. His laptop was gone. He tore the room apart searching for his work, but it was nowhere to be found. They must have taken it. He raced out of the room and straight into the arms of security.

"Let go of me."

"Not just yet," the larger of the two muscled men said and shoved Sam back into the room. They looked just as confused as Sam when they discovered no body. "What's going on?"

"They've run out and taken my things with them. We've got to find them."

Sam tried to sidestep the men but they restrained him easily.

"Let's go down together," the man said.

Sam ran off an explanation as the security men escorted him to the elevator, but they weren't listening. They were more interested in the hotel's reputation. All the while, his presentation to CalBank slipped further from his grasp.

The desk clerk and two police officers, one a sergeant, met Sam in the lobby. They asked the same damn fool questions hotel security had asked. They might have been more responsive, if Sam had kept the hysteria out of his voice.

"There's no one up there," the larger security man said.

"Because they're gone," Sam said.

"The room is clean," the other security man added.

"He saw them. Ask him," Sam said and pointed at the desk clerk.

"I'm a little confused," the desk clerk said.

"What's to be confused about?" Sam demanded.

"You checked in alone."

"What the hell are you talking about?"

"What I said. You checked in alone. This woman you're speaking of, I've never seen her."

"She paid for the room with a credit card."

"Is that true?" the sergeant asked.

"No, he prepaid with cash. I can prove it."

The desk clerk led a procession, which drew stares from everyone in the lobby. Sam's heated explanations had turned this debacle into a spectator event. The desk clerk called up the reservation and pointed to the screen. The reservation was indeed in Sam's name, and the room had been prepaid in cash.

"Is this some sort of joke?" Sam demanded.

The desk clerk raised himself up. "I have no idea what you mean."

"I'm obviously being used as the scapegoat for something."

"What are you talking about now?" the tired-sounding sergeant asked.

"They've got a body on the premises, and they don't want the bad press."

"So what are you saying?" the desk clerk said. "That we made off with a body?"

"That's exactly what I'm saying, but you screwed up. I had room service delivered. I admit you work fast, but not that fast. I bet you didn't have time to brief everyone."

The sergeant asked for the room service waiter who had brought the food to Sam's room. He knew the cops were only humoring him at this point, but he didn't care. They'd be whistling a different tune in a moment.

"Do you remember me?" Sam asked the waiter.

"Yes. I delivered a fruit platter and pot of coffee to your room."

The news failed to impress anyone, but Sam smiled nevertheless. "Do you remember the woman in my room?"

"No. You were alone."

"No, I was with . . ." Sam let his words trail off. He remembered he had answered the door while Fran was in the bathroom.

"I think we've heard enough," the sergeant said. "Time to go."

The cops grabbed Sam by the arms and guided him toward the exit. Sam protested and demanded they speak to the room service person who had taken the order from Fran, but no one was listening. The desk clerk made sure the inconvenience left with the authorities and led the way out.

"Sorry for the trouble," the cop said.

"These things happen," the desk clerk replied.

"You're a lying son of a bitch," Sam fired at the clerk. He shrugged off the policemen's hold and grabbed the desk clerk by the lapels. "You're in on this, aren't you?"

"That's it," the sergeant said and pinned Sam against the wall while the other officer cuffed him. They dragged him out to a patrol car and shoved him in the back.

His cell rang, but in his current predicament, he was unable to answer it. He knew who it would be—his team wondering where the hell he was. All wasn't lost yet. As long as he got himself under control and explained himself to the cops, he'd still make it over to CalBank, but he'd be without his laptop. He had to face facts. There wasn't a chance in hell of getting that back in time. Why had they taken it? To sell? By mistake? None of it mattered. CalBank was history.

Luck didn't fair with Sam. The cops booked him on a misdemeanor, and it was evening before they released him. More than a dozen messages filled his cell phone's voice mail. He listened to his colleagues then the senior partner blast him for his no show at CalBank. The senior partner punctuated his rant by telling Sam he was fired. Sam wanted to be angry, but it had been too long a day, and he just didn't have the fight left in him.

Between the tirades, Sam gleaned that Rennie Creative Partners had won the lucrative contract. A nice win for RCP. They were zero and ten against Sam. One and ten now, he supposed. He deleted his messages along with his career. He paused when he came to the last message. The caller left no name, but he recognized Fran's voice.

"If you want your laptop back, come to the Ferry Building. We'll be waiting outside."

Sam had his explanation. He'd been scammed. Fran and company had conned him out of his laptop. If they thought they could extort anything out of him, they were dead wrong. They'd killed his career. He'd go along though, just so that he could tell them the computer was worthless.

He walked the short distance to the Ferry Building. People were filing past the historic building to make their journeys home after a hard day's work. He scanned the faces for Fran, Lieber, and Burke, but failed to see them. It looked like he was being stood up and was about to leave when a hand settled on his shoulder. He turned and faced not Fran, Lieber, or Burke, but Lucas Rennie from RCP. Pieces of the puzzle fell into place.

"I hear you've had quite a day," Rennie said, smiling.

"Likewise," Sam answered, "but for entirely different reasons."

"Let me make it up to you and buy you dinner. I've got a table. It's not too far."

After the day he'd had, why not? "Lead on."

"Good. Shall we?" Rennie pointed in the direction of the restaurant, and they set off at a leisurely pace.

"I was expecting someone else."

"I bet you were."

"Who were the three stooges?"

"Investigators from a private security company. They've been shadowing you for the last few weeks. You're a pretty clean-living guy, Sam. They could only come up with two chinks in your armor. One was your weakness for the ladies. Nothing creepy, mind you, just a girl watcher."

"And the second?"

"You're a creature of habit. You're ritualistic when it comes to pitches, and you don't trust your team. You keep all the important stuff in your possession. That gave them an opening. The plan practically devised itself."

"Well done. That scam is the most imaginative thing RCP has come up with in years."

Rennie belly-laughed. "You're not wrong there. They tell me the desk clerk's cooperation really swung things."

"So this has all been about discrediting me and you winning a much-needed client? It's no secret that you've been hurting for business."

"You're close, but not quite on the nose."

Another turn of the screws? Sam wondered.

"You're right insofar as I wanted to prevent you from pitching to CalBank, but I also wanted more than that."

"More?"

They turned off the Embarcadero and headed toward a waterfront restaurant.

"Yes. Our CalBank pitch was weak. Even with you out of the running, I doubted that the CalBank board would go for it, so I pitched them your proposal."

That sucked the air from Sam's lungs. Not only had Rennie ruined him today, but he'd used his own hard work against him to do it. "You son of a bitch."

"Don't get flustered. I haven't gotten to the good part yet."

The good part? What did Rennie have in store for Sam now? The guy really wanted his pound of flesh and then some. "What's the good part?"

"You."

"Me?"

"I want you to join us. You're smart, talented. You've got everything we need. Join me, and I'll make you a partner. I've got all the paperwork drawn up. All you have to do is sign."

"So today has been one big job interview?"

"More like head hunting. You should be flattered."

"Should I?"

"Yes, I went to a lot of trouble."

"It felt like it," Sam said. "You could have just offered me the job and dispensed with all the theatrics, you know."

"Yes, but we're in the game of selling people products they didn't know they needed. A simple taste test wouldn't have swayed you. You needed convincing."

They arrived at the restaurant. Rennie held the door open for Sam. "Are you going to join me?" he asked.

Sam paused for a long moment before stepping inside.

Parental Control

Preston's long, loping, rhythmic strides beat an impressive tattoo on the sidewalk. Each elegant footfall connected effortlessly with the concrete. Although he was tall and his gait was long, he floated a couple of feet beyond his stride. A sheen of sweat clung to his lean black body. He exuded strength, confidence, and grace. He seemed to glide when he jogged, riding on a wave of self-belief. It was a sight to behold, unlike my lumbering attempts.

Preston and I were night and day. My footfalls slapped the sidewalk, sounding like wet meat tossed against a wall, sending lightning bolts of pain through my bones and into my groin. My corroded knees popped every other step, and air struggled to make it into my lungs. Hell, Preston made me feel old.

The key to Preston's superior form had little to do with better diet, a good night's sleep, protein formulas, or the elixir for eternal youth. No, he was riding a tidal wave of good fortune. Life, private and professional, was going his way. I don't begrudge him, though. If ever a guy deserved good luck and good fortune, it was Preston. He was a stand-up guy, and not many of those find themselves ahead of the game these days.

We used to be the perfect running partners, just two guys trying to fight off the effects of middle age, kidding ourselves that we could beat Time. That was cool with me. I didn't run to keep in shape, to keep my wife interested, or even to attract the eye of other women. I ran with Preston because he was my neighbor and my buddy. We were the same age, we liked the same things, and it was a mark of our relationship—a guy thing, if you will. An unsaid bond between men.

But Preston and I hadn't been on the same page—hell, the same chapter—for quite some while. In the last eighteen months, I watched my friend grow in stature, leaving me behind to stagnate in my own pond. But the disparity in our performances hadn't all been one way. As Preston stretched out in front, I slid back. I'm definitely not the man I was six months ago or the six months before that, for that matter.

Time hasn't been the only thing that has caught up with me, even the general day-to-day has trampled over me. My checkbook doesn't balance. My expenses get higher as my income gets smaller. The kids demand more. My wife seeks and receives more gratification from television than she does from me. It's sad, but no different from many American lives, I'm sure. Preston has a secret to his success. I just wish I knew what it was.

"C'mon, Jack. Pick up the pace. I'm running at half speed."

I panted in apology.

"This isn't you. What's up?"

I tried to answer, but I couldn't. My response stalled in my chest, trapped in the syrupy air jellifying in my lungs. It was a particularly bad run for me. Current events were weighing me down more than most, and my speed showed it. I shook my head, flicking sweat in all directions as my breath whistled in my throat.

Preston glowed. The lucky S.O.B.

"C'mon, spit it out."

He slowed his pace to allow me to catch my breath. I still seemed to be running full tilt, while Preston was doing the running equivalent of treading water.

"Kids, marriage, job, life, everything. Tell me, what isn't hitting the fan these days?"

"Me." He grinned. "Everything is cool in the house of Preston Barnes."

Preston couldn't have been more right. He was living the American dream. There wasn't a thing in his life out of place. If he fell, it would be into his wife's loving arms. If I fell, I'd crack the sidewalk and be sued for the privilege.

But it hadn't always been like that. About two years ago, Preston had trudged through the same quagmire the rest of the suburban world had and then some. His life was a blight no one in the neighborhood envied.

"I know," I wheezed. "You don't have to rub it in." Starbursts speckled my vision. "Well, we can't all be as lucky as you, Press."

Preston barked a short, sharp laugh. "Luck had nothing to do with it. I was losing the battle with life, so I took control. Now that I'm calling the shots, life couldn't be better."

"Easier said than done."

"I wouldn't say that. Once you make that first step toward resolving your problems, you'll be amazed at the results. Tell me what's up, and I'll tell you what to do about it."

To be honest, I'd been hoping Preston would reveal his secret. He'd never offered before, even when others and I had asked. A feeling trickled over me that he was only telling me now because I was at rock bottom and I couldn't fall any lower. But I didn't care what he thought about my life. If he wanted to throw me a bone, I wasn't so proud that I wouldn't gobble it up with glee. Now I would learn the Preston way and become a devout disciple.

"Jenny's been upset for days and dragging everyone down over her cat," I said. "It went missing last Thursday. The damn thing was probably hit by a car."

"Tragic, but that doesn't sound too disruptive."

True, it wasn't. My daughter's problems weren't the reason for my despair. They were just several in a never-ending laundry list of minor irritations that were draining my spirit. No, Jenny wasn't the problem—my son was.

"It's Kevin. He's going through the teenage thing. You know the drill. He goes out, but doesn't tell us where, then follows it up with the silent treatment. Lately, he's stepped up the pace. He's coming in after midnight on school nights, and he's skipping classes. We've already met with the school principal, but it doesn't seem to have any effect. It's gone too far, but I don't know what to do about it. It scares me, Press. It really does. I have visions of where this is all going to end. Well, you know . . ."

"I know," he replied.

And Preston would know. He would understand my fears and problems. His son, Nathan, used to be every suburban neighborhood's nightmare, a black kid caught up in a street gang. No one dared to give Nathan a sideways look when his gangbanger friends came visiting. Paranoia was a flag flown from every home's porch. Those were rough times for Preston and his wife. They felt the tension the neighborhood was feeling, but they turned that boy around. The kid was now a poster boy for everyone's child. At the moment, the nearest my Kevin would come to a poster boy would be on a milk carton.

"How far has he gone?" Preston asked.

"He was suspended last week for smacking a kid with his helmet during football practice, and next week, he's got to answer to a petty shoplifting case. I'm hoping that I can get the store manager to drop the charges."

Preston nodded, assessing the information. "So it hasn't gone too far."

"Too far for me. Tracy's ready to wash her hands of the boy."

"You're a long way from bottom, my friend."

"It doesn't feel like it."

"Trust me, you are."

"So how did you sort things out with Nathan?"

"Parental guidance, pure and simple."

I snorted. "It's a bit too late for timeouts and spankings."

Preston laughed. "Ain't that the truth? Kids grow up so fast I wonder who the parent really is sometimes. No, you can't use the techniques our parents used on us. It's a new millennium and that calls for new millennium solutions."

We came to a major intersection. Jogging in place, Preston hit the pedestrian crossing button. I slumped forward, resting my weak arms on trembling knees. The specks of light in my vision were gone, replaced by a wave of nausea.

"It comes down to respect," Preston continued. I looked up at my friend. "We give them unconditional love. They give us unconditional respect. But as they start growing up and their little brains develop, we, as parents, are in trouble. It's inevitable that they're going to see chinks in our armor. They come to realize we aren't gods. We aren't perfect. You just have to reinforce their first impressions. They were right—we are gods."

Don't Walk changed to Walk, and Preston set the pace again with me trailing a stride and a half behind.

"So what did you do to teach Nathan that you and Amber are gods?"

"As soon as we saw the company he was keeping and respect they were getting from him . . . we took his CDs away."

That was it? I was disappointed, to say the least. I'd been hoping for more, a lot more. Up until then, Preston had impressed me. His approach sounded bang on, but the execution was weak.

"Did it work?"

"No. It pushed him further away from us and closer to his friends."

"So what did you do instead?"

"You have to understand, we were desperate and I did things that I wouldn't normally do, but we had to get through to Nathan. We had to leave a mark that he wouldn't forget. So I sat him down with his CDs and I told him that Amber and I loved him, but he had to be taught a lesson for his actions. Obviously, he went to smart-mouth me, but before he could, I smashed his CDs to pieces with a hammer."

Again, I wasn't impressed. I know what Kevin would have done if I'd done that to his music collection. Hell, I know how I would have reacted if Preston smashed up my music. I understood Preston's motivation. He was trying to strike at the kid's heart, to make him realize the effect he was having on his family, but it wouldn't have turned me around.

"Not surprisingly," Preston said, "that didn't work either. I was pushing Nath further away . . . any further, and I'd lose him forever. I had to think, really think, about my next move."

Preston was reliving these moments, these trials, these decisions. His voice took on a reverential tone. He'd gone to the mountaintop to find his faith and had been rewarded. I stepped up my pace to catch sight of a side of my friend that I'd never seen.

"I knew I was losing Nathan. I could feel my son slipping through my fingers. Well, you know what they say about drastic times requiring drastic measures? I did what I had to do and it worked. I killed his dog in front of him."

Preston's last comment was a hammer blow, so much so that I stumbled and stutter-stepped a couple of times before I found my running rhythm again. He'd let his admission slip out so casually that I wasn't expecting it. My mind didn't have time to comprehend the viciousness of the act.

"How?" I asked. This wasn't what I'd meant to say, but Preston had knocked my brain out of gear and my mouth was freewheeling. I'd meant to say, "You killed your son's dog? Get away from me, you freak."

"Well, Nathan isn't so big that I couldn't pin him down and tie him to a chair in the kitchen. Then, we called in Hunter for his dinner as usual. Amber made the dog's dinner, and I mixed in the rat poison."

"I thought you said the dog had died from a tumor."

I pictured it all. Preston and Amber's immaculate custom kitchen with the beautiful tiled floor that I'd helped Press lay, and Nathan duct-taped to an Ethan Allen chair as Preston, my friend, lowered the poison-laced bowl to the retriever. I closed my eyes to blot out my vision, but only gave it greater clarity. I tasted bile.

"He thought we were bluffing, of course. He thought I was trying to scare him and all I was mixing into Hunter's food was crushed oatmeal. I told him, as parents, we were deadly serious about poisoning. This was a wake up call to the fact that there were consequences for his actions. And this was an indication of how serious we were. Thinking about it now, I saw a flicker in his eyes. He was taking me seriously. I could have stopped there, but I could see Nathan's resolve wasn't rock solid. A threat wasn't going to do it this time. So, I gagged Nathan, gave the dog the food, locked him in the kitchen with the dog, and took Amber out for dinner. Do you know it took that mutt over twenty-four hours to hemorrhage its last?"

"My God, I can't believe you did that!"

My horrified condemnation was misinterpreted. I could barely put into words my disgust for what Preston understood to be good parenting, but he took my remarks as a compliment. The son of a bitch actually smiled.

"Yeah, well, we had to do it. We were losing our son to a life of crime and eventual corruption. It had to be done. Obviously, we made our point to Nathan. Having been tied to a chair for twenty-four hours, he'd messed his pants, but we didn't let him clean himself up until he'd cleaned up the dog and its mess. You wouldn't believe the amount of blood and puke a poisoned dog will produce."

That was it. I couldn't run anymore. I was lightheaded to the point of unconsciousness. An ocean a time zone away sloshed in my ears, and my vision dissolved to block shapes and primary colors. My response to Preston's parental guidance was to vomit. I yakked up a light breakfast into the gutter, much to the disgust of the coffeehouse's outdoor customers across the street. Splashing vomit speckled my ankles, but I didn't care. It took all my strength to prevent my feeble legs from collapsing.

Preston patted me on the back. "Steady on there, buddy. Drink too much water this morning? That stuff'll bite you in the ass. C'mon, let's run it off. It's the best cure."

I couldn't believe Preston. The man didn't have a clue what kind of monster he'd become. I wanted to rip him a new one, let him have it, but my stomach hadn't finished unloading its remaining contents. Mercifully, I stopped and I breathed like a bull ready to charge, with thick gobs of sputum trailing from my lips. I wiped a hand across my mouth before straightening. Preston called out. He was a hundred yards ahead. Although he'd taken a baseball bat to my emotions, I followed. I had to learn more.

"We pretty much cracked it," Preston said, when I'd caught up with him. "We did have a couple of setbacks, but I took care of them."

I didn't know what Preston meant by "setbacks" and I wasn't sure I wanted to know. Not yet, anyway.

"Yep, in a couple of weeks, Nathan was our son again. The respect was back. The bad influences were gone. You must have noticed the change?"

"And everyone lived happily ever after," I said.

Preston's smile slipped. A serious demeanor took over his features. Obviously, not all was perfect in Neverland.

"My tactics only work for so long before there is a call for further reinforcement."

I couldn't imagine Nathan slipping back after the trauma of Hunter. If it had been me, I'd never have put a foot out of line with Preston again. I couldn't help feeling sorry for the kid. His fear of screwing up must have been intense.

"Nathan's been slipping back. I've discovered that he's hooked up with some of his old associates. But I'm going to handle it."

Preston's words struck a chill in me. Never had I heard that simple promise sound so malicious.

He went to say something, but caught himself and a smile spread across his lips. "This might be good practice for you, Mike . . . to see how I handle matters. You never know, you may be able to use my tactics on Kevin. You up for it?"

I said yes. Yes, out of fear for what Preston would think if I said no. Yes, out of fear for Nathan. And yes because, let's face it, I was curious.

"Good. I'm pleased," Preston said. "I'll be 'round for you at nine."

The knock came right on the button. Preston was dressed causally in dark clothes, as was I, as instructed. We got into Preston's car, but not his Infiniti and not Amber's SUV. Preston had pulled up in an ancient Crown Victoria with a broken taillight. I had no idea where the car had come from. It was like nothing I'd seen him use before.

"Where are we going?" I asked once we were on the expressway. Funny really, I didn't want to know what we were up to while we were in our neighborhood. Subconsciously, I didn't want my home tarnished by what Preston had planned. Although Preston hadn't made any disclosure, I knew, just knew, it wasn't going to be good.

"We're heading over to the warehouse district. A couple of Nathan's friends deal out there."

Deal what? I didn't think it was cards.

"How did you find out?" I asked.

"I followed Nath. He'd been late home from football practice a few times and from a study session once. We have ground rules in our house. He's allowed to stay out to a prearranged time. When he stopped obeying that rule, it was time to investigate. Parenting isn't like having a Chia Pet. You can't just feed it once and leave it to do its thing. Parenting requires constant diligence. Tonight will be a good example." Press turned to smile at me. "Trust me, follow my lead and Kevin will be snapping to attention before the month is out. And once that happens, you'll see your world following suit."

I didn't smile back. I couldn't. Fear coursed through my veins like a virus. The best I could do was nod in agreement and wait for the heat of Preston's gaze to leave me.

We entered the decaying warehouse district. The properties became seedier the further we were from the expressway. Ripe for redevelopment, it was ignored by the city and left to descend into a haven for every kind of criminal activity available on the books. At least crime was contained in a confined space, making it easy for the cops to mop up after the event.

Driving through the decaying streets, my heart raced. Although he had the air going, I was sweating. He was determined—the focus apparent on his face. He didn't plan on taking prisoners tonight. I knew this, and I could have avoided the event, but I still came along for the ride. I had to see.

Preston parked a car length from a four-way stop with weather-beaten striping. The street was deserted, except for a couple of junkers skulking on the cross street. Interrupted streetlight peppered the neighborhood thanks to burned or shot out bulbs. I didn't feel safe, even with the Crown Victoria's engine still running.

"This is it," Preston said, gazing at a three-story, graffiti-scarred warehouse with most of its windows missing. "This is where I followed Nath to. Let's hustle."

Preston switched off the engine, but left the Ford unlocked. He strode across the four-way without heed to any possible oncoming traffic. Not so bold, I followed in his footsteps, keeping an eye out for traffic or anybody else.

Preston stopped by a side door, which looked secure until he put his shoulder to it and it caved in with little resistance. From the silent street, the sound of the fracturing lock was deafening. I expected that we'd disturbed every dealer and chop shop in the district, but my fears were unfounded. Preston's never-ending stream of good luck knew no bounds.

We stepped inside. Shattered glass crunched under foot. Sinuous electrical wires hung from the ceiling like exposed veins. A muffled baseline throbbed in the distance.

"They hang out on the floor above," Preston said.

He led the way to an emergency access stairwell and a flight of steel stairs. Our footfalls clanged on the metallic surface, but the music masked our intrusion. I eased back the second floor door. A jerry-rigged light feebly lit an area. Three figures shifted in the shadows at the center of the warehouse floor. I went to ask Preston our tactics but he brushed by me.

He walked toward the group of three. His cool was astonishing. There was no haste or excitement to his pace. Fear was not an emotion that existed inside him. Being spotted was not an issue. As observer to this demonstration of parental guidance, I followed.

"I know we don't have a sign posted, but no trespassers," a shadow said before we were halfway across the floor. Laughter followed the quip.

"I'm here for Nathan," Preston commanded.

"Dad?" Nathan managed.

"Dad?" the comedic shadow echoed. "Is it your curfew, Dawg?"

More laughter followed. Nathan mumbled a curse.

When we reached them, the light exposed Nathan's bad influences as being not much older than Nathan, just a couple of punk kids. One wore a Raider Nation sweatshirt, and the other was a walking advertisement for FUBU. What elevated them from punk kids were the bags of dope, pills, and weed sitting on top of a wooden, upturned packing case. None of the three made any move to hide their stash. The dealers flopped into a couple of worse-for-wear loungers. Nathan remained standing, rigid in his fear.

"Nathan, I thought we had an agreement," Preston said.

FUBU cranked the volume on the boom box. He swapped a mischievous glance with Raider Nation. Preston wasn't to be trifled with and kicked the boom box clear across room. The CD player skittered across the floor, pieces breaking off as it disappeared into the gloom. With the boom box dead, an oppressive silence squeezed

the standoff.

"Hey, man," FUBU said, jumping to his feet.

Preston thrust him back down into the lounger. FUBU didn't get up again. He swapped another glance with Raider Nation. This time, there was no mischievousness present, only shock.

"Is this what you want, huh?" Preston demanded, ignoring the dealers.

Nathan said nothing.

"We had a deal. You don't associate with drug dealers."

"Hey, we ain't no drug dealers. We're businessmen," FUBU said, but not with the conviction I'd heard when we'd first arrived. He sounded more like a whining child.

"Did you think for one minute I wasn't going to find out? Was what I did to Hunter not example enough to show you how far I will go to keep you on the straight and narrow?"

Fire burned in Nathan's eyes. I felt the pain of that event. I'd only heard the tale second hand, and it was a raw wound to me. God knows what it was like for Nathan who'd lived through it.

"Do you think being a drug dealer makes you special, huh?" Preston flung his arms wide before stuffing them in his jacket again. "Do you think it's cool or something?"

Nathan still said nothing. I felt the escalation in the air. Preston was building to something. I willed Nathan to say something to calm his father down.

"I want an answer."

Nathan mumbled something inconsequential.

"Do you know what happens to drug dealers, Nathan?"

Before Nathan could answer or FUBU and Raider Nation could mouth off, Preston jerked out a small revolver and shot the two dealers. FUBU took one in the forehead, killing him instantly and Raider Nation took one in the throat, mortally wounding him as blood geysered from the wound. He clutched at his neck. Pleas for help were reduced to gurgles, but they didn't last long. He was dead within a few seconds.

I hadn't been prepared for what Preston had done—none of us had, least of all FUBU and Raider Nation. The look of shock and stunned amazement on Nathan's face mimicked my own. Preston had crossed a line, but it was obvious by the way he talked and acted he didn't believe he had. To him, this was parenting plain and simple—just good old-fashioned methods to keep a kid on the right track.

Preston turned to me, the gun still in his hand. For a glimmer, I thought I'd been brought there to create a scenario—drug deal gone bad—but the gun wasn't aimed at me.

"You see, Mike," Preston said. "There are no limits. You have to do what you have to do. If not, you'll always be at someone else's mercy."

"You killed them, Press."

Preston smiled the kind of smile intended for dense children. "No, these boys were on a slippery slope to this end. If anyone is responsible, then Nathan is."

"No," Nathan protested.

Preston gabbed his son by the shoulders, the gun still in hand, muzzle inches from Nathan's head. "Yes. You are responsible for what happened here tonight. You were told what would happen if you didn't keep your end of the bargain."

Nathan tried to interrupt, but Preston shut him down.

"Nathan, listen," Preston commanded. "You promised to stay in school, not to smart mouth your mom and me, stay away from bad influences, not to drink or do drugs, and I promised not to take action. I've been true to my word. Haven't I?"

Nathan couldn't look at his father when he replied. "Yes."

This was tough love at its harshest. Preston, whether you agreed with his methods or not, was a devoted father. I am too, but my devotion has never caused me to go this far. He was certainly a father among fathers.

"Let's get out of here. C'mon, Nath." Preston rested a hand on his son's shoulder and escorted him out of the building.

As I hit the street, the cool night air struck me. I'd hoped it would refresh me and clear my head of what I'd just witnessed, but it didn't. Instead, nausea overwhelmed me. But I wasn't the only one suffering ill effects. As I helped Nathan into the back of the Crown Victoria, he was shaking. I wanted to tell him it was okay and not to worry, but I knew Preston would negate that. Tonight was a demonstration that things weren't okay if Nathan carried on this way.

On the drive home, Preston got me to ditch the gun down a storm drain and told me to dispose of the clothes I was wearing. He detailed other measures I should take to ensure that nothing came back to connect us to the killings. I listened and took it all in.

As Preston parked, I glanced back at Nathan. The kid was broken. He was clay to be molded into whatever shape Preston desired. I couldn't see Nathan breaking the rules again. If he did, then he deserved Preston's special form of parental guidance.

"You go on in and apologize to your mother," Preston instructed as we got out of the car.

Nathan said nothing and traipsed inside.

"Good kid, really," Preston said, as Nath closed the door. "Just needs a few taps in the right direction. Know what I mean?"

I nodded. I did.

"Thanks for tonight," he said. "I really appreciate the support. I hope you learned something."

I nodded. I had.

"I just need your help with one more thing."

"Sure."

"I have to dump the car. Can you pick me up from this address in an hour?"

He handed me a scrap of paper, and I read the address. "I'll be there."

"Good." My friend smiled at me. The smile scared me, but I welcomed it. Things had been leading up to this point. This had been what I'd been waiting to hear. "We should talk about how we're going to solve your problems."

"I'd like that," I said.

"I'm glad. Did you know these skills can be adapted to suit any problem? It's totally universal." Preston sidled up to me conspiratorially. "My boss kept taking credit for my ideas, but since I cut the brake lines on his car, he gives credit where credit is due, and now I have his job. My father-in-law said I was a good for nothing. It's not a tune he likes to sing since his house burned down."

Once Preston started, he didn't stop. He proceeded to catalog his triumphant successes, describing in minute detail how he'd won battles with his church pastor, store clerks, car mechanics, and a bank manager. As wrong as it sounded, I took it all in, never once questioning his ethics.

"Like I was saying, it comes down to respect. Once you have respect, the world is a much finer place. I think if you take my approach, you'll see a marked improvement in your quality of life." Preston spread his arms wide. "Aren't I proof enough?"

Yes, he was, but I didn't respond. I still wasn't sure I wanted to follow my neighbor's path, irrespective of its successes. For all Preston's stories and his demonstration, I couldn't decide whether I was that kind of a man. Could I inflict the same ruthless love on Kevin? I needed something to push me.

"Fall is certainly upon us now," Preston said.

"Er, yeah." Preston knocked me off guard by the observation. I was still preoccupied with his teachings. My mind was thick with the visions of Hunter writhing on the kitchen floor and Nathan's face when Preston killed the two drug dealers.

"Leaves are getting everywhere. Sidewalks are covered in the things. I'd hate to see my gutters right now."

Preston was right. Drifts of leaves were everywhere, and who didn't have a lawn hidden under a blanket of nature's castoffs?

"The problem is, I don't have a leaf blower."

"Yes, you do."

"Oh, I know I do, but I don't have it." Preston turned to face me. "You do."

"Sorry, about—"

"I lent that blower to you last winter, and you still haven't returned it."

"I'll get it back to you," I promised.

"Mike, would you like to know what happened to Jenny's cat?" Preston's eyes were hard. "I can tell you, you know, but it won't be good news, I'm sorry to say."

"That's okay. I understand."

I returned home full of Preston's teachings. Things were going to change—and for the better. Preston had shown me the way.

The Real Deal

"So, in conclusion, yes, this has been a bad year for Casper Industries. Profit and revenues are down, as is return on investment. This doesn't mean a slide. The economic environment is tough, and we're weathering the storm better than most."

Kenneth Casper searched the sea of investors' faces. He was losing the crowd. Frowns and headshakes were everywhere in the packed auditorium. He hadn't seen an annual stockholder's meeting this well attended in a decade. There was a reason for that. In the investors' minds, Casper Industries was on a death spiral and they blamed one man, the man in charge—him. If he didn't turn things around in the next few months, there would be a call to oust him. How embarrassing was that? To be kicked out of the company he had created fifty years ago. At least this torture was nearly over. After this address, the meeting would be at a close.

He turned to the final page of his address, using his talon-like, arthritic hand. The sheet slipped from his feeble grasp and fluttered to the ground. He groaned when he bent to pick it up, and his back seized on the way down. Mark Clinton, vice-president of operations, dashed to his rescue, snatching up the sheet and passing it to him.

Kenneth wished the stage had a trapdoor that would open up and swallow him. This was just the kind of display that would destroy him. Everybody knew his health was poor and that was where the problem lay. Nobody looked beyond the surface. Everybody associated Casper Industries' crumbling empire with his own physical decrepitude. Okay, he was the first to admit that his physical problems drained him of energy, but his mind was as sharp as ever. No one cared about that, though.

"Come on, Kenneth, we're nearly through."

The situation wasn't helped by Mark's rescue. The tableau only played to everyone's fantasy that Casper Industries was being held together by a younger, stronger man. If the stockholders kicked him out, it would be Mark who would succeed him. Kenneth wasn't unduly stressed by Mark's aspirations. Whatever the investors thought, Mark was Kenneth's greatest and most fervent supporter. It wasn't something he could say about the rest of his board.

"Thanks," Kenneth said and smiled.

"Let me help you up."

"No. Let's not give them the satisfaction"

Mark nodded and retreated to the wings.

Kenneth straightened as quickly as he could, endeavoring to show a spark of youth, but his spine screamed under the load. He hadn't fooled anyone. He completed his address and tottered from the stage to a damp smattering of applause. It was the least they could do for all the years he'd lined their pockets.

Meg welcomed him off the stage with a smile that matched his physical pain. She didn't help him. She waited until he made the short, tortuous distance from the lectern to the stage wings. She was a great kid and just as beautiful as her mother. She hugged him when he reached her.

"You look done in, Dad," she whispered into his ear. "Let's get you out of here."

"Do you have the plane tickets?" he whispered back.

"Yes, everything is ready, and the car's waiting outside."

"Let's go then."

Meg ushered Kenneth through a side door, helping him avoid his fellow executives and stockholders. He didn't want to be waylaid. He had a flight waiting, and nobody was to know what he was doing until it was done. This was his last shot at saving his career. She led him along a service corridor, and they burst through the door at the end.

Out in the rain-soaked alley, Mark paced alongside the waiting limo. He opened the door for Kenneth the moment he appeared and helped him inside.

"Good luck, Kenneth. Come back a new man."

"Thanks, Mark. You don't know what your help means to me." Kenneth failed to hide the emotion and tears welled up. He grabbed Mark's hand and shook it two-handed.

"Trust me, I do know. Now get out of here before your flight leaves."

Meg slid into the limo next to Kenneth, and Mark closed the door. Before Kenneth had buckled himself in, the limo blew out of the alley. Thirty minutes later, it pulled up in front of international departures at LAX, and they were in the air an hour later on a LanChile Airlines flight bound for Lima, Peru.

Although Lima offered nothing but hope, Kenneth couldn't relax, and the nine-hour flight seemed longer than it was. He stayed awake while Meg slept soundly. Late afternoon stretched into night, and Latin America faded into meaningless dots of light. All he could think about was failure. The treatment, successful for so many, would surely fail in his case. He would return home in time to see his company slip from his arthritic grasp. He was stupid to believe in anything else. The airliner touched down in Peru's capital city after midnight, and he disembarked, feeling older than he ever had in his life.

Even at that late hour, the city was alive. Exiting the arrivals lounge, taxi drivers mobbed anyone and everyone. Locals jostled Kenneth while trying to secure his business. Meg knew Spanish and dismissed all comers, but they ignored her.

"Don't worry, Dad, we'll be out of this soon. Someone's here to collect us."

Passengers from another flight poured out of the arrivals lounge feeding the taxi drivers' frenzy for business. The resultant force halted Kenneth and Meg's progress. Sweat prickled Kenneth's brow, and air trickled from his chest. His grip on consciousness loosened.

A man wearing a Giants baseball jacket pulled two men apart. "Señor and Señorita Casper?"

"Yes," Meg replied.

"I am Jorge," he said in crude English. "Come with me, please."

Jorge took the luggage cart from Meg and used it to plow a furrow in the crowd. He didn't take any prisoners, giving anyone in his path a single warning in Spanish before forging ahead. His technique was effective, and Kenneth, aided by Meg, followed in his wake.

Jorge loaded their bags into a well-preserved, red and white Nissan Maxima from the Eighties. He opened the rear passenger door for them, and they slithered onto plastic sheathed seats. Kenneth guessed this was what passed for a limo in Peru, but he didn't care too much for absent luxuries. He was free of the zoo and on the road.

Hitting the city streets, Jorge said, "I take you to hotel."

Meg leaned forward. "Where is Señor Escobar?"

While searching for a reply, Jorge veered into another lane to avoid a slow moving bus, cutting off an ancient Mercedes in the process. The maneuver was worthy of a New York cabbie, but not of Kenneth's heart, which fluttered with nervous agility.

Jorge failed to make a coherent answer in English, and Meg re-asked in Spanish. Happy to speak Spanish, he reeled off a rapid-fire reply. Meg leaned back in her seat.

"What's happening?" Kenneth asked.

"Escobar will meet us for breakfast at the hotel at ten tomorrow."

"Is Escobar the shaman?"

"No, he's our guide. He will take us to the shaman."

Out of this chaos, there was finally some order. Kenneth felt a portion of his stress melt away, and he wound the window down for some air, leaving Jorge to his crazy driving. Meg clasped his hand and gave it a comforting squeeze.

In spite of all the pollution and car fumes, the air smelled sweet. It wasn't bleached of its personality like its U.S. counterpart. Something still virgin and untouched scented Lima. He smiled.

"A penny for them," Meg said.

"I just have a good feeling about this." He lifted her hand in his and kissed the back. "Thanks for all your help. Without you, I wouldn't have this chance to regain my strength and my company."

"You don't have to thank me. You're my Dad. What daughter wouldn't do this for her Dad?"

Jorge turned onto a residential street and stopped under a neon sign announcing "Hotel," although guesthouse was a better description. A six-foot stucco wall hid the hotel's entrance from view, and a wrought iron security gate made sure unwelcome visitors didn't get in without a fight.

"We here," he said.

Jorge pulled their luggage from the trunk and banged on the iron gate for attention. A withered man of late middle age with jet-black hair exchanged words with Jorge and opened the gate. The men shared the burden of the bags, and Kenneth and Meg followed them inside. Abundant plant life filled a well-kept courtyard, and Kenneth's apprehension left him. At the check-in desk, the withered man introduced himself as Miguel. He spoke in English, although his soft cadence made it difficult for Kenneth to understand him.

While Meg checked them in, Kenneth scanned the hotel. A small lounge area constituted the lobby. Squishy and mismatched sofas were pushed together in a U-shape. Local and American newspapers covered a table that filled the gap between the sofas. It was a so-so affair.

Jorge left them. Meg offered a tip, but he refused it, saying he had been properly compensated for his efforts. Miguel carried their bags with the aid of his son, a clean-cut man in his twenties. He then led them through a beautifully tended garden courtyard in the rear, which doubled as their restaurant.

The climb up two flights of stairs felt like a mountain ascent to

Kenneth. His decrepitude embarrassed him, especially considering how easily the spry Miguel completed the obstacle. Kenneth guessed there had to have been only a handful of years between them. Everyone was polite though and waited for him to reach the second floor. He hated their pity and hoped to God that the shaman was worthy of his reputation.

Miguel had placed Kenneth and Meg in adjoining rooms. Meg stayed and helped him settle in.

"We should be staying here just tonight, but I've decided to keep these rooms until we leave for LA," Meg explained while unpacking his bag. "We can leave some of our things here. We'll need to travel light."

Kenneth sat on the edge of the bed, waiting for the throbbing in his head and the aching in his legs and hands to pass. He would have liked to have been in the cosseted surrounding of a Hilton or some such, rather than this place, but he understood the reasons for their low profile. No one was to know about his recovery plan.

"Hey, what's this?" Meg asked with a smile. She held up a small bottle of Burgundy Kenneth had brought with him. It was from his favorite French vineyard and a very good year.

"You weren't meant to see that. It's a little surprise for later," he replied and smiled back. "It's for a little celebrating, if the shaman does his trick."

He was lying, of course, but Meg believed him, and that was all that mattered. Fifty years of business made him a good liar. If the shaman turned out to be a charlatan, then Kenneth wasn't going back. There was no point. He was finished, and there was no way he would return to LA to see his empire pass into someone else's hands. He'd poisoned the wine, and when the time came, he would drink it and die in a shabby hotel in a third-world country. It was a pitiful end, but death was rarely glorious. That was why everyone feared it.

"Well, have no fear, you'll be drinking this before the week is out."

Meg finished unpacking and left him alone. Still dressed, he collapsed into a heavy sleep.

Daylight through his window woke him around nine. Sleep had done him a lot of good. His aches and pains had receded to a low-level hum and were all but gone after a long shower. Meg knocked on his door as he was toweling off.

"Escobar is waiting for us downstairs."

"I'll meet you down there."

Kenneth found Meg and Escobar having breakfast in the garden patio. They stood as he approached. Escobar smiled and offered a hand, which Kenneth took.

"Mr. Casper, it's an honor to meet you," he said in clear but heavily accented English.

Escobar had a professional air to him. His wore an expensive shirt and slacks, but no tie. He sported a brush-cut hairstyle and a fashionable goatee. He exuded Latin suave. But his laid-back professionalism was a façade. His calloused hands said much of past careers, and the crescent scar above his left eye looked to have been the work of a beer bottle. Whether he was a man to be admired or feared, Kenneth wasn't sure.

"Mr. Escobar, you flatter me."

Escobar shrugged off the compliment and sat.

"I'll get you some breakfast, Dad," Meg said and went over to the buffet.

Kenneth settled into a chair next to Escobar. "When do I meet the shaman?"

"Straight to business, eh, Mr. Casper?"

When Escobar said this, he wasn't looking at Kenneth, but at the patio's only other occupants, a couple eating breakfast half a dozen wrought iron tables away. They were South Americans, certainly not from the U.S. by the look of them. They didn't seem too interested in what Kenneth had blurted out.

"Maybe I should be more discreet," Kenneth said.

Escobar dismissed the suggestion with a wave of his hand. "Nothing to fear, my friend. People here understand and respect the shaman."

Meg returned and slid a plate of fresh fruit and a tall glass of orange juice in front of Kenneth. He speared a cube of papaya and ate it. It was the freshest he'd tasted anywhere.

"So when do I meet the shaman?" Kenneth asked again.

"Two days from now," Escobar replied. "We leave after breakfast and ride to Caraz."

Kenneth didn't relish the long overland ride. He didn't know much about Peru, but he knew enough to know it wasn't miles and miles of gleaming freeways.

"Can't we charter a plane?" Kenneth asked.

Escobar shrugged. "We could, but it won't get you to the Caraz drop-off point. The terrain isn't suitable for airplanes to land, and, even if it was, you'd still have ride with the shaman's people to meet him."

"You aren't taking us to him?" Meg asked.

"No," Escobar replied.

"Why?" Kenneth asked.

"His location is secret. Even I don't know where he is."

It sounded tedious. Kenneth just wanted to get the shaman's cure and get out. This wasn't meant to be a quest for El Dorado.

"I thought you knew the shaman," Kenneth said.

"No," Escobar corrected. "I know his people."

"How do you know he can do what he says he can do?"

"I have brought the shaman many people, and he has cured them. You have nothing to worry about, Mr. Casper, the shaman will help you."

Kenneth didn't like all this palaver. He knew he'd let his heart rule his head in coming here, but now his head wasn't too keen on letting his heart have control. He was a businessman unaccustomed to superstition for answers. That was the domain of rich widows and daytime talk shows. He could call it off, but if he did, then Casper Industries was over. He had to see it through, even if it killed him, because not following through was a sure ticket to the grave.

"I don't think we should waste any more time, Mr. Escobar," Kenneth said. "We should leave immediately."

Clogged Lima streets slowed their progress, not that the battered Toyota Space Cruiser was rapid transport. Once out of the city, their pace didn't increase. The pockmarked coastal highway had to be negotiated rather than driven. The Toyota's air conditioning failed to keep the cabin temperature tolerable. Escobar cracked a couple of windows to cover the deficit. Dust and the drone of worn bearings washed in. Escobar didn't drive. He acted as navigator while a barrel-chested local did the work.

Meg stared at the Peruvian landscape washing by and smiled at the unfamiliar world. She looked so happy. For her, this was a trip of a lifetime, not Kenneth's last hope at survival. He reached out to her and took her hand.

"What do you think about this?" he asked.

"The shaman, you mean?"

He nodded.

"I think he's going to do wonders for you." She squeezed his hand. "Don't you?"

If something seems too good to be true, then it is, he thought. He wasn't sure why he was being so negative. He'd spent months looking for a cure, and the shaman seemed to be the answer, but as each mile closed in on that answer, he feared he was chasing rainbows. He smiled at his daughter and lied.

"Of course the shaman will do wonders." He squeezed her hand. "I just wanted to see if you felt the same way."

"Oh, Dad." Meg nestled against him, and he slipped an arm around her. "I believe in this more than anything."

The first day's drive ended at some shantytown Kenneth couldn't find on a map. They stayed in a hostel not as well kept as the guesthouse in Lima, but Kenneth was glad to be free of the minivan. His head and muscles throbbed from the constant pounding of the shot suspension over two hundred miles of broken roads. A simple meal of rice and beans restored his spirits, and he was somewhat ready for the drive ahead. Caraz wasn't far, but the mountain climb on pink dirt roads made the second leg of the journey slow. The spectacular scenery was hard to enjoy. The change in elevation hurt his chest and gave him a headache, but Escobar produced a bag full of coca leaves for them to chew on.

"It's good medicine for altitude sickness," Escobar announced.

If taste was anything to go by, then the leaves had to be good medicine. Kenneth found the sour tang and tough texture nearly inedible, but they did their job. His head cleared, and his breathing settled.

The rest of the drive went without incident until nightfall. It had been dark an hour when Escobar's driver stopped the Toyota in the middle of a mountain pass.

"You have to get out now," Escobar said, leaning over the back of his seat.

"Is this the drop-off point?" Meg asked.

"Yes." Escobar hopped out of the Space Cruiser and opened the side door.

"How long will we have to wait?" Kenneth asked.

"Not long. Come, please. If they see the van, they won't come."

Kenneth and Meg clambered out of the van. Meg brought her daypack with her.

"We will be back for you in the morning," Escobar said, getting back into the van.

They watched the Toyota's taillights recede into the darkness. Both of them shivered the moment they were alone. South America wasn't warm at these altitudes. LA had to have a thirty-degree advantage. Civilization was out to lunch permanently here. Once the minivan was out of earshot, a blanket of silence enveloped them until a howling, bitter wind kicked up and cut through them. Instinctively, both of them backed up against the mountain face for shelter. Airborne and ground-based nightlife staked their territory with penetrating shrieks. Within an hour, a terminal sounding diesel engine came growling from the east.

"I think this is it," Meg said, her teeth chattering.

"I hope so," Kenneth replied.

An ancient military truck screeched to a halt in front of them. A man jumped out of the passenger seat, while two others climbed down from the rear. All three of them brandished flashlights. Kenneth's heart rate leapt, and sweat broke out across his forehead, despite the frigid conditions.

The man from the front passenger seat introduced himself as José in English, before spouting a volley of rapid-fire Spanish. Meg responded. José indicated to the rear of the truck, and the others helped them in. There were no seats in the truck, and Kenneth and Meg had to make do with sitting on the dirt-streaked flatbed.

The man in the passenger seat fired off more Spanish.

"No," Meg shrieked.

"What is it?" Kenneth demanded, snatching her forearm.

Before she could reply, he had his answer. The two other men produced blindfolds. Kenneth and Meg fought the men as they tried to tie the blindfolds over their eyes. José shouted angry Spanish at Meg. She responded and relaxed.

"Let them, Dad." She sounded defeated. "The shaman's location is a secret. They won't take us to him unless they blindfold us."

Kenneth complied, letting the stale rag be tied over his eyes.

The commotion over, the shaman's people climbed aboard the truck and they set off with a lurch. The two men left in the rear of the truck with Kenneth and Meg exchanged muffled Spanish with each other. Kenneth guessed they didn't want Meg to hear since she spoke decent Spanish.

"Can you hear what they're saying?" he asked in a low voice.

"No," she replied. "Not over the engine noise."

"Were you expecting this?"

"No."

Secrecy was one thing, but this felt like some entirely different. *Kidnapped*, Kenneth thought. It made sense. He was desperate for a miracle cure, and the shaman was the perfect bait to lure him out here. No one would find them in the deserted Peruvian mountains. Escobar knew all this and how much Kenneth was worth. Casper Industries would have a ransom by morning. Who wouldn't pay a million dollars to get their CEO back? Casper Industries wouldn't, that was for sure. Escobar hadn't done his homework. With the future of the company at stake and Kenneth being the only obstacle, this was the board's chance to fumble the ball and get rid of him. A tightness constricted his chest that had nothing to do with the altitude. He kept his theory to himself; he didn't want to scare Meg.

As the truck scrabbled for traction on the mountain road, Kenneth contemplated their possible escape. There wasn't much they could do right now in the dark and cold. A daylight break for freedom was possible, but people who knew this terrain well would easily find them. He surmised their best bet was an evening break when they could get a meal inside them and some blankets for warmth. By the time a rudimentary plan was in place, the truck stopped.

Kenneth's fear abated when their blindfolds were removed and José's sidekicks helped them from the truck. They hadn't been on the truck long, an hour at the most, so it was still dark and their eyes didn't have to adjust to the scene before them. To say they had been brought to a village was an overstatement. The shaman and his people lived in what Kenneth considered to be an encampment, no more than a collection of feeble structures and outhouses clinging to a hillside. Lights glowed from gaps under doors and drape-covered windows.

José led the way with his flashlight. Kenneth didn't feel welcomed, but he didn't feel he was being held against his will either, which puzzled him. He couldn't see why anyone would want to keep this place a secret. They stopped in front of a ten-by-ten building, and José announced their arrival. A diminutive woman, bandaged in layer upon layer of clothes, opened the door to a room lit with propane lanterns. Several people occupied the corners of the room while one man knelt at the center, arranging colored stones on a multicolored rug. José followed Kenneth and Meg into the room and closed the door, leaving the other two men to stand guard.

The man with the stones stood and said something in Spanish.

"He wants you to lie down on the rug," Meg said.

Kenneth guessed the shaman had just introduced himself. He wasn't what Kenneth had been expecting. In all honesty, Kenneth wasn't sure what he had been expecting. The idea of a shaman conjured images from elaborate ethnic dress and face paint to a hooded figure who was half-brother to the Grim Reaper. He definitely wasn't expecting the man dressed in threadbare Levis, tennis shoes, and a hand-woven jerkin over a Simpsons T-shirt. Bemused, Kenneth lay on his back on the rug as instructed.

The shaman selected several polished stones from a pile to the left of him and placed them on various parts of Kenneth's body. He rested a duck-egg blue pebble on Kenneth's forehead between his eyes, a fist-sized hunk of granite over his heart, and a number of colored stones over his abdomen near his stomach, spleen, and liver. He positioned a number of flint pebbles, scarred with imperfections, over Kenneth's knees and the backs of his hands. By the time the shaman was finished, Kenneth resembled a human pool table. The shaman spoke Spanish to Kenneth, and Meg translated.

"These stones," Meg said, "will give the shaman great insight into your ailments."

The shaman touched the stone on Kenneth's forehead with his right hand and closed his eyes. He muttered an incantation. Kenneth glanced over at his daughter for a translation. Meg shrugged and shook her head. These were not words of Spanish. Although they were only words, fear wormed through Kenneth's veins. The magic frightened him.

The shaman moved from stone to stone muttering various chants. The chants had a lullaby quality to them that massaged Kenneth clear through to his soul. Aches and pains spawned from his age and the tiring journey drained from him and into the rug. He'd never felt so relaxed. After an hour or so, the shaman removed the stones and replaced each one with a highly polished, white crystal. He spoke.

"He has felt your pain," Meg translated. "He understands it and has brought it to the surface. He will now draw the sickness into the crystals."

The shaman began a new series of incantations. As soon as his chants began, the people packing the room, so far redundant by their presence, became a choir. Their voices fell into place with the shaman's, with instant synchronicity. Their combined voices turned the chant into a song to cure him.

The power of the voices stunned Kenneth, but he didn't feel a change in his health. He felt rested and excited by the shaman's words, but the arthritis in his bones hadn't magically disappeared. The miracle cure he'd hoped for wasn't forthcoming. He would remain a sick man. Disappointment seeped into him.

The chanting and singing ended after several hours. The shaman removed the crystals, pocketing them in his jerkin. He said a final blessing over Kenneth before gesturing for him to stand. It took three people to help Kenneth to his feet. He was dusting himself off when the shaman said something to him.

"He says, expect changes," Meg said. "Your pain will not last."

I won't hold my breath, Kenneth thought, but he smiled politely at the shaman and thanked him. As Kenneth left the hut, he wondered who was humoring whom.

"How do you feel?" Meg asked.

"Okay." Kenneth saw the disappointment on his daughter's face. She'd put so much faith in this moment, and it didn't seem to have worked. He reacted to salvage her hope. "I am at peace."

"That's good." She smiled, but he saw the sadness in her eyes.

José led Kenneth and Meg back to the truck. Just as Kenneth climbed back aboard, Meg broke away, dashing over to the shaman. She exchanged words and handed the shaman an envelope that looked thick with cash. The shaman took the envelope with grace and handed something small to Meg, but Kenneth didn't get to see it. One of the shaman's people slipped the blindfold over his eyes. He fought against the man, tearing the rag away, but it was too late. Meg was trotting toward the truck.

During the ride back to the drop-off point, he asked her, "What did the shaman give you?"

"A surprise." Hope filled her voice.

"Meg, I'm too old for surprises."

"It's a medicine. I saw that his ceremony hadn't gone far enough, so I asked him for something else, and he gave it to me."

It sounded like another carrot for the donkey to chase and an expensive one by the wad of cash she'd given the shaman. Not that it mattered. He was too tired to care.

Sunrise had cracked the horizon when Escobar returned to collect them. He asked questions and Meg answered them. Tired of the questions, Kenneth just asked Escobar to get them back to Lima. Silence underlined much of the drive back to the capital. Despite the atrocious roads, Kenneth slept for most of the journey. When he was awake, he and Meg didn't discuss much, at least not in front of Escobar. They did discuss the shaman's "miracle" powder, once, during a rest stop.

"You look wasted, Dad," Meg said.

"Maybe I should try the medicine." He watched a heavily laden bus trundle past, kicking up rooster tails of dirt.

Meg frowned at him. "I think we should wait until we're in Lima, where we have some privacy."

Back in his room, he examined the medicine Meg had given him upon their arrival in Lima. It wasn't much to look at, just a candy tin filled with an oatmeal-colored powder. He rubbed the coarse granules between his fingertips. He sniffed it; it didn't possess a discernable odor. The stuff reminded him of a bulk fiber laxative. It probably was. He smiled at that. He'd come all this way for a laxative.

Well, he wouldn't know for sure unless he tried it. He turned over a glass on his dresser and emptied a reasonable measure of the powder into it. He had no idea of whether that was too much or not enough, but that was the shaman's instructions according to Meg. He cracked open a bottle of water and filled the glass. He stirred the mixture with his finger. It didn't exactly dissolve into the liquid, but the solution would make it easier to drink.

He shot back the shaman's brew. It tasted like dirt and wheat chaff. He gagged on the unpleasant concoction, but he fought it down.

"Anything that tastes that bad has to be good," he said to the empty glass.

Kenneth's grip on the glass tightened. His knuckles shone white through his papery skin. His strength astounded then frightened him. He couldn't control it. His grip intensified and the glass shattered, spraying shards everywhere. Pain coursed up his arm followed by a strange sensation in his hand. It spread throughout his body. His left side went rigid, freezing his left lung. His bones seemed to want to fold in on themselves. Unseen forces latched onto his face and dragged it down. Trying to yell for Meg, he bit his own tongue, and drool and blood drizzled from his contorted face. Something inside his right eye popped sending a searing jolt of agony to the center of his brain. Paralyzed, Kenneth collapsed, striking the floor with a resounding thud. A part of him broke, but he was unable to tell which part it was as his body seized.

What had the shaman done to him? What the hell was in that powder? Other questions piled in on each other as his hijacked body tried to destroy him. But all those questions became irrelevant when Meg entered his room accompanied by Mark Clinton. Kenneth grunted, trying to speak.

"Don't get up on my account," Mark said. "I bet you're wondering what the hell is going on."

This didn't make sense to Kenneth, none of it. The world had turned itself on its head. Mark and Meg seemed to be together by the way she was holding his hand. Kenneth grunted.

"I think that's a yes, hon," Meg said.

Mark crouched before Kenneth. Meg stood behind Mark and steadied him with her hands.

"I don't have much time before that brain of yours turns to so much rancid pudding." He prodded Kenneth's head. "So I'll give you the abridged version."

The malice in Mark's eyes was unmistakable, as was Meg's. Kenneth wished he would go blind.

"Newsflash, Kenneth, I hate being your number two. I'm not meek and mild, willing to wait for you to stand down. The problem was the stockholders still had faith in you, even after I orchestrated this year's appalling downturn in business. They were never going to vote you out. I've been feeding you a line for some time to make you believe they were against you."

Meg knelt by Kenneth's side. "And I helped him, because I love him, which is a feeling I've never had for you." She patted his face. "You should have been there for us instead of the company, then Mom might not have drunk herself to death."

He couldn't believe he'd been blind to Meg and Mark's hate. If the poison hadn't already struck Kenneth dumb, then their vitriol would have. He was almost glad this nightmare had happened. At least he knew the truth now. Drool oozed between his lips.

"Kenneth, you looked so scared," Mark said. "Don't worry, you're not going to die. We're not killers." They both laughed. "The powder has caused a debilitating stroke, from which you'll never recover."

"Dad, if you can hear me, the shaman wasn't part of this. He was the real deal, if you believe in that sort of thing. I have no idea what that powder was for, but it can't overcome what I spiked it with."

Kenneth tried to move a hand to show them he wasn't finished, but the severed connection between his brain and body failed to produce any movement, so he gave up trying.

Mark stood and checked his watch. "Another minute before we call the paramedics should seal it."

"Let's celebrate while we're here," Meg announced.

"What with? I didn't bring anything."

"But Dad did."

Meg rummaged through his suitcase for the Burgundy. Mark took the bottle from her, and after reading the label, nodded in admiration.

"You always had good taste in wine, Kenneth."

Meg handed Mark the bottle opener, and he did the honors.

"I know we should wait for it to breathe, but we don't have that luxury."

Mark poured the wine out into a pair of tumblers Meg took from the dresser. They toasted each other and drank the wine down. Kenneth would have liked to have told them about his poisoned wine, but they would find out soon enough, especially at the rate they were guzzling the stuff.

Kenneth couldn't help thinking that the shaman was the real deal if his final words were anything to go by. He'd said to expect changes. They weren't the kind Kenneth had been hoping for, but he'd seen them. And the shaman was right about the pain too. He couldn't feel his arthritis. He couldn't feel much at all, but he could take pleasure in Meg and Mark's pain as the poison took effect.

Officer Down

Webber zeroed in on the suspect. Even weighed down by his street cop paraphernalia and boots, he still had the legs on the kid in the baggy jeans and hoodie. People on the sidewalk parted to watch the street performance, with stunned fascination. He radioed in his position again and asked for a unit to cut the kid off at Bush.

The kid had other plans and ducked down an alley between two apartment buildings. Backup wouldn't be necessary. The kid had just screwed himself; the alley dead-ended. Webber smiled. Sometimes perps made it too easy. He drew his weapon as he charged into the alley.

Before he got the chance to issue a warning, a length of pipe smashed him across the chest. The impact felled him, and he crashed down hard on his back. His Glock leapt from his grasp. The searing pain in his back and his chest overwhelmed him, and he forgot his training. He ignored his weapon, but the suspect didn't. The kid snatched it up, and the pain in Webber's chest and back ceased as he stared down the barrel of his own gun.

"Take it easy, pal," Webber said, raising his hands slowly. "Put the weapon down."

Webber saw trouble in the kid's eyes. Amongst the mist of fear and panic was the killer's gleam. There was no way he could talk this kid down. The decision had been made. Before Webber could say anything more, the kid pumped two rounds into his chest. The bullet strikes snatched his breath away and his heart twitched from the impacts. How could two 9mm slugs feel like two MUNI buses being dropped on his chest? He tried breathing, but nothing worked. The suspect studied his work then bolted out of the alley with Webber's gun in hand.

His vest saved him, of course. It smothered the bullets like a catcher's mitt swallowing a fly ball and dissipated the impacts according to its design, but each slug still felt as if it had punched a fist-sized hole through his spine.

Sirens filled the air, smothering the screams of people in the street who did nothing to help him. Webber's radio squawked, and he brought it to his mouth and keyed the mic, but no words came out. He gave up until help came.

"How do you feel?" the department shrink asked.

"Sore," Webber replied.

It was two days after the incident. The hospital had discharged him the same day. The wonders of modern technology. Even a near death experience warranted only a couple of hours of hospital time. He couldn't complain. The vest had turned the double tap into a pair of handprint-sized bruises. The Vicodin did a decent job of dulling the pain, but left him fuzzy headed, so he stopped taking them.

"Besides sore?"

"Sore with myself."

The shrink, a thickset woman around fifty, liked that reply. She smiled, exposing neat, gleaming teeth. Webber wondered if she'd had them bleached to cover up her smoking habit. The stink of cigarettes clung to the cramped office's interior. "Explain?"

"The son of a bitch dented my pride, as well as my breastplate."

The shrink's smile widened into a grin.

"I have five years on the job, and I got sucker punched by some street punk like I was in my rookie year. It cost me my weapon and nearly my life."

"Okay, it was a mistake on your part. You survived. You'll learn from this. You can move on."

"Yeah, but—"

"No buts. The but you're inserting into this situation is of your own devising. The criminal investigation underway is not focused on you, but your attacker. No blame has been attached to you. Your colleagues are hard at work tracking down this person. All you have to do is heal and get back out there."

Yeah, yeah, yeah, it all sounded nice and reasonable, but the harsh reality of the situation was that there was a black mark against his name. He'd lost his weapon to a perp. He'd put a gun on the street and not taken one off. It was hardly the image of protect and serve. He tried not to imagine his gun being traced back to a killing. He'd feel no different than if he'd pulled the trigger himself.

"This situation troubles you, doesn't it?" she asked.

"Of course it does. What kind of cop would I be if it didn't?"

"A poor one."

"Now you're getting it."

"Understandably, you're upset by this encounter, but don't let it take over. Accept it and move on. You're bruised physically and mentally, but bruises fade." She smiled and checked her watch. "Our time is up. Can you drop by the same time tomorrow?"

Webber crossed the city to hook up with Murphy, his old training officer, at Murphy's favorite haunt, Tara Hills Irish pub. Murphy had a Guinness waiting for him when he arrived. Webber had built a tolerance for the stuff, he had to as one of Murphy's ex-rookies, but he'd never learned to love the black beer. He took his place at the bar.

Murphy asked the same questions the department and the shrink had asked. Murphy was a friend, but Webber was no more comfortable answering the questions than he had been in the more formal interviews. Webber guessed he'd be answering these questions for some time, at least until something fresher came along.

"It's the gun, isn't it?" Murphy asked.

Webber shrugged.

"Okay, you lost the weapon. It's a mistake, but we'll recover it. This perp isn't smart enough to lie low. We'll pick him up by the end of the week."

"It's not that." Webber rolled the buckled slugs from his vest in his palm like they were lucky dice. He hadn't put them down since the doctor gave them to him.

"Then what is it?"

"This kid drilled me twice in the chest. He wasn't doing it to disable me. He intended to kill me. Fortunately, he was too stupid to realize I'd be wearing a vest."

"That's why I say we'll pick him up before the end of the week. The kid's a hothead and very likely a killer in the making. He'll be caught. Relax."

"I know that."

"Then what's the problem here?"

Did he want to say it? Admit to it? His Kevlar vest had prevented the kid from killing him, but he still felt like he'd died that day. His life had been snatched away when those two 9mm bullets pounded his chest. He'd felt less than himself ever since. He was hollow. There was only one way to restore himself. He had to find the kid and get his weapon back.

It hardly made sense even to him, so how could he tell Murphy? Murphy was an old hand at this. He was a seventeen-year veteran who said he'd seen it all. But had he seen this? Would he understand what Webber was going through? Webber tried to put it in terms the guy could understand.

"I want to bring the guy in."

"That's natural, but don't let it get to you. You survived, and you have the whole SFPD behind you. They want a piece of this guy as much as you. We'll get him for you. Look at what happened when Garcia got shot in the Haight. All of us were out there looking for that son of a bitch, you included, and we got him. This is no different. Take my advice. You've got some days coming to you, so take them. Watch TV; catch up on *Springer* and *Judge Judy*. By the time you're back on the streets, we'll have the guy."

Webber tried to sound enthusiastic, but failed. "Sure. Whatever you say."

Murphy snatched the slugs from Webber's palm. "And take these to a jeweler and get them put on your keychain. They're your lucky charms. Hang on to them."

The shrink talked, and Webber fingered the charms in his pocket. She was probing again, trying to get him to open up like Murphy had tried the night before. He wanted to talk, but Murphy wasn't the right person to unload on. Neither was the shrink. She had the department's interests at heart, not his. The last thing anybody wanted, including Webber, was a cop running around with a nasty dose of post-traumatic stress disorder, but that wasn't his issue. He just wanted his life back. The shrink announced their time was up.

"So, Doc, am I cleared to go back to work?"

She looked Webber over before answering. "I think this event has hit you harder than you're willing to accept. You'll have to deal with it. You'll have no choice in the matter. Stress needs an outlet."

"Are you saying I'm going to go wacko?"

She shook her head. "I'm saying you're fine. I'm going to recommend that you return to active duty."

There was a but coming. He heard it in her voice.

"But, I'm also recommending that you continue visiting me once a week for the next month. You're holding back, and I don't want to let you go until I see that change. Now how does Thursday at three sound?"

He cursed himself as he left her office. The façade he'd put up hadn't allayed her suspicions. He would have loved to see her notes. Well, at least she was recommending him for activity duty. That was what he wanted. He needed to get back in the saddle.

But the saddle didn't fit as well as it once had. His colleagues treated him differently. Worse than that, he felt different. He saw spooks where there weren't any. They all had the same face—the kid with his gun.

On the second day of active duty, he called in and took two weeks off. He came by in person and used the opportunity to get the latest update on the case. No one had come up with much. They had no name on the perp. The liquor store he'd attempted to rob had failed to ID him from mug shots. The best they'd come up with so far was a video image taken from the liquor store's security tapes. It had made the TV news. He asked for one of the printouts.

"Why?" the detective had asked.

"Call it a memento."

Instead of resting, Webber spent long days knocking on the doors of gun stores and pawnshops. It was a long shot that the kid had tried to hock the gun. The video image and the gun with its serial number had been used in the newspapers and on TV. It was unlikely anyone would touch the gun now, but it didn't mean the kid wouldn't have tried. He didn't strike Webber as a criminal mastermind. Finally, his perseverance paid off.

"This is personal, isn't it?" Myles Cathcart of Cathcart's Armory asked.

"What makes you say that?"

"You guys have already been in here about this gun."

"Consider this a follow up."

"It was you this punk blindsided, wasn't it?"

"Look, do you have any information on this or not?"

"Okay, okay, don't get excited. I just want to make sure who I'm talking to."

"Now you know."

Cathcart shrugged. "No, I haven't seen your guy. If I had, I would have turned him in. I do my level best to keep on the right side of the law, got me? You guys made a mistake advertising that guy on TV. Now, he can't take the gun anywhere, except underground."

It was a good point. "Who would he go to?"

Cathcart asked for a business card. Webber handed him one, and Cathcart wrote an address on the back with a name. Webber examined the information.

"Do I tell this Friedkin you sent me?"

"Not unless you have to, and if you do, tell him you roughed me up."

"Will do."

Webber had to put off visiting the person Cathcart had given him in favor of his appointment with the shrink. They talked, covering the same topics as before. By the time he left her office, it was the height of rush hour. He crept along with the traffic until he reached the 10th street address underneath the 101 off-ramp. Parking wasn't hard in this part of the SOMA district. There was no reason for most people to come here. None of the businesses were active, not to the general public leastways. Not all parts of the SOMA district fell into the trendy, rejuvenated portions.

Derelict cars littered the streets, except for a very respectable-looking Mercedes sedan parked in front of Friedkin's address. The custom wheels would have bought the block. Obviously, Friedkin didn't live here. He knocked on the door to what was once an antique furniture store. No one answered, but Webber had the distinct feeling he was being watched and spotted a CCTV camera from inside the store aimed his way. He waited for action but none came. He pulled out his shield and pressed it against the glass door in clear view of the camera. A moment later, the door unlocked. He let himself in, passed by the fake store, and opened another door to the rear of the place.

"Stop right there," a voice cloaked in shadows instructed.

"I've come to see Friedkin."

"What do you want?"

"Information, to begin with."

"To begin with?"

"If you can help, I might need your services."

Silence filled the shadows. If Webber hadn't flashed his badge, he might have been scared. They were considering their next move, but he doubted it had anything to do with killing him. They wouldn't kill a cop in their own backyard.

"You're that cop, aren't you?" the voice said. "The one that got shot."

"Yes."

"So this is a private matter we're talking about."

"Very private. Very personal."

"Come up then."

Webber followed the figure up a flight of stairs and through a door into an office. He caught the closing door. It was made from steel. He was entering a strongbox.

Two men were in the windowless room. An elderly man with little muscle tone and even less hair sat behind a Chinese lacquer writing desk that was in beautiful condition. Webber put the man's age in his early seventies. The voice turned out to be a man of similar age to Webber. He was very unassuming—the kind of guy most people wouldn't give a second glance. Webber did though. The guy possessed an average build and dressed in nondescript clothing, but underneath, he was a coiled spring, all bottled potential energy just waiting for someone to tug out the cork.

"You're Friedkin?" Webber asked the older man.

"I am."

"Has this person come to you?" Webber pulled out the artist's rendering of the kid that shot him and went to give it to Friedkin, but he had his hands up already.

"First things first."

The voice came over and patted Webber down, then removed his jacket and shirt, exposing his bruise-stained chest. Webber made no objections.

"He's clean," the voice said and stepped back.

"As you can appreciate, I have to take every precaution."

"Totally understandable," Webber said and redressed himself.

"You didn't bring a weapon," Friedkin remarked.

"I don't need one to ask a question."

Friedkin smiled and asked for the picture. He put on his narrow spectacles, brought the picture close to his face, and studied it for a long while.

Webber looked over at the voice. He had fixed him with an unwavering stare.

"Have you seen him?" Webber asked Friedkin.

"Yes."

"When?"

"Why the interest?"

"You've seen the bruises, why do you think?"

"And this has nothing to with an official investigation?"

"Like I said, this is very personal."

Friedkin pondered the point for a moment and satisfied himself. "Yes. He came in here the day after the shooting. He tried to offload the Glock."

"Do you have it?"

"Like I said, he tried to offload the Glock. I stay current. I knew the gun was hot. I told him to hurl it off the Bay Bridge."

"Does this kid have a name?"

"Yes."

"Can I have it?"

"Yes, but I have conditions. I'm sure you can appreciate that a person in my position can't be seen to roll over at the first sign of a badge." Friedkin waited for Webber to comment, and when Webber didn't, he carried on. "I won't give you information, but I'll trade information."

"What is it you want to know?"

"Nothing yet, but I'm sure a time will come when I'll need something from you."

"I'm a street cop. I don't walk on carpet. What I know is limited."

"Of course, but someday I may need a favor. Do we have an understanding?"

Friedkin was a snake, Webber decided. If he agreed to the snake's terms, he'd be selling his soul to this criminal. Unfortunately, that was the price of doing business in this matter. "Yeah, we have an understanding."

Friedkin smiled. "Good. You're looking for Brandon Manning. I believe he lives over in Potrero Hill, I don't know where, but you'll find him working at Fisherman's Wharf during the day."

"Doing what?"

"Picking pockets. Pushing stolen merchandise. Selling fake Rolexes and Chanel perfume. Brandon has many talents. I believe he was moving up to knocking over liquor stores, but after his run-in with you, I think he'll stick to what he knows best in the short run."

Webber reached inside his for his wallet. He pulled out a wad of fifties and began counting them out on Friedkin's desk.

"You have no need to pay," Friedkin said. "We have a trade agreement."

"I'm not paying for the information. I'm buying a weapon from you. If Brandon didn't take your advice and still has my Glock, I want to protect myself."

"What do you want?"

"Something untraceable."

Two hundred dollars got Webber a throwaway in the form of a six-shot .32 automatic pistol produced by Davis Industries. It was small, cheaply made, poorly maintained, and likely to blow a hole in his hand the first time he pulled the trigger. It would do.

With the gun in his pocket, Webber checked in with the shrink. She picked away at him with her noninvasive manner. She liked his answers this time around. She wasn't going to let up on his sessions until the month was up, but she was positive about his recovery. Leaving the office, he wondered what he had said different to warrant her optimism. He considered his answers and it came to him. She was positive because he was finally positive. He was doing something about his problem and wasn't leaving it in the hands of Murphy or the others at the SFPD. He hadn't mentioned this to her, but his attitude must have shown.

Feeling good about himself and his luck, he went down to Fisherman's Wharf. It was late afternoon and the tourists were out but Brandon Manning wasn't, so he went home. He spent the evening there, screening his calls through his machine. Murphy called around eight to ask him to join him and a few others at the Tara Hills. He fought the urge to go, fearing that he'd tell them about Manning. Once they knew, SFPD would pick him up in a heartbeat and Webber didn't want that. He wanted to be the one to find him. He needed to be the one to find him.

The tourists started trickling into Fisherman's Wharf around nine in the morning. There wasn't a lot of action, so he wasn't surprised he didn't see Manning. He spent a couple of hours wandering up and down the piers, stopping for coffee and a snack, waiting for the main flood of tourists to wash in.

Just after noon, Webber spotted him. He felt his presence before he saw him. Something preternatural in him sensed the kid. He put it down to his subconscious picking up on Manning's mannerisms or movements. Regardless, he picked out the punk in the crowd like someone had shone a spotlight on him.

Manning was standing in line with the dozens waiting to buy

tickets for the Alcatraz tours. When everyone inched forward, Manning picked the back pocket of the man in front with practiced skill and natural finesse. Manning slid the tourist's wallet up the sleeve of his baggy hoodie. He completed the theft by bitching about the wait and busting out of the line. He checked over his shoulder to make sure he'd gotten away with his crime and transferred the wallet to his own pocket.

Webber shadowed Manning's escape as he headed along Jefferson toward the Marina District. Webber liked that. The gaudy attractions of Fisherman's Wharf trickled out by Ghirardelli Square, and the tourists never ventured any farther. He would have Manning to himself.

Manning's hood was up. It was a stupid move, in Weber's opinion. Sure, witnesses would find it hard to recognize Manning if called on, but wearing it created a huge blind spot. Webber used the blind spot to creep up on Manning, and the dumb son of a bitch never even noticed.

Turning up Leavenworth, Manning stole a look over his shoulder. Webber failed to react in time, and the kid noticed him. He hesitated before turning back around and continuing up the steepening street. Webber wondered if Manning had recognized him. Considering his gait, Webber didn't think so. Panic hadn't crept into the kid's stride. But Webber couldn't take a chance, so he moved in.

He broke into a jog and threw an arm around Manning's shoulder. "Hey, Brandon, how's it going?"

Confusion and shock contorted Manning's expression. Webber jammed the .32 against Manning's ribs.

"Recognize me, don't you?" Webber asked with a leer.

Manning stiffened. "Hey, man, I didn't know. I didn't know."

"You didn't know what?"

"About the gun. I didn't think it would fire." His voice jumped a couple octaves.

"Jesus, you can't even lie straight. You pulled the trigger twice.

Pulling it once is an accident. Twice is intent."

"Yeah, yeah, you're right. I want to turn myself in."

Manning wasn't as dumb as Webber had thought. He recognized that this wasn't a conventional bust.

"It's a bit late for that. We have to do things differently now."

"Yeah, sure. Whatever you say."

"Where's my gun?"

"At my place. I tried selling it, but that piece is white hot. No one wants anything to do with it."

"Take me to it."

"Sure thing, man. Just take it easy with that thing."

Webber ground the little .32 against Manning's ribs to let him know his advice wasn't needed. He didn't have to worry about spectators. He'd bided his time. Foot traffic was occasional. Cars slipped past and if they thought they saw anything suspicious going down, they were a block away and by then, it was too late to do anything about it. Nobody stops to turn around in San Francisco traffic when it's moving.

Manning told him that the gun was at his place on Potrero Hill. Webber's car was parked at the Bay Bridge end of the Embarcadero. It was too far to walk, and Webber couldn't afford take a cab ride with Manning and be remembered being with him. He cursed his own shortsightedness. This was a two-man job. He wished he'd confided in Murphy.

"Got a friend?" Webber asked.

"What?"

"Got a friend? A scumbag like you that you can trust. A friend."

"Yeah."

Webber dragged Manning to a phone booth, shoved in two quarters, and told him what to say. Manning dialed someone called Link. Link got curious and asked questions. Manning, at the .32's urging, slapped Link down.

"Just do as you're damn well told," Manning barked. "You feel me?"

The phone call over, Webber led Manning to the drop point, Black Point Battery at Fort Mason. It was a secluded point that attracted only the occasional visitor to sit on its single bench. A few joggers traipsed by, too intent on their run to take notice of anything around them. He shoved Manning into the surrounding trees to keep out of sight while they waited for Link. Manning broke the silence that had built up between them.

"What happens when you get the gun back?"

"You'll find out."

"You ain't reporting this. No way. I can dangle after you get your piece back, right?"

"I'm not reporting you."

Manning sniggered. "Yeah, I didn't think so. The embarrassment factor, right? This is all about your cop pride, isn't it?"

Webber ground his teeth. Manning was getting cocky.

"You should have seen your face before I pulled the trigger. You knew it was coming. You thought you'd seen your last sunrise."

Webber jerked out the .32 and pressed it against Manning's eye. "Did I look anything like the way you look now?"

That shut Manning up.

Link arrived a few minutes later in a battered Grand Am. He drove up to a trashcan next to the sign for Black Point Battery, as instructed. He looked around him before he powered down the window and dropped a cloth-wrapped parcel in the can. He didn't wait for an okay and drove off.

When the Grand Am was out of sight, Webber sent Manning ahead of him down to the trashcan. He kept the .32 trained on the center of Manning's back just in case he got courageous.

"Take it out," Webber said. "Nice and easy."

Manning reached inside the can and removed the parcel, holding it like he was holding precious jewels.

"Show me."

Manning peeled back the paisley rag to reveal Webber's gun. Webber took the weapon and took a piece of himself back. He tucked the Glock into his waistband. It felt good—right.

"So we're cool, yeah?" Manning asked.

No, they weren't. Claiming his weapon back healed only one part of the hole created by Manning. Manning had to do one more thing to make amends. Webber indicated with the .32 to move back into the trees.

"Hey, man, we're done."

"We're done when I say we're done. Now, move."

Manning did as he was told and returned to their hiding place.

"What more do you want?"

"I want to take from you what you took from me."

"I gave you the gun back, didn't I?"

He didn't get it. Just the way the shrink didn't get it. Murphy might have understood, but he'd never gone through what Webber had gone through. None of them had.

"Keep moving."

"No, man."

Manning dug in his heels like a little kid. That was fine. They were far enough in that they wouldn't be seen from the street. They would be heard, but that couldn't be helped. Webber swiped the .32 across the back of Manning's head. It lacked the mass to do any real damage, but he fell to his knees all the same. Webber pushed him onto his face with his foot. Manning rolled onto his back. Webber held Manning in place with the .32 aimed at his face.

"What? What do you want?"

"My life."

"What?"

"You killed me. The vest might have stopped the bullets, but you killed me all the same. You meant for me to die, and I did."

"You're alive."

"Not really."

"Sorry. Is that what you want to hear? Will that make things better?"

"No."

"Then what will?"

"This."

Webber fired once and put a hole in Manning's face. The report registered on the car backfire level. It was loud enough to draw attention but not someone's curiosity.

Seeing Manning dead restored Webber. It filled the void and repaired the damage. He was himself again. He could move on.

He left Manning where he lay. It didn't matter who found him or when. Nothing would lead the investigators back to him. He returned to his car and drove out to the Golden Gate Bridge. He parked at the observation center on the Marin county side of the bridge and walked back across the span. When he got a third of the way across, he stopped. When no one was watching, he tossed the .32 and the Glock through the railings.

A father of a family of British tourists caught a flicker of something going over the side. "Make a wish?" he asked.

"Yeah," Webber answered, "and I think it came true."

The Fall Guy

Part 1: Fender Bender

Todd raced back to his car, cursing the ATM all the way. Why was there always a line? His job packing boxes for a firm in Oakland wasn't much, but he didn't want to lose it by being late again. They'd find a way of firing him sooner or later anyway. Although a monkey could do his job, they'd be better off hiring one. His workmanship, even by his own admission, sucked. But this was his plight. When it came to him and jobs, they never lasted. Okay, he lacked the interest, but irrespective, he also lacked the skill set for any job he undertook.

He hopped back into his car, glad not to see a parking ticket glued to the windshield, and crunched it into reverse. The Honda Accord was way overdue for an overhaul, although an overhaul wouldn't do much for its ancient transmission. It was toast. Half the time, he didn't know what gear he was selecting. The Accord stuttered in the parking spot.

"Get in there, damn it."

Gears snarled as Todd struggled to find a forward gear. He jumped off the clutch and the car leapt backwards, slamming into a Porsche Boxster's headlight.

"Shit," he muttered.

His antics had drawn quite a crowd, and they'd all witnessed his screw-up. *Nowhere to run*, he thought. He found first gear without effort and eased the Accord forward to assess the extent of the damage.

Everyone had an opinion and had no problem telling him where he'd gone wrong and how much it was going to cost him. He crouched in front of the Porsche and picked at the broken headlight and buckled bumper. There was a couple hundred dollars of damage to the average car, but on the German exotic, he was looking at thousands. His car, the piece of shit that it was, didn't exhibit any signs of damage—just like Todd, who didn't exhibit any signs of insurance.

"Does anyone know who the owner is?" Todd asked.

No one did.

"You'll have to wait," someone suggested.

"I can't. I'm late for work."

"I don't think you have much choice," someone else said.

"I can't. I've been late twice this week already." Todd delved inside his car for a scrap of paper and a pen. "I'll leave a note."

He wrote: *People think I'm leaving you my contact and insurance details. I'm not. Sorry.*

Todd folded up his note, wrote sorry on the outside, and stuck it under the windshield wiper. He shrugged, hopped inside the Accord, and raced off.

He felt guilty for shafting the Porsche driver, but at the same time, he was buzzing with the thrill of his lawlessness and his speedometer showed it. He was accelerating past forty-five on Telegraph. He took a deep breath and eased off the gas.

In the scheme of things, what he'd done wasn't so bad. It was an accident, and it was more likely the Porsche driver's insurance could afford the repairs than he could. *Anyway, with a car like that*, he thought, *you're asking for trouble*. Todd pulled into his employer's parking lot, safe in the knowledge that the matter was over.

Todd liked to take Sunday mornings easy. He lounged in bed until ten then took a walk to the newsstand to pick up the Sunday paper. He wandered back through the apartment complex, pulling out the color supplement and flicking through the magazine, ignoring the front-page splash about some big drug bust. He took a different route back to his apartment and passed close to his assigned parking space. He slowed as he got close to his car. At first, he'd thought his windows had steamed up overnight, but the weather conditions hadn't been right for that. As he closed in, he realized he'd been way off. Every one of the Accord's windows had been smashed and all four tires had been slashed. He ran a hand over the scarred paintwork. A hook end of a crowbar protruded from the front windshield, and a note was sticking out from under a wiper. He pulled it out and read it: "Guess who?"

Todd didn't need to guess. He hadn't forgotten about the fender bender, but it had been days since it happened, and he thought it was over, a stunt that would dissolve in his memory over time. Well, he just found out his stunt was insoluble.

He'd screwed up this time. Someone must have taken down his license plate before he'd driven away. He was going to pay big for this one. He tugged out the crowbar and tossed it on the backseat through a glassless side window.

Returning to his apartment, a thought dogged him. Someone may have reported him to the police or the Porsche driver, but how did the Porsche driver know where he lived? He opened the door to his apartment.

"Mr. Todd Collins, I presume," the small man said, getting up from Todd's couch.

Two linebacker types, one black, the other Hispanic, flanked the small man. The small man seemed genial, but the linebackers looked ready to tear Todd's head off. He could have bolted, but judging by the bulges under the three men's jackets, he didn't expect to get far. He guessed he was meeting the owner of the Porsche.

"I'm Todd Collins." Todd stepped inside the apartment and closed the door.

"Do you know who I am?" the small man asked.

Todd went to say, "The Porsche owner," but decided against it. He thought it best not to antagonize the situation any more than he had already. He shook his head, finding that his vocal chords had failed him.

"Good. That makes things simpler. It's probably not a good idea that you do. It's only important that I know who you are. Understand?"

Todd nodded.

"I bet you're wishing you'd left your insurance details now, aren't you?" the small man said.

"I can make up for it. I can pay."

The small man held up a hand and shook his head. "It's far too late for that." He looked Todd up and down. "Besides, I doubt you could afford to pay. The damage is incidental, but the consequences of your misdemeanor have been severe. Put the newspaper down."

Todd, confused at first, hesitated before doing as instructed. He placed the newspaper on the chipped coffee table. The small man separated the newspaper from the supplements and opened it out. He tapped the front page with the back of his hand.

"See what you've done."

Todd glanced at the headline: Drug Dealer Busted During Routine Traffic Stop.

"The car you hit belongs to an employee of mine. Driving home the other night, he was pulled over for a busted headlight. The cops discovered two kilos of cocaine in his possession. He's in a lot of trouble, and I'm minus an employee, not to mention a lot of money. Do you see now? Do you see what you've done and why it has led us to your door?"

"I'm sorry."

"That's not important."

"I didn't know."

"I wouldn't expect you to know. But I've lost a valuable employee who had a job to do. Now he can't do it. This is where you come in." The small man stabbed a finger in Todd's direction.

Todd's stomach twitched. He didn't like what was coming. He knew it was retribution for what he'd done, but it wasn't the kind he wanted. Points on his license and a fine he could accept. He'd even take a beating. But the small man's kind of retribution filled Todd with dread.

"Me?" Todd stammered.

"Yes. You'll have to fill in."

The linebackers wrinkled their noses. They knew Todd wasn't the right man for the job, and he agreed with them.

"What do you want me to do?"

The small man beamed. "That's the attitude. These two said I was making a mistake."

The linebackers frowned.

The small man dug in his pocket and threw a set of keys to Todd. Todd caught them and examined them.

"Those fit a black Jag. You'll find it outside Danko's restaurant in the city. Bring it to me in Oakland."

"When?"

"Oh, I like you. I debated about just beating the crap out of you, but I wanted to give you a chance to make up for your error, and you've done that. You've assessed the situation and decided to stand by your mistake. I admire that." The small man stood and dropped a note on Todd's newspaper. "Bring the Jag to me tonight. Addresses are on the paper. See you at midnight."

The black linebacker brushed Todd aside to open the door. It was a petty gesture, but Todd wasn't going to tell him that.

Todd grabbed the small man's arm on his way out. The small man stared at Todd, his look piercing. Todd knew enough not to touch him, but he didn't care. He knew what was being asked of him was illegal. He just needed to know how illegal.

"Will I find drugs in that car?" Todd demanded.

The linebackers stiffened. The small man nodded at his arm. Todd released his grasp.

"Unfortunately, you don't have a choice, Todd," the small man said, his tone barbed. "Be at the Oakland address at midnight."

Todd resorted to public transportation to get him into San Francisco, seeing as the linebackers had finished off the Accord. He was looking at a couple of thousand to replace the tires and windshield. It was cheaper to get another car.

A combination of BART, MUNI, and good old-fashioned walking brought him out on the corner of Bush and Powell. Danko's was classy and unique for the city. It had its own parking lot. Strictly, it wasn't a parking lot. To the right of the restaurant was a dead-end alley, which had been cordoned off to make a parking lot. Two valets protected it. They looked as if they were relations of the small man's linebackers. Obviously, the small man was making Todd work hard to make up for the fender bender. It wasn't going to be easy, but it was doable.

He breezed on by the restaurant, counting his steps, then turned right at the next block onto Powell. He turned right at the next cross street and counted his steps again. When he counted eighty-seven, he stopped in front of a narrow apartment block that looked squeezed by its neighbors. The door was locked, but there was a buzzer entry system. Todd pressed the first one his finger fell on.

"Yes," a woman answered.

"Pizza delivery," Todd said.

"We didn't order any pizza," she barked.

"Sorry, is this 3A?"

"No, 4A, moron."

"Sorry. Can you buzz me in?"

She growled, and the door clicked.

Todd let himself in and bounded up the first flight of stairs. The good news, as he had hoped, was the landing window opened out onto the restaurant's alley parking lot. The bad news was that there were no fire escapes. They were all on the front of the building. He flicked the safety latches and slid the window open. Surprisingly, it opened with ease.

One of the valets trotted up the alley to collect a Range Rover. Todd waited until the SUV and owner were reunited, then he climbed onto the ledge and jumped out. He connected hard with the ground. Electricity crackled through his legs, intensifying in his groin. He bit back a scream and crumpled onto his knees. The valets didn't notice him. They were too busy hustling for a tip. Todd crawled behind the nearest car to survey the lot.

Todd had a new problem. There were two black Jags in the parking lot, one a XK8, the other an S-type. The small man had told him to pick up a black Jag, but he hadn't told him the model or license number. He fumbled in his pocket for the keys. He aimed the remote in the direction of both cars and pressed the unlock button. The S-type chirped and blinked its lights. The valets whipped around at the noise. Todd burst out of the shadows, charging for the Jag. The valets did likewise. Todd was lucky on two counts. First, the valets were big, but not fast, and second, he was closer.

He reached the car, jumped in front of the wheel, and gunned the engine, all before the valets were halfway to him. He cranked the steering and hit the gas. The Jag leapt forward, smearing its fender across the back of a Lincoln Navigator, setting off its alarm. The Jag bounced off another car before he gained control.

One of the valets raced back to the gates while the other blocked the alley with his body. He made himself wide by crouching and splaying out his arms. If they were playing chicken, Todd knew he had the upper hand and floored the gas.

"Time to jump, buddy," Todd said, grinning.

Todd's grin slipped when he realized the second before he hit the guy that the valet wasn't going anywhere. He smashed into the windshield and disappeared over the roof.

The remaining valet had closed the gates, but hadn't locked them and Todd blasted them open. They slammed back against the side of the restaurant, busting its neon sign. Todd jumped on the brakes to prevent the Jag from slamming into the apartment block opposite. Traffic slithered to a screaming halt, and he floored the gas pedal, fishtailing down the street and jumping the first red light he hit.

His heart out-revved the S-type. Neat adrenaline raced through his veins, and sweat poured off him. Heading toward the Bay Bridge, his grip on the steering wheel softened, and his foot eased off the gas.

He laughed. His panic and fear changed into exhilaration and excitement. His crime-fueled buzz was hard to deny. He liked being a criminal. It beat stacking boxes.

The drop-off point was in Oakland's warehouse district, near the rejuvenated Jack London Square, except the address wasn't in the fancier end of the neighborhood. Todd pulled up in front of a whitewashed building that was in desperate need of a fresh coat. The building had an address, but no sign giving any clues as to its business.

Todd got out of the Jag and banged on the rollup door. Before he was finished banging, the door retracted. He hopped back into the S-type and drove the car in.

The warehouse's interior was in marginally better condition than the exterior, but was well lit. The place was barren, except for a scattered collection of Snap-On tool chests and half a dozen car lifts. Cars Todd couldn't afford occupied the lifts. The small man stood in the middle of the warehouse floor with the familiar linebackers and a few new friends. Todd parked and got out.

"Christ! What the hell have you been up to?" The small man examined the busted headlight and scarred paintwork. "Do you do this to all the cars you drive, or just mine?"

The rollup door closed with a bang. The noise echoed off the walls.

"It wasn't easy getting the car out. You didn't say anything about stealing it."

"I didn't say anything about smashing it up either. Or were you just trying to impress me?"

"Sorry." Todd didn't know what else to say.

The small man waved the issue aside. "Don't worry, I just wanted the car back. The condition is unimportant. Dalton, park that thing."

The black linebacker shifted the Jag over to the lifts, and the rest of the hired help set about stripping the car.

"Are we square? Can I go?" Todd sounded tired, more tired than he felt.

"Not yet." The small man patted Todd on the shoulder. "You're close. There's just one more thing before accounts are squared away. Vasquez, give him the keys."

The Hispanic linebacker tossed a set of keys to Todd, and he caught them.

"Those fit that Lexus over there. I want you to drive it to Dallas."

"Texas?"

"The one and only. Don't look so worried. This job is a lot easier than the last one. All you have to do is drop it off at Ruskin's. It's a dealership. Your contact is Charlie Ruskin. Then you're done, and our business is concluded."

"That's a good two day drive. I can't do that. I have a job."

The small man's irritation evaporated his grin. He yanked out an automatic pistol and jammed it in Todd's face. "You drive or you die. Your choice. You've cost me a lot of money, and I think I've been damn charitable giving you this chance to redeem yourself. So what's it to be?" He snapped the safety off the pistol.

"Drive," Todd managed.

"Good. You said two days, but I'm going to be generous. You have three days to get this car to Texas."

The preamble was over. A minute later, he was on the road, Texas bound. The euphoria he felt stealing the Jag seeped away with the prospect of the boring drive ahead of him. The small man had really screwed him this time. He'd given him a schedule that meant no time to pack any clothes or leave a message. He hit the road as he was dressed. He couldn't blame the small man too much. If he'd done the right thing in the first place, he wouldn't be on I-580 now.

"You're a dumb, dumb man, Todd," he said to himself and turned the radio up.

The miles passed swiftly at that time of night, but compared to the length of the drive, he seemed to be crawling. Fatigue got to him by the time he reached the Arizona state line, and he pulled off the highway and slept in the car. The sleep did little to rejuvenate his spirits. The small man's vice grip around his nuts forced him to drive hard. His fellow freeway users received no charity from him. They were on his road and in his way. He flashed his high beams when someone moved into his lane and never conceded an inch to anyone who wanted to merge or change lanes. He didn't stop to eat or drink. He took a piss when he filled up with gas. His bad mood lasted as far as New Mexico.

Evening was descending, and he was driving into another night. His stale breath cloyed at the back of his throat to the extent that he could taste its noxious odor. His BO was so ripe that its stench permeated the inside his skull. He'd washed up as best he could in a gas station restroom, but his clothes were rancid. He pulled off at Gallup and raided a Wal-Mart for a change of under shorts and a couple of T-shirts. At a diner that boasted all-day breakfasts, he changed into his fresh clothes in the restroom and tossed the dirty ones in the trash. He decided to eat there too. Having only eaten his own stomach acid along with the junk food he'd gotten from gas stations, their sausage and egg skillet tasted like Heaven. He couldn't help but groan with pleasure with every swallow of coffee. He drooled over their pies, but resisted. He wanted to get on the road again. He'd spent too long indulging himself. Besides, on a different day under different circumstances, this meal would have rated only a couple steps above pet food.

He hit the roads in good spirits, which improved the closer he got to the Texas state line. Sure, he'd screwed himself with the small man, but that would soon end. Texas was a big state, but he'd be in Dallas by this time tomorrow, and then he'd be a free man again. It didn't matter that he didn't have any way of getting back to the Bay Area. All that mattered was that he would be out from under the small man and wouldn't that first inhale of air taste sweet? Forgetting himself, he took in a practice breath. It jolted him from his reverie.

The Lexus's interior stunk with his odor. He wouldn't be surprised if it had impregnated the vehicle linings and leather seats. If Ruskin's couldn't get it out, the small man would exact his wrath.

Sweat, hot and persistent, leaked out from under his arms and down his spine, ruining his fresh clothes. The hairs on the back of his neck bristled and gooseflesh broke out underneath it. *Payback*, he thought. Delivering this car was payback for screwing over the small man. One of the small man's lieutenants had been taken down by Todd's mistake. Stealing one car and transporting another seemed like a small price to pay for the potential loss in revenue he'd caused and the subsequent heat provided by a police investigation as a result. It didn't make sense. It wasn't enough. The small man wouldn't let him get off this easily. What Todd had done hardly measured a pound of flesh. There had to be more.

He sniffed the car's rank air again. It didn't smell right. He powered down the windows for twenty minutes and let the night air flood in and wash the stink away. When he powered the windows back up, he sniffed again. The smell was still there, just as pungent and persistent, and it didn't smell like sweat or bad breath.

His hands trembled as a thought punctured his brain. He fought to keep them steady. At the first off-ramp, he pulled off I-40 and drove along some poorly maintained county road until he found an abandoned strip mall. He parked around back, out of view of passersby. He popped the trunk and walked to the rear of the vehicle. He didn't have to guess what he'd find. The stench rammed a fist through the sweet night air.

Shrink-wrapped in plastic was the contorted shape of a man. The corpse's bulging eyes and tongue pressed against the tight plastic. Decomposition had set about its merry work, and the body had bloated, stretching the plastic beyond the breaking point. The plastic seams had snapped in several places, letting out the stink. Even through the distortions, Todd recognized the dead man from his picture in the newspaper. He was the Porsche owner the cops had picked up after Todd had hit his car.

Todd sighed. The small man wasn't going to let this slide. Todd should have seen the setup. Stealing the Jag was merely a ploy to keep him busy while the small man took care of the Porsche driver. The cops would know the Porsche driver worked for the small man, and he couldn't let a loose end like that exist without cutting it off. The cops didn't know about Todd, but he was another loose end that needed trimming.

He wondered how this was supposed to go down. Had the small man set up a tit-for-tat sting? What and who was waiting for him in Dallas? The cops? Thugs? No one? For all he knew, Ruskin's dealership had nothing to do with the small man. Maybe the dealership was a name plucked from the Yellow Pages purely as a carrot for Todd to follow while the cops picked him up along the way.

Todd could have been angry, but he smiled instead. Credit where credit was due. The small man had almost put one over on him. Todd had been eager to believe he could climb out of the hole he found himself in and was willing to accept any crap the small man wanted to feed him. It had almost worked. He guessed highway cops were supposed to pick him up long before he reached the Lone Star state. Instead, luck, in its twisted and cruel form, had intervened. He was still in the game. He might just get away with it. He slammed the trunk down on the body. There was a lot to do.

Todd rejoined I-40. He had to get rid of the body and car. The car had to be on the hot list, but he couldn't dump it—not just yet. He consulted the maps he'd picked up in a gas station, then drove to Santa Rosa. It was a small town with an infrastructure just big enough to swallow up a stranger.

He pulled off at the freeway exit and trawled the downtown. He parked across the street from a chain motel he had no intention of staying at. He looked for security cameras in the parking lot. He didn't see any. It wasn't surprising. This was the New Mexico equivalent of Green Acres. Crime just didn't happen here. He scanned the rows of docile vehicles for a Lexus and found none. It would have been nice, but it wasn't important. Any vehicle would do. He dropped to his knees behind a rental car with Texas plates, jerked out his penknife blade, and unscrewed the license plate. Local plates were all he wanted. The cops would be looking for a Lexus with California plates. Okay, it wasn't perfect. An inquisitive cop would see through that, even expect that, but it was the best he could do under the circumstances. Stealing from a rental car also bought him some time. The renters wouldn't give the missing plate a second thought, not like if it had belonged to their own personal vehicle. Who would care? The renters wouldn't. They wouldn't know the license plate number even if Todd parked next to them. It was flawed, but close enough for government work.

Keeping to the shadows, Todd scurried back to the Lexus and swapped plates at a diner a couple of miles away. He stopped for coffee and time to think. Disposing the body had to be done right. He couldn't be rash. That would get him caught. No, he wouldn't dump the corpse tonight. Besides not having any tools, he didn't know where to dump the body. He needed somewhere remote, not only for today but for the next decade. No, he'd sleep tonight, tool up in the morning, spend the rest of the day finding a burial site, and dig a deep dark hole tomorrow night. He paid his check, and there was a confident bounce to his step on the way out.

He could have driven back to the motel where he'd lifted the license plates, but he decided against it. Fate didn't need tempting. He picked up the freeway again. He didn't have to be careful about the roads he used now. To the outside world, he was a Texas native in his Texas-bought Lexus, as long as they didn't look too closely.

He fancied staying the night in town for no good reason other than he liked the idea of sleeping in a bed. It sounded like a good plan. He settled into his drive. He switched on the radio and searched for a station that didn't play country or Mexican music. He couldn't find one and settled for country. He racked up the miles, listening to people having the kinds of troubles Todd only wished he had.

"You think that's bad," he said to the hapless cowboy lamenting the loss of his girl. "You should walk a mile in my shoes."

Headlights lit up the Lexus from behind, and Todd deflected his rearview mirror to shield his eyes. He'd thought it was some jerk who didn't know when to dip his high beams until he recognized the familiar outline of a police car. He hadn't seen them, not that he'd been keeping an eye out. He'd been playing it safe, keeping to the speed limit and using his turn signals. He shouldn't have registered on anyone's radar. All the spit in his mouth escaped to somewhere safe.

Now he wished he'd dumped the body back in Santa Rosa. He'd take the stint for grand theft auto and not bitch about it, but he didn't want to go down for the body too. Not that it would ever come to that. The small man would have connections. Todd would never see the inside of a courtroom. He held his breath, waiting for the light bar to burst into life and bathe him in red and blue.

But the lights never came.

The state troopers were checking the license plate with the one on the hot car list. It wouldn't match up. He thanked God he'd switched the plates already.

"I'm not the person you're looking for," he murmured at the car reflected in his rearview mirror. "Don't stop me. Go by."

As if by magic, the troopers granted his request. The driver killed the high beams and sped past.

Todd released a mammoth breath he'd been holding. That was too close for comfort. Time to get off the road for the night.

He pulled off at Tucumcari and checked into a motel. He had to show ID, but paid cash and hoped that wouldn't leave a trail for the small man or anyone else to find.

"No one pays cash these days," the sleepy-eyed clerk said.

Todd smiled. "Never a lender nor borrower be."

The clerk shrugged, handed Todd a cardkey, and went back to the TV he had playing behind him.

Todd found his room and slept the sleep of the innocent, so much so, he didn't wake until housekeeping knocked on the door. It was after eleven. He couldn't remember the last time he'd slept that well. He was sure this was a sign. A sign of what though?

He picked up a late breakfast at a drive-thru burger joint and tracked down the nearest hardware store. The Lexus stood out next to all the pickups, but there wasn't a lot he could do about that. He trawled the aisles with his cart and filled it with a pick and shovel and bunch of unnecessary crap for cover. The last thing he needed was to be remembered by the staff as the guy who bought a shovel then asked for directions to a large chunk of nowhere. So he made it look like he was a greenhorn handyman who watched too much DIY TV, embarking on a landscaping project he couldn't possibly pull off.

Standing in the checkout line, he examined the contents of his wallet. The hotel and this purchase drained him of most of his cash reserves. He'd have to make some money soon, but that would have to wait until the corpse was in the ground.

He paid and loaded up the Lexus. From his maps, the best place for a drug dealer burial was out at the parklands surrounding Ute Lake State Park. It was an hour or so from Tucumcari using the local highways. After last night's run-in with the state troopers, Todd wanted to avoid the freeways.

He reached the state park by mid-afternoon. He left the Lexus on the road and explored the areas north of the park on foot. If anyone came snooping, Todd had his cover story. *Sorry, Officer. I drank three cups of coffee, and nature took its course. You know how it is when you're miles from anywhere. I had to go somewhere.*

He climbed a small rise and surveyed the land around him. The place defined nothingness. Wildness spread in all directions marred only by the empty roadway he'd traveled. It was stunning to think that the U.S. could still have places as unpopulated and undeveloped as this, considering how high property prices were in the Bay Area. Undeveloped or not, it was going to make for a perfect burial site.

Chain link fencing cordoned the land off from road users and signs stated the land was private property, but the land was so vast that the owners would need a herd of security officers to enforce the penalties threatened on the signs.

He didn't see much point in driving off and coming back under the cover of darkness. He busted off the padlock on the gate and drove through and relocked the gates with a padlock he'd brought with him. He picked his gravesite and parked the Lexus out of the view of the roadway. He retrieved the shovel and the pick from the car's trunk and broke ground. Digging a grave wasn't as easy as in the movies. This wasn't Hollywood dirt. The sun-baked ground yielded little to his pick. It bounced off the dirt leaving behind a minor dent in comparison to the effort he exerted. To soften the ground up, he poured all his bottled water onto the dirt. The thirsty earth sucked up every last drop without giving anything back in return. He was in no mood to be screwed over now when he was so close and smashed away at the ground until it finally succumbed.

The sun had long set and the day's heat was waning when he had a person-length hole just under two feet deep. It was a shallow grave fit for a drug dealer. How his blistered and bleeding hands and aching back wished that were true. But two feet wasn't anywhere deep enough. Scavengers would be chewing over the remains in no time. Six feet was too much to ask, but four, that sounded like a reasonable depth to him. It got no easier the deeper he dug. The ground was softer and gave way to his pick and shovel more readily, but it was a damn sight harder to hurl the dirt to the surface from that depth.

When the hole reached chest deep, Todd stopped. He tossed the shovel out of the hole and tried to straighten. His lower back screamed as each vertebrae failed to pop back into place. It took him three attempts to clamber out of the grave. How ironic would it be if he ended up digging his own grave? He imagined the small man would get a kick out of that.

He hefted the plastic-clad corpse from the Lexus. He possessed enough strength to lift the body over the seemingly mile-high trunk lip, but not enough to stop it from rolling out and crashing to the ground. On his knees, he rolled the dead drug dealer to the edge of the grave. He went to give the corpse one final roll when he stopped. He couldn't bury it with the plastic on. It would take forever to decompose. He'd have to remove the drug dealer from his packaging. It was a simple task, but Todd didn't relish it. The stink associated with releasing the three-day-old corpse from its shroud turned his stomach, but it had to be done. He retrieved the box cutter from his purchases and sliced open the plastic. He didn't allow time to psyche himself out of doing this. He just dropped to his knees in front of the corpse, stuck the blade in at the head, and ran the keen edge all the way down to the feet. There was no finesse or skill to this action, and he took no care to avoid cutting the clothes or the body. He held his breath as the stench poured from the rapidly expanding slit. He gagged, but the moment the body was free of the plastic, Todd rolled it into the grave. It struck the bottom of the hole with a satisfying thud.

Fluids rested in the folds of the plastic sheeting. Todd gagged again, and he kicked the plastic in with the body. There was no way he was taking that back with him.

The drug dealer's leaking residues galvanized Todd. He snatched up the shovel and thrashed at the freely dug earth, piling it back onto the stinking body. His disgust petered out when he'd filled the grave three-quarters full. After a short break, he piled on the rest of the dirt and smoothed it over. It looked pretty good, even under moonlight.

He fell behind the wheel of the Lexus and drove off the property. Hitting the road, he realized that half his problems were over. He just had to offload the car, and he was free. He wondered if the Lexus came with any papers—crooked or straight. He reached over to the glove box and popped it open. A nickel-plated .357 fell out into the passenger side foot well.

Todd slammed on the brakes. The gun slid across the carpeting. He picked it up. *Another present from the small man?* he wondered. He rifled through the glove box's contents. No registration, but there was a cell phone. The phone would come in handy. He switched it on and slipped it into the door pocket.

He examined the revolver. It was loaded and well maintained. He didn't like guns, but like the phone, it would come in handy. "You really want to see me burn, don't you?" he said to the absent small man and returned it to the glove box.

Todd went to pull away but hesitated. His gut churned. Something still wasn't right. It wasn't enough. He felt there was more. Anything less was beneath the small man. The car concealed another unseen surprise. He smelled it as strongly as he had the corpse.

He shined his flashlight under the car. Nothing dangled underneath, and he didn't find anything in the engine bay or hidden in the trunk. He turned his focus to the Lexus's interior. Still, nothing. He knew he wasn't wrong. His punishment wasn't over. Kneeling on the ground, he thumped the rear seat in frustration. His fist bounced off the rock-hard backseat.

He looked at his fist and the seat. His blow hadn't left a dent. This was a Lexus, a luxury car, providing quality and a refined ride for all its occupants. He felt that in the driver's seat, but not the rear. He examined the seat up close with the flashlight. The seams were machined stitched, but the stitching differed from the rest used in the vehicle.

"Gotcha," Todd said.

With the box cutter, he slit the seams. A cloud of white puffed up through the incision. The powder dusted the black leather. He wiped up the powder on his fingertips and tasted it. The powder tasted bitter with a medicinal kick. Moments later his tongue went numb where the powder had touched. He didn't recognize the taste but he knew what it was—cocaine. He smiled. It was fitting. He had to hand it to the small man. He knew how to twist the blade.

Todd spent the next twenty minutes carefully cutting open the backseat's leather to reveal six bricks of white powder, each weighing around a couple of pounds . If this coke was supposed to hang him, the small man had just screwed up tying the noose. He'd just made Todd rich. That euphoria passed the moment it arrived. He'd dug himself a big enough hole hitting that Porsche. What kind of shitstorm would he conjure up if he tried to push the small man's dope? He tossed the packets on the roadside, got in the car, and left two long tire marks getting the hell away from that accident waiting to happen.

He got a hundred yards. He left an equally impressive pair of tire marks stopping the Lexus. He couldn't leave all that coke on the highway. Like the gun, it was useful. Not to sell of course, but useful in other ways. That amount could be a valuable bargaining chip. He backed the Lexus up and stored the cocaine in the trunk with all the landscaping equipment.

He'd been on the road twenty minutes when the phone rang. He'd forgotten that he'd left it on. He answered it.

"There you are," said the small man. Todd almost choked on the sarcasm. "I would have thought you'd have dropped the car off by now. I was frightened you'd fallen off the radar."

"Yeah, well, I ran into a couple of problems."

"Tell me about them."

"Nothing to tell, seeing as you were the cause."

The small man laughed. "So you found my gifts."

"Some quite expensive."

"I know."

"Well, none of them were to my taste, so I gave them away."

"You shouldn't have done that. I would have taken them back."

"Too late now. They're all gone. No one will ever find them."

"I've misjudged you. You have an aptitude for this work. You've proven to be much smarter than I expected."

"Yeah, I know." Todd powered down the window and tossed the phone into the night. "And I'm getting smarter all the time."

Part 2: Detour

Todd's aching muscles woke him. Every one of them expressed their annoyance at their mistreatment and now exacted their revenge. He groaned when he rolled out of his motel bed. He'd checked himself in when he realized he didn't have to run anymore.

He schlepped over to the bathroom and stood under a shower for far too long. While the hot water picked away at his knotted muscles, he thought about the small man. This distracted him from the pain in his overworked body. He recalled the small man's final words before he tossed the cell phone out of the Lexus's window.

"You have an aptitude for this work."

Todd found it hard to disagree with this. Less than a week ago, he was working a dead-end job, going nowhere with his boring and annoying life, but now, who knew? His life was a blank sheet. He could do anything. He could relocate. Start afresh. Reinvent himself. He still had to get a few things out of the way first, namely the coke, the car, and the gun. The gun was easy. There were plenty of storm drains. He fancied trading the Lexus in. That would rectify his pitiful money situation. The coke. That was the tricky one. He'd vacillated over that one all during the drive and through the night. He could flush that shit down the drain or go into business for himself. One was a smart idea and the other was the worst known to man. There was an even more appealing idea. Use the coke to stick it to the small man. Yeah, he liked that. But that didn't have to happen over night.

Revenge took time. He needed to get the measure of his opposition. At this point, he didn't know jack about the small man, and that was like taking a ripe banana to a gunfight. No, the coke wouldn't get dumped down a drain or sucked up a nose. It would rest awhile.

He'd holed up in a place called Grassmore, a small town thirty minutes east of the Texas border. He checked out of the motel and drove into town where he breakfasted at a down-on-its-luck diner that served pretty decent food. He bought a cheap backpack at a drugstore and deposited the six packets of cocaine inside it. The pack weighed more than its twelve-pound cargo when he walked into the bus station with it slung over his shoulder. He expected everyone to instantly know what he was carrying. He nodded to the cop standing sentry at the main entrance to the station. The cop gave him scant regard. Todd found the lockers and stuffed the backpack in one. The locker slammed shut with a satisfying bang. He pocketed the key and slipped out of the station's side door.

That out of the way, it was time to say goodbye to his faithful steed, the Lexus. He tore a page out of the yellow pages listing dealerships and drove out to them. They all looked to be respectable. A respectable dealer wouldn't touch the car, especially with a shredded rear seat.

He needed a nonrespectable dealer, but where would he find one? On the rough side of town? He wouldn't know the rough side of town if it bit him on the ass. He picked up a local newspaper and flicked through the pages. The news loved to dish the dirt, and he found it. The Texan, a bar on the outskirts of town, had been busted again after two roughnecks took a bar fight to the next level. The winner of the battle was facing a manslaughter charge. The newspaper alluded to drug dealing and other crimes too heinous to mention. It sounded like the perfect place to move a hot car, as long as no one broke a pool cue over his head.

The Texan didn't reach simmer until eight o'clock that night, when a motley crew filed in to drown their sorrows. Todd struck up a couple of dead-end conversations at the bar at the cost of a couple of drinks. His stranger status closed verbal doors.

His latest shunning drew the attention of the bartender. He'd been watching her bartending prowess all night. She worked the bar with effortless efficiency and kept the clientele in check. Todd developed a large measure of respect for her, but this respect wasn't mutual, judging by the glare she shot him. They made eye contact, and she wandered over to him.

Todd cast an appreciating glance over her. He guessed she was in her late-forties, and she was clinging on to her good looks and figure by a thread. She'd thickened in the waist, and her sun-damaged skin could never be repaired, but she worked her remaining assets. Her bust was still to die for. She sported a number of tattoos on her wrists, biceps, and shoulder blades, and they looked to have adorned her skin long before tattoos proved to be en vogue with the pretty young things. Todd found her personality her most attractive trait. She exuded strength and self-assurance. She must have been a dynamite package in her day.

"Looking for a friend?" she asked in a tone that offered little friendliness.

"What makes you say that?"

"You've bought just about every idiot in here a drink."

"Is that a problem?"

"It can be, if you're buying those drinks for the wrong reasons."

"I'm just after a little help."

Some guy well on his way to drunkdom, although the clock had yet to chime ten, yelled out from three stools down, "Ginger, leave loverboy alone. I need a beer."

"And you can wait for it," Ginger barked back without taking her eyes off Todd.

The drunk looked wounded and sat back down. His drinking buddy patted him on the shoulder to console him.

"So why don't you tell me what you need?"

"I want to sell my car. I'm not local, I'm passing through, and I wanted the name of a dealer who wouldn't stiff me. Know anyone?" Todd threw in a smile to sweeten the deal.

He failed to melt Ginger's heart.

"If you're passing through, aren't you going to need that car?"

No pulling the wool over Ginger's eyes, but Todd had it covered. He'd spent the day coming up with cover stories. "The thing is costing me too much money. I'm working on a budget these days."

"Is that right?"

Todd nodded and tried the smile again with no success.

"I'm sure any dealer in town can help you out." She paused for effect. "Unless there's a reason why you can't go to any dealer."

Todd noticed how green her eyes were. Amber flecks acted as contrast to bring the green out even more. She noticed him looking at her eyes and not her "go to" tits. That seemed to smooth the edges a bit.

"You're right, I can't go to just anyone. I'm ducking a bad relationship, and the loan company still has dibs on the car. You know how those bastards can be when you're down on your luck. I'm looking for someone that's not too fussy about paperwork." Todd paused for dramatic effect this time, hoping for a little sympathy. "Can you hook me up?"

Ginger scrutinized him with a piercing stare that cut through bullshit at fifty paces.

"You know what I think?" she said.

"No. What do you think?"

"I think you're a cop."

If only she knew the truth. Todd shook his head in protest, but she ignored this and plowed on.

"This place has a bad reputation, and you sons of bitches want to find any excuse to shut me down, regardless whether you have to invent one or not."

"Look, honestly, I'm not a cop."

"I don't care. You're not welcome. Get out."

Todd pleaded his innocence again until Ginger reached under the bar for a small Billy club. This was coupled with a significant number of supportive patrons rising from their seats. He raised his hands in surrender and backed away toward the exit. He made it unmolested and broke into a jog when he felt the hot night air close its arms around him. Even though no one followed him out, he didn't slow up until his reached the Lexus. He got behind the wheel and gunned the engine.

Before he could leave a trail of dirt, a young Hispanic guy blocked his path. Unlike Ginger and many of her compadres, this guy possessed the build of a twelve-inch ruler viewed edge on. If he wanted to tussle, Todd liked his chances.

Seeing Todd hesitate, the kid raced to the passenger side and jumped into the seat next to him. "I heard what you said."

"Which was what?" Todd asked.

"You want someone to take this car."

Todd mulled over Ginger's assumption. The cops were looking to shut the Texan down and didn't care how they did it. Entrapment seemed like a minor twisting of the law, and this kid could be a cop. Ginger may have sized him up all wrong, but he had the measure of this kid. He wasn't a cop on his first undercover job. He could trust him.

"You know someone?"

"Yeah. Is it worth something to you?"

"Of course. Who?"

"Larry Vandrel. He'll take care of you."

The kid rattled off directions, which seemed simple enough to follow. Todd thanked the kid and pressed a twenty in his hand when he shook it. It wasn't much of a thank you, but it satisfied the kid, and he returned to the Texan's loving embrace.

The kid's directions took Todd out of town and past the residential areas into the desert. Vandrel had to be the real deal. The warehouse he worked out of, formerly an aircraft hangar at a disused landing strip, possessed no sign—just a security light spraying a cone of light in the darkness.

Todd pulled up next to a grime-encrusted tow truck and went up to the hangar doors. He thought he heard voices, but realized it was a radio playing. He leaned on one of the doors and slid it back. A good ole boy sporting bib overalls and a shotgun appeared from behind a car lift.

"Can I help you, son?"

Neither the gun nor the good ole boy's placid tone bothered Todd. He was beginning to take this kind of treatment in stride. "I'm looking for Larry Vandrel."

"You've found him."

"They tell me you take trade-ins."

This explanation failed to prompt Vandrel to lower his shotgun. He did take a number of measured steps to take him within range of Todd. If he set off the shotgun, it would punch a hole the size of a melon in Todd's chest. "And who exactly is they?"

"Some Hispanic kid at the Texan."

"This Mex got a name?"

"I didn't ask, and he didn't tell."

"I don't like unannounced arrivals. You should have made an appointment."

"Sorry, I didn't get your phone number."

Vandrel dropped the shotgun's muzzle to his side. "Let's see what you've got."

He brushed by Todd and looked over the Lexus. The security light failed to bring out the Lexus's best, and he instructed Todd to bring the sedan inside the hangar. Vandrel hit a switch, and a bank of florescent lights flooded the hangar. The light revealed rows and rows of vehicles in various states of disrepair. There looked to be a spray booth in the far corner.

Vandrel surveyed the Lexus, circling the car like he was examining an antique with his nose inches from the paintwork and his hands tucked behind him with the shotgun in his grasp. After he circled the Lexus three times, he straightened and faced Todd.

"Don't no one buy American these days?"

"I think Lexuses are made in the U.S."

"Don't give me that. A Jap car is a Jap car wherever it's built."

Todd let the subject of foreign trade drop. A heated debate could affect the final price.

Vandrel opened the rear passenger door and peered in at the shredded backseat. He paused in contemplation before slamming the door shut.

"So what's the story, son? Why have you driven all the way out to me?"

Todd fed him the same line he'd spooned to Ginger about the bad breakup and the repo man. Vandrel mulled the lie over.

"Finance companies. They're your friends when you're riding high and the enemy when you're on the skids," Vandrel said.

"Ain't that the truth."

"And the backseat?"

"Vandals. The bastards broke in and tore it up."

"They didn't go to town on it."

"They were probably disturbed in the act. I suppose I should count myself lucky."

"That you should. Anyway, it's getting late, and I still have things to do. Let's talk numbers. Blue book on this is around twenty grand, even with the torn-up backseat," he began.

Todd failed to hide his delight. Twenty grand would go a long way. It was the stuff that fresh starts were made from.

"But I'll give you five hundred," Vandrel finished.

Vandrel's punchline forced a gasp out of Todd. He should have known this wasn't going to be easy.

"If you're not interested, why don't you say, instead of wasting your time and mine?" Todd hadn't intended on unleashing such a venom-filled response, but Vandrel shouldn't have jerked him around. He brushed by the guy to get to the driver's door, but Vandrel blocked his path with the shotgun.

"Son, this car is worth five hundred bucks because it comes with twenty grand's worth of trouble attached to it. Correct me if I'm wrong."

Todd invoked his Fifth Amendment right and said nothing.

"I didn't think so," Vandrel said and lowered the gun. "Have you got papers for this vehicle?"

"No."

"Is there anybody looking for it?"

"Not in this state."

"That's good. That just tacked on a couple of hundred."

Seven hundred bucks. That wasn't worth wiping his ass on.

"So what's the real story on this?" Vandrel nodded in the direction of the Lexus.

Todd didn't see much point in bullshitting. Vandrel had it all worked out except for the finer details.

"As far as I know, the car's stolen, and I was supposed to deliver it to Dallas."

"Dallas? I don't know if you've noticed, but you're a half a day's drive from there. What changed?"

"Circumstances."

"Circumstances might just bite me just as hard as they've bitten you. I think I'll take that two hundred back."

"Back to five hundred then?"

Vandrel nodded. "I'll ask again. What's with the backseat?"

"An unexpected bonus for my time. It's gone. You don't have to know about it."

"But it sounds like I should worry about it. I'm getting the idea that I should keep my five hundred and let you be on your way."

Funny what a few minutes did. The five hundred deal had insulted Todd. Now he lamented its loss like an old friend. "If that's the way you want to play it, fine. I'll take my business elsewhere."

"Now then, cool your heels, son. What's your name?"

"Todd."

"Todd, I like you. Yeah, you can give me that look, but it's true. You're a straight shooter, and I appreciate that. I deal with a lot of scum. Not that that bothers me, mind. It comes with the territory. I find it refreshing to find someone who doesn't see bullshit as necessary as air. I'll tell you what. I'll give you ten grand for the Lexus. I know that's not what you were hoping for, but you're not in a position to bargain. You're in a hole, and me throwing you a line does me no favors unless you do something for me in return. Ten grand is good money, you've got to agree?"

Todd did agree. In all honesty, he was expecting a couple of grand and hoping for five. Ten, although not as pleasing to the ear as twenty, still possessed a natural beauty he could admire. But it also seemed generous to the point that it gave Todd pause. There was something coming and he speeded its arrival.

"Ten grand is very generous, considering the situation," Todd replied.

"Yes, well, the money isn't just for the vehicle."

"No?"

"No. You're going to have to do a job for me first."

"What job?"

As mayors went, Lyle Moran was no Rudy Giuliani. Then again, Dumont was no New York City. Four thousand souls called Dumont home, and the city clung to its incorporated status by its fingertips thanks to Moran. The town was so small, his mayoral status was a part-time position. Most of the city's services were subbed out to county agencies. Moran earned an income from his hardware store and after a hard day's graft from selling two-by-fours and chainsaws,

Dumont's residents could find their mayor at the Yellow Rose tavern. Despite this, Moran was a popular figure. He swapped near-the-knuckle jokes, slapped backs and, on occasion, the behinds of women a decade beyond their prime, and everyone loved him for it. Lyle Moran was the people's man, albeit a good couple of steps out of stride with the big city world. Being Dumont's mayor wasn't a sign of civic duty but a popularity contest, and Moran won hands down.

Todd came up with this assessment after shadowing Moran for a day and a half. He'd done a pretty good job fitting in. The unrelenting sun had darkened his skin and the absence of air-conditioning left a permanent shine of sweat. He disguised his stranger factor further by bunking down at Vandrel's chop shop instead of checking into a motel. He'd even managed to mimic the local accent. It was far from perfect. People knew he wasn't local but guessed he was from the vicinity. He wouldn't have gone to all this effort if the job Vandrel had given him had been of the wham, bam, thank you ma'am variety.

That was the easy part. The tough part was getting close enough to Moran to clean out his safe. Vandrel had been vague as to the reasons why he wanted Todd to rob Moran. Todd couldn't see how this man was connected to Vandrel, and he didn't care too much either. He just wanted the ten grand Vandrel had promised him.

Dusk was handing over the reins to night, and the Yellow Rose had been well patronized since quitting time. Country western music leaked from an aging boom box. Two ceiling fans stirred the hot air, failing to cool it. But no one seemed to mind the heat as long as Grady, the Yellow Rose's owner, kept supplying the beer.

Todd had concealed himself in the shadows. He was on his third bottle of Bud Lite and cleaning the bottom of a chili bowl. He wouldn't have credited Grady with the ability to come up with good Tex-Mex, but he pulled it off.

He'd done enough surveillance. It was time to make contact. He drained the Bud and approached the bar. He stood behind Moran and the three other guys he was shooting the breeze with. There was a gap at the bar rail for him to stand at, but he wanted to be noticed.

Moran, heavy from riding a barstool too often, felt Todd's presence at his shoulder and turned. He wiped back his thick graying hair, which had slipped across his forehead. "Can I help you?"

"No, I'm just after a replacement," Todd said and held up his empty bottle.

"I don't know you, do I?"

"No reason you should."

Grady acknowledged Todd's request and reached for a replacement.

"You could argue that I do have a reason."

"Why argue? It's too hot to argue."

Moran liked that one and laughed. Moran's drinking buddies laughed too.

"You're right. No reason to argue."

Grady handed over the beer to Todd. Todd reached for his wallet and fiddled with the bills.

"I've got this," Moran announced.

"You don't have to do that," Todd countered.

"I think it's only fair that the mayor buy everyone in town a beer."

"You're talking to the honorable Lyle Moran," one of Moran's buddies said.

"You're the mayor?"

"Three terms and counting," Moran said.

"That's very generous of you."

"Not really, that's how I get re-elected."

"I like a politician who's a straight shooter," Todd said and held up his beer to Moran.

This got another round of laughs from Moran and the boys.

Moran swiveled on his barstool to face Todd full on. He smiled, but his cool stare examined Todd with snake-like intensity. "Now that we've established who I am, who are you?"

Todd stuck a hand in Moran's direction. "Todd Collins."

Todd shook hands with Moran. His drinking buddies introduced themselves as Charles "Chuck" Baker, Theo Masterson, and J.G. Thorpe.

"Am I buying Dumont's latest voter a beer?"

"Sadly, no, I'm just passing through."

"Then I've got a good mind to ask for that beer back," Moran joked.

Laughs came fast and easy after that. Todd fell into a rhythm with Moran and his buddies. After twenty minutes, he was parked on a barstool next to them. He trotted out his cover story he'd spent the day inventing, and Moran and company bought it as gospel. It didn't take long for Moran's examining stare to recede. This gave Todd confidence to keep pushing with his cover story, but he kept it to the right side of cockiness. Moran might be on Todd's side now, but his radar would be scanning for slipups.

Last call came, and Todd eased himself off his barstool. The combination of too much beer and heat that squeezed the sweat out of him left him lightheaded when he took his first steps.

"Thanks for your hospitality, and I hope our paths cross again," he said.

"Where do you think you're going?" Moran asked.

"It's closing time."

"For the unfavored," Chuck remarked.

"Do you play poker?" Moran asked.

"Sure do."

"Then you're welcome to join us."

While Grady closed up, Moran led everyone to a back room filled with cleaning products and a card table at its center. They settled into a five-handed game of stud poker. Todd feared these guys were scamming him, but after ten minutes, he realized that not even card sharks played this badly. Todd could have cleaned them out, but he wasn't here for that. He followed their lead and lost enough hands to keep the game square.

In some respects, this was a high-powered game. Chuck ran a real estate agency, although Todd couldn't imagine he made much money at it in Dumont. J.G. doubled as the head of the Chamber of Commerce and owned a market on Main Street. Thorpe acted as city clerk while also being a practicing attorney. The game was an excuse to shoot the breeze. They talked about life and business. They probed Todd on his reasons for being in Dumont, and he fed them more of his cover story about working his way back to Oklahoma.

"Where were you looking to pick up work?" Moran asked, dealing fresh cards out for a new hand.

"Dallas."

"Have you thought of staying on around here for a spell?"

"No, offense, but I'm not sure your town can spare it."

"Oh, you'd be surprised. We can rustle up something to put a young man to work. Can't we, boys?"

A chorus of approval followed.

"If you've got work, then I'm happy to do it—whatever it is."

"Good. Then come by the hardware store in the morning. Say nine?"

Todd smiled. He'd hooked Moran. "Nine it is."

"You don't look any worse for wear," Moran said when Todd walked into Moran's Hardware. "Youth is kind to the young."

Todd nodded, careful not to disturb the hangover skulking in the recesses of his skull. Moran could decry the virtues of youth, but he looked real sharp for someone who had put away the amount of booze that he had, not to mention that Moran's Hardware had been open since seven. The guy couldn't have had more than four hours sleep. Todd leaned against the checkout counter from where Moran piloted a cash register with no customers.

"Fighting fit and raring to go?" Moran asked.

"Sure am. What do you want me to do for you?" Todd smiled, and his face ached.

"Not for me—not directly, leastways. Chuck's all ready for you."

"Chuck?"

"Yeah, I talked it over with him after the game. He's at his most persuadable about then. He gets real charitable when he's down a hundred bucks and full of bourbon."

Todd masked his disappointment well. His plan had just gone to the wall. He'd expected to work alongside Moran and when he had the man's confidence, he'd reward him by cracking his safe, just as Vandrel wanted. Time to switch to Plan B, which he'd put into action as soon as he thought of it. "Thanks, Lyle. I really appreciate it." Todd did well to keep the sarcasm out.

"Don't thank me. Chuck's the one paying you."

Todd returned to his pickup parked next to Moran's Cadillac CTS. *Not a bad set of wheels for this neck of the woods*, he thought and pulled out of the parking lot. He checked his rearview mirror and the reflected image of Moran's Hardware without a customer in sight. *How do you make your money, Lyle?*

Chuck's realty business wasn't hard to find. Nothing was hard to find in Dumont. Todd parked and walked in. Chuck's offices were small, taking up one half of a commercial unit shared with a coin laundry. Pictures of unsold properties hung in the window and for the most part, they'd always hang in the window. The office furniture, which included a secretary, dated back to the 80s.

Chuck looked how Todd felt, but Chuck put on a good front and was all smiles and bonhomie. He sat Todd down with a much-needed cup of coffee.

"Thanks for the job, Chuck."

"Don't thank me yet. You don't know what it is." He laughed his half-man/half-donkey laugh that Todd had acclimated to the night before.

"Doesn't matter. Work's work in my book."

Chuck slapped a hand down on his desk. "Good to hear. Not enough people have that attitude these days. Isn't that right, Jolene?"

Jolene nodded while her gaze remained fixed on the world outside the window.

"Like I always say, hard work never killed anyone," Chuck added.

"Unless you work for a bomb disposal unit," Todd tossed in.

It took Chuck a moment before his face lit up, and he laughed again, this time, three parts donkey to one part man. Once Chuck had dispensed with the anthropomorphic side of himself, he slid over a map and a stapled sheaf of papers.

"Up for a management job?"

Management job? Todd hadn't been expected that. "Yeah, sure."

"Good. You're my new Property Manager."

"Wow."

"Do you hear that, Jolene? The kid's excited."

"He sounds ecstatic," Jolene said, sounding anything but.

"Don't get too excited, Todd. The job sounds impressive, but it isn't," Chuck said with sincerity.

Don't sugarcoat it, Todd thought.

"The job is pretty simple. I maintain a number of rental and unoccupied properties. These need to be checked out regularly to ensure the renters haven't trashed the places and that unoccupied ones haven't been vandalized. Sound good?"

"Sounds good."

"Great. I've highlighted the ones Lyle, J.G., Theo, and I own. Take special care with our nest eggs."

Todd flicked through the pages listing the properties owned by Moran and his drinking buddies. If they were nest eggs, then they didn't have much to look forward to in their dotage.

"Will do," Todd said and stood.

Chuck raided the petty cash for a hundred dollars gas and eating money and told him to come back when it ran out. He promised to pay Todd two-fifty a week, cash, with Fridays being payday.

After returning to the pickup and looking up the first address, Todd hit the road. Within a handful of miles, a dark cloud settled on his shoulder. Two-fifty a week. He was in a dead-end job again. Worse still, he had less than he did when he was back in the Bay Area. Sure he possessed six kilos of cocaine and a Lexus, but both were worthless. Making matters worse, he was in deep again. He was supposed to be shedding his old life to start anew, but Vandrel had him over a barrel. All Todd's rebirth money was tied up in this job.

He wasn't totally penniless. He did have the hundred bucks gas money. It wouldn't get him far, but it was enough to cover the price of a bus ticket. He could start afresh somewhere else. Again. Okay, it might mean dead-end jobs for awhile, but he could get out from under. He wasn't in as deep with Vandrel as he was with the small man. Vandrel had nothing on him. He could get away clean.

He sensed getting away clean would become his mantra. Even if he hadn't been saying it in the past, it was certainly his modus operandi in recent years—screw up, run away to start all over again. He guessed he could do that a few more times, but there was only so much road. Eventually, he wouldn't have anywhere to run. He'd stick this one out and hope the small man's assessment that he had an aptitude for this kind of work held true.

The first property Todd came to belonged to Moran. It consisted of a dilapidated farmhouse with a collapsed barn on four acres of desert scrub. A county road gave up on connecting the property to civilization.

What the hell did Moran want with a piece of crap like this? Moran had probably bought it for a song, but it was hardly a song worth singing. He bounced over the dirt drive to the farmhouse, parked, and inspected the 'nest egg.'

Todd walked the perimeter of the farmhouse. He was no building inspector, but this place was a tear down. The siding curled away from the frame. Shingles dotted the ground where they'd fallen off the roof. The house possessed a slight list that screamed imminent structural failure. He would have liked to have checked out the interior, but couldn't courtesy of some pretty impressive padlocks. Even the windows had been nailed shut.

He had no idea why Chuck had wasted his time sending him out here to check on the place. You'd have to be a pretty desperate vandal to come out here and trash this crap. He didn't see any point in noting down the condition of the property for Chuck unless the place fell down. He had reached the pickup when he noticed a set of well-defined tire tracks leading to the barn.

Maybe there was good reason to have this place inspected regularly. He retrieved the .357 from the glove box, glad he'd brought it along with him, and followed the tracks to the broken-down barn.

He aimed the .357 inside the crooked doorway and peered inside. Light penetrated the gaps between the wood planks to give him a reasonable view of the interior. He ventured inside. Nothing of interest presented itself. The tires tracks went only as far the entrance. Not that that was a surprise. The structure creaked every time the wind blew. He knelt and scooped up a handful of straw from the thin layer scattered on the ground and brought it to his nose. It was fresh.

"Who's been coming out here?"

His curiosity was getting the better of him, but it would have to wait. There were other Moran properties to inspect. He wondered if he'd find more of the same. He dropped the straw and returned to his pickup.

The distance between properties was vast, and he didn't make it out to all of them. He managed to check out one of Chuck's properties, two of J.G.'s, and two of Moran's. In most cases, the properties were of the same ilk as the first—large parcels of land in the middle of nowhere. One of Moran's holdings proved to be a true rental though. He logged the renters' complaints of a rundown six-unit complex about a mile from the Texan. Instead of driving back into Dumont to drink away the night at The Yellow Rose, he drove to Vandrel's. He found the old man there, but not the Lexus.

"Where my car?" Todd asked entering the hangar.

Vandrel had his feet up on a desk in a small space that passed for an office, listening to his country western spilling from a radio perched on a shelf. He turned the radio's volume down. "Your car? I distinctly remember you saying it was stolen."

Todd saw this was going to be one of those conversations. "Okay, the car I brought you. Where is it?"

"Gone. Sold. Got good money for it too. Better than I expected. I guess Jap cars are popular."

Todd leaned against the desk next to Vandrel's dust-encrusted work boots. "Do I get any of it?"

"That weren't the deal, son. You get paid when you bring me the contents of Moran's safe."

Todd said nothing.

"How's it going with the son of a bitch?" Vandrel asked.

"It's going."

"That bad, huh?"

"Not as bad as you think."

Vandrel smirked.

Todd wasn't going to allow himself to be drawn into an argument and tried a different tack. "I'm assuming you know Moran well."

Vandrel nodded.

"Why would he buy up undeveloped parcels of land with rundown shacks on them?"

Vandrel took his feet off the desk and straightened in his seat. "He wouldn't. He doesn't spend a penny until he knows he's getting a dollar back. What have you found out?"

Todd told him. When he finished, he asked, "Mean anything to you?"

Vandrel shook his head. "Keep digging, son. I think you could be on to something."

"I might need something other than the pickup. Have you got anything else I can use?"

Vandrel tossed Todd the keys to a late model Buick Century and an aging Cadillac Seville. "I don't need to move them any time soon. They run good. What are you thinking?"

"I don't know yet."

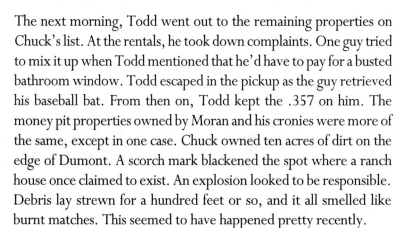

The next morning, Todd went out to the remaining properties on Chuck's list. At the rentals, he took down complaints. One guy tried to mix it up when Todd mentioned that he'd have to pay for a busted bathroom window. Todd escaped in the pickup as the guy retrieved his baseball bat. From then on, Todd kept the .357 on him. The money pit properties owned by Moran and his cronies were more of the same, except in one case. Chuck owned ten acres of dirt on the edge of Dumont. A scorch mark blackened the spot where a ranch house once claimed to exist. An explosion looked to be responsible. Debris lay strewn for a hundred feet or so, and it all smelled like burnt matches. This seemed to have happened pretty recently.

Todd drove back to Chuck's to report in. He wasn't there, and Jolene directed him to the Yellow Rose. Chuck was in his usual spot with his usual friends.

"There's our boy," Moran announced. "We missed you last night."

"I'm a working man now. Early to bed and all that."

"How did it go?" Chuck asked.

"It went okay. I do have bad news. The Parker place, it's been destroyed."

"Oh, that's okay." Chuck ordered a beer for Todd. "I should have told you that before you went out there. Lost the place about a month ago. Damn propane tank took the place out."

Todd was no fire investigator, but he knew Chuck was lying. The explosion had obviously originated from inside the house, and it had blasted the propane tank from its mounts. The tank was still intact.

"I was going to demo the place anyway. The fire saved me the job," Chuck said and laughed. "Other than that, all good?"

Todd handed over the paperwork Chuck had given him. "I've made notes for you."

Chuck leafed through it. "You've done a nice job. Take the rest of the day off, and I'll give you some new addresses tomorrow. You've done well."

"I know a hard working guy when I see one," Moran said and patted the stool next to him.

Todd sat and reached for the beer in front of him. It tasted good after a day cooped up in the pickup with no air-conditioning. He didn't put the beer down until it was half empty.

"How you liking the job?" Moran asked.

"Fine. It's simple work."

"Nobody likes complications."

"Amen to that." Todd raised his bottle, and Moran clinked his bottle with Todd's.

"You look worried, son."

"No, it's nothing."

"Don't give me that, Todd. We're all friends here."

"Yeah," Chuck said, and J.G. slapped Todd on the back.

"Okay. I'm grateful for the job and all, but . . . " Todd hesitated.

"'But?" Moran urged.

"It's just that I feel I'm taking your money. I mean, most of the properties I've been out to don't need me checking up on them."

"I know they're aren't much to look at," Moran said, "but they're ours, and it means a lot to us. It's natural for us to have someone keep an eye on them."

"I guess," Todd said. He wondered if he was playing this hand a little too hard, but didn't think so. He could afford to push a little more. "But why all the rundown properties?"

"Investments," Chuck said.

"They might'nt look it," J.G. said, "but give it time, and every one of those properties will make us rich. Ain't that right, boys?"

The boys harrumphed—except for Moran. He'd turned on the snake eyes again. Todd dialed it back and let the subject drop. He needed to get off Moran's radar and announced he needed something to eat, since he hadn't eaten anything all day. Before he could slip out, Theo said dinner sounded good. Chuck seconded him. They left the bar telling Grady not to give up their seats.

Chuck led the way to the Buckeye, a steak house two blocks up from the Yellow Rose. While Moran's boys laughed and joked, Moran just brooded with a storm front for an expression. Todd cursed his stupidity. He'd pushed it too much, and Moran was suspicious. He'd have to move things up now.

They ate, and Moran added to Todd's discomfort by picking up the tab for everyone. *Nothing like being made to feel like a Judas*, Todd thought.

After the meal, Todd blew off the idea of going back to the Yellow Rose. Moran's boys bitched and whined at him to share a barstool. Todd insisted he couldn't.

"Why?" Moran asked. He put an edge on the question that gave Todd the feeling he was asking more than one question.

"I need an early night is all. I promise tomorrow that I'll make it a late one."

"Whatever you say, tenderfoot," Theo said.

They ribbed him some more, but they let him go. Todd returned to the pickup and drove back to Vandrel's. He exchanged the pickup for the Seville and drove out to Chuck's burnt out property.

He lit up the site with the Caddy's high beams and approached the scorch mark that had once been a house. The stench of charred matches still radiated off the remains as fresh as if the fire had been yesterday and not weeks ago. He kicked over the remains, but unable to connect the dots, he drove off. Maybe Moran's property with the mysterious tire tracks and nailed shut windows might yield more.

During the drive, he wondered if he was making a big mistake. What did the burnt matches smell have to do with anything? And what did he expect to find at Moran's place? Squatters? It could mean something or nothing. It certainly wasn't getting what Vandrel asked him to get. Well, if he turned up nothing but squatters at the other property then he'd do as Vandrel had asked.

As soon as Todd spotted light leaking from the windows of the house, he doused his headlights and stopped the Seville. He left the car on the dirt road and approached the house on foot.

An Econoline van sat parked in the dilapidated barn. No other vehicles were in the vicinity. Todd went up to the van. It was unlocked, and the key was in the ignition. Obviously, the unofficial tenants had no fears about security. He touched the van's hood. It was lukewarm.

Music penetrated the house's walls and made it easy for Todd to creep up on the house without being heard. The drapes, essentially sheets nailed up inside, not only failed to keep the light out, but failed to keep him from looking in. He peered through the tears in the thin material into the living room. Two men and a woman, all wearing bandanas, worked furiously around a crudely constructed bench covered with glassware and containers. Todd made out the writing on one container: anhydrous ammonia. Bulk size containers of paint thinner sat next to the ammonia. On the floor, there were enough broken open cold medicine packages to cure a hospital wing of the sniffles.

It was time to go.

"A meth lab," Vandrel said after Todd had filled him in on the night's discovery.

"I didn't see all the chemicals, but that's what it looked like, and it explains the burnt out house. Not only are meth guys unstable, so is the manufacturing procedure."

Todd peeled back a length of masking tape around the window frame of a Mercedes S-class and tore off the plastic sheeting protecting the window from its new paint job. Vandrel inspected the paintwork for imperfections.

"Okay, someone is setting up meth labs in Moran's abandoned properties. So what are you saying—Moran is a meth producer? Because I don't see it."

"Neither do I. I think he's taken being a landlord to a new level. He's taking on tenants who don't mind the cockroaches and mold, as long as they don't get disturbed. He's letting these tweakers do whatever they do for a slice of the action, and if anything goes wrong, well, who cares? Someone will replace them."

"And how does this help me?"

"Now you have something on Moran."

"I don't have spit on him. We cry foul, and he's gonna say the drug labs are the work of squatters."

Todd sighed. He'd fallen on the same conclusion on his ride over to Vandrel's chop shop. "What are you saying—we just give up?"

"You can give up if you want, but you won't get your ten grand. No, we need something tangible on Moran."

"Like what?"

"Paperwork." Vandrel handed Todd a VIN plate to affix to the Mercedes. "Moran might not look it, but he's a packrat. He never throws shit away. That's how he got me. If Moran has dealings with anyone, he makes a record of it."

Todd pop-riveted the VIN plate in place. "Even with drug dealers?"

"Even with drug dealers. You need to break into that safe."

Safecracker. Another talent to add to his résumé. He'd hoped to get the combination before this eventuality. What was it with everyone? They all seemed to think he was capable of any crime. He couldn't crack a nut let alone a safe. Then again, hadn't he proved that he did have special talents and aptitudes? A week ago he was struggling to pack boxes in the shipping department. Now he was a pretty successful criminal. He'd yet to make any money, but he'd certainly settled into his new career without too many issues. While he'd failed to make an impact on the corporate world, he'd showed he had the smarts for this dubious career change. If Vandrel wanted a safe cracked, then he was the man to crack it.

"When do you suggest I do this?" he asked.

"If you're right and Moran is on to you, like you say, then there's no time like the present."

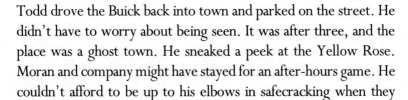

Todd drove the Buick back into town and parked on the street. He didn't have to worry about being seen. It was after three, and the place was a ghost town. He sneaked a peek at the Yellow Rose. Moran and company might have stayed for an after-hours game. He couldn't afford to be up to his elbows in safecracking when they staggered back from the bar. Luckily, the bar exhibited no signs of life.

He went to the rear of Moran's hardware store. If Moran did have any secrets he wanted protecting, he didn't invest too much in security. There was no visible sign of an alarm system. The door was a solid core model with a deadbolt. Todd could bust his way in with a crowbar, but he didn't want to leave a mess. He liked the look of the restroom window. It was small, but not so small that he couldn't squeeze his way through. He stripped off his sweatshirt, pressed it against the opaque glass, and smashed the crowbar over the window. The glass splintered after the first blow, but the sweatshirt muffled the earsplitting crack. He brought the crowbar down for a second time, and the window fell away. He cleared the glass from the frame, climbed up, and clambered through.

Moran didn't have an office. The area behind the counter and cash register was as close as it got. Todd found the safe against the back wall. It wasn't much. To Todd, it looked to be the next model up from what hotels used. It was pedestal mounted with four bolts securing it to the floor. If worst came to worst, he could simply unbolt the thing, take it with him, and crack it open with a cutting torch back at Vandrel's. But he didn't want to go that route, if he didn't have to. He didn't want to keep taking the sledgehammer approach to his newfound career. Okay, busting the window wasn't a good start, but he could work on that. He would pick up a set of skeleton keys and practice on locks. Reading up on safecracking would be another task. He sat down in front of the safe.

He wished he knew Moran better. If he did, it might clue him into a likely combination. He spun the dial to the lock hoping to sense the tumbler falling into place. Sadly, he didn't. It was looking more likely that he'd have to unbolt the safe and take it with him, but that was the great thing about ripping off a hardware store. The place was full of tools.

He picked out a power drill and armed it with a half inch bit. He plugged it in and positioned the drill just to the left of the dial. He was about to squeeze the trigger when he heard the unmistakable snap-snap of a pair of hammers going back on a double-barreled shotgun.

"I'd prefer you didn't ruin the safe like you ruined the crapper window," Moran said.

The blood in Todd's veins turned to ice, freezing his body rigid. The .357 was still in the pickup's glove box at Vandrel's. Even if he had it with him, it might as well be at the North Pole for all the good it would do him. Moran had the drop on him.

"You really should clear a building before getting down to business."

"I'm sorry." Todd wanted to say, "it's not what you think." But it was. There was no ducking what he was doing.

"The combination is ten, twenty-seven, sixty-seven," Moran said. "That's my son's birthday, if you're wondering."

Todd raised his hands slowly and carefully above his head.

"You can't open the safe with your hands above your head."

"You want me to open it?"

"You want to see inside, don't you?"

Not really. Not anymore. But Todd did as he was told and fed the combination into the safe. He put his hand on the lever and wondered if this would be his last action on earth. Moran could claim he was stopping a thief with the safe broken open. Todd pressed down on the lever and opened the door.

No buckshot tore him to shreds.

"Remove the contents," Moran ordered.

Todd removed a number of sealed manila envelopes and a small amount of cash.

"See what you're looking for?"

"I don't know."

"Well, take your time. Give everything a good look over before you decide."

"I'm sorry I betrayed you."

"You never betrayed me. It takes a friend to betray someone, and you, son, are no friend."

The insult cut deep. In truth, Moran was no friend of Todd's either, but the jibe made him feel inches high.

"The best way to get to know a stranger," Moran said, "is to welcome the stranger. You can't get to know them if you keep them at arm's length." Moran came around the counter with the shotgun barrel and got himself close enough that he couldn't miss. "You're not too smart, are you, son?"

"It doesn't look that way."

"No, it doesn't. This is a small town with only one motel, and you weren't checked into it."

"I could have been bedding down in my pickup."

"Yeah, you could have been, but no one saw your pickup parked on the streets, and if you were, the moment you were offered a job, a sensible man would have asked for a room or a handout, but you didn't."

Moran was handing Todd his ass in a hat, but at the same time, he was giving him a valuable lesson. He was new at this game, and he would make a few mistakes along the way, but he wouldn't make the same mistake twice. That was, if he ever got out of this one.

"You're not a cop, Todd, are you?"

"No."

"Is Todd your real name?"

"Yes."

"Good. I'm glad you didn't lie about everything. You aren't an opportunist, so who are you working for?"

"Me," Vandrel answered, emerging from the restroom with a 9mm in his hand.

Moran swung the shotgun in Vandrel's direction, and Todd felt the sweat dry on his back.

"After all these years, you finally got off your ass."

"Is it there?" Vandrel asked Todd.

Todd shone his flashlight on the sealed envelopes. Nothing was marked "incriminating evidence on Vandrel" or "meth labs." All the envelopes were seemingly for monthly invoices. He ripped the envelopes open and poured out the contents. Invoices. Nothing but invoices.

"There's nothing here," he said.

"What?" Vandrel said.

Moran laughed. "What did you expect? That I'd lock everything up in a pissant lockbox? I ain't a fool, Vandrel. You know that."

"Then where is it?" Vandrel demanded, taking two steps forward, his grip tightening on the pistol.

Todd didn't like this. Something was brewing. These guys' feud had been simmering for God only knew how long, and he was caught in the crossfire.

"I have a safety deposit box in San Antonio. Everything I've gathered over the years is there. There are a lot of skeletons gathering dust there. Yours included, Vandrel."

"And I've got one of yours," Vandrel answered. "We know all about your little meth lab sideline. Isn't that right, Todd?"

Thanks, Todd thought, *just put me back in the firing line.*

"Is that right?" Moran said swinging the gun back in Todd's direction.

"You're buying shitty properties out in the middle of nowhere to rent out to scum to make meth," Todd said. "Judging by the scorch mark and the stink, one crew barbecued themselves. But hey, it doesn't matter. There are plenty of tweakers looking for a new place to set up. It pretty good business too. It's getting harder to set up mobile labs these days, especially in the cities, so why not come out to big open nowhere where there are no cops and no snoopers to worry about?"

Todd hadn't intended to spill so much. He put it down to nerves. He doubted anyone else had expected the speech either. It was a long time before anyone spoke again.

"You're right. There aren't any snoopers—except for you."

"Don't take it out on him, Lyle," Vandrel said. "He was doing a job for me. If you need to blame anyone, it's me, but you've been blaming me for years."

Moran swung the shotgun away from Todd and aimed it squarely at Vandrel's gut. Todd sensed a violent change in Moran's demeanor. A deep-seated rage melted away his cool. One wrong word, and he'd open up with the shotgun.

"You don't know much about our friend here, do you, Todd?" Moran's teasing question squeezed out through gritted teeth.

Todd said nothing.

"Vandrel likes to use people. Young people. Get them to do his dirty work and hang them out to dry when it turns to shit."

"That's not true. What happened to Jesse was an accident."

"My boy died stealing cars for you," Moran bellowed.

"I made a mistake, Lyle. I was fed bad information on the owner. You know how much Jesse meant to me. I loved him like a son."

"But you weren't his father. You don't know a father's pain."

"Then how can you help these killers make their poison? How many other fathers have lost their sons and daughters because of it?"

Todd had to defuse this situation. Guns were going to be used tonight. Whatever information Vandrel hoped to get back, it wasn't going to happen. That left only one alternative—gunplay.

"How do we get to your safety deposit box in San Antonio?" Todd asked.

"You don't," Moran replied.

"We can if you come with us."

"I know what Vandrel wants, and he ain't getting it. Do you understand me?"

Moran wasn't talking to Todd anymore. Vandrel answered that he understood.

"Todd," Vandrel said. "I think you should leave now."

"I think that would be a good idea," Moran said.

"Hey, it doesn't have to end this way. It's not over."

"It was over a long time ago," Moran said.

"Todd, if you go back to my shop, you'll find the money I owe you, and you can take your pick of the cars," Vandrel said, his tone clipped and abrupt as if his words were holding back a breaking dam.

"Vandrel," Todd insisted.

Vandrel turned his automatic on Todd. "Go."

Moran stepped back from the counter, unlocked the main door, and pushed it open for Todd. He squeezed by Moran. In the doorway, he stopped. Moran and Vandrel had turned their guns on each other.

"I'm sorry I let you down, Vandrel."

"You didn't. We're finally going to get this problem resolved."

Moran closed the door.

Todd raced back to the Buick and gunned the engine. He pulled a U-turn to get back to Vandrel's. As he headed out of town, he passed by Moran's hardware store. As the store receded into the distance, two flashes of light from inside it reflected in his rearview mirror. He didn't stop to check that everyone was okay. It was too late for that. There was only one thing to do now.

Get out of town.

Part 3: Trading Up

Todd rode the Greyhound into Dallas. This hadn't been the plan. He'd collected the ten grand from Vandrel's warehouse and hit the road in the Buick. He was going anywhere except Dumont. He was about fifty miles out from town when good sense sank in. Moran and Vandrel had taught Todd a lot about his new life. One thing he'd learned was never to go anywhere without a gun. Everyone needed insurance. He was swapping carriers from State Farm to Smith and Wesson. He might never have to use his insurance, but it was good to have it with him. The second and more important thing he'd learned was a grudge was a grudge was a grudge.

The small man had gone to a lot of trouble to bury Todd because Todd had screwed up his operations. He'd cost the small man money, personnel, and credibility, and he wasn't about to forget that in a hurry. It didn't matter where Todd went or what he did to cover his tracks. He was sure the small man would find him and get his pound of flesh.

Todd couldn't risk driving the Buick to Dallas. The car was hot, and it would be even hotter when Moran's first customer found the bodies. He couldn't afford to leave a trail all the way Dallas. He dumped the Buick in Amarillo and caught the bus.

The Greyhound got in early. Over breakfast at a diner, Todd skimmed the yellow pages for Ruskin's dealership. His breakfast partner at the counter remarked he wouldn't go to Ruskin's if he had the choice. Todd had no intention of buying a car from Ruskin's, but he did need wheels. He asked his breakfast partner where he would go to buy a car if he had to choose. He recommended a dealership out toward Rochester Park.

After breakfast, Todd phoned for a cab to take him out there. He picked up a ten-year-old Toyota Corolla from a nearby lot for three grand. It wasn't much to look at, but the engine was sound. It would do, and it still left him seven grand in his pocket. Ready for action, he drove out to Ruskin's.

Ruskin's wasn't a franchise dealership catering to one of the big-name car manufacturers. Instead, it was a secondhand dealership catering to the prestige market. Their cars were lightly used. Mercedes and BMWs took up most of the inventory. A fully loaded Infiniti claimed the bottom rung of the For Sale ladder.

Todd parked on a side street, slipped out of his jeans and T-shirt, and pulled on a pair of dress slacks and a button-down shirt. If he was going to pretend to be a prospective buyer, then he had to look like one. He crossed the street and entered the lot. He cast an eye over a Mercedes C-class and wondered if the Lexus he'd been bringing here would have ended up on this lot. It seemed likely.

It took just under a minute before a salesperson smelled blood in the water and zeroed in for the kill.

"Hi," the young, clean-cut woman in her early thirties said. "I noticed you admiring that C-class."

"It certainly looks like my kind of car," Todd remarked.

She presented Todd with her card and introduced herself. "Charlie Ruskin."

Todd fought to keep his surprise in check. Charlie Ruskin was the small man's contact. He'd never said it was a woman.

"So this is your dealership?" Todd asked.

"Sadly, no. It's my father's, but it'll be mine some day. Would you like a test drive?"

"I thought you'd never ask."

She was slick. Todd had to give her that. Instead of running back to the office to grab the keys off the board, she produced them from her pocket and handed them to him.

They got in the car, and Todd guided the Mercedes onto the street. Charlie outlined a route she wanted him to take. It took several minutes to thread the vehicle through the choked streets onto the freeway. This provided Charlie the perfect opportunity to wax lyrical about the qualities of German engineering and craftsmanship. She slipped price into the conversation, which was a bitter pill to swallow, but she sweetened the taste by mentioning the C-class's great resale value. On the freeway, Todd whisked the C-class up to eighty-five without feeling a thing. It drove how a Mercedes should drive.

"How does it grab you?" she asked.

"By the balls and doesn't let go."

"So I can take from that statement that you're interested."

"Very much so. The price is in my range."

She beamed. "We have a deal then?"

"We have a deal."

"How will you be paying?"

"Cash."

"Excellent." She wasn't fazed, or if she was, she didn't show it.

"I had intended on trading in my previous car, but I had to sell it. Sadly, for well below its Blue Book value."

"If you haven't finalized the sale, and it's our kind of automobile, I'm sure I can make you a better offer. What's the model?"

"A black Lexus with six kilos of cocaine stitched into the back seat and a corpse in the trunk. Interested?"

The color drained from her face, washing away that car-savvy saleswoman persona to reveal a frightened little girl. Todd piled on the pain by producing the .357. He didn't aim it at her. He just let her know that he wasn't going to be a pushover.

"I didn't have anything to do with it. You have to understand that."

"We need somewhere where we can talk."

Charlie directed Todd to Sargent Park. It was small and pleasant, even though a railroad ran through it. They stayed in the car, since Todd didn't want to be overheard. Charlie called the dealership. She told them the sale was a done deal, and she was showing Todd around since he was new to the city. Charlie carried off the lie with conviction. She hung up and clipped the cell phone to her belt.

"What do you want?" she asked.

"To know how it all works."

"Simple really." Her eyes were on the gun. "I receive a call. They tell me a car is coming. When it arrives, I call a number."

"What kind of number? Local? Out of state?"

"Local."

"And what happens when you make the call?"

"We make an arrangement to meet. My contact comes, removes whatever is being transported, and goes."

"Who is he?"

"He calls himself Fox, but I don't think that's his name."

"What happens to the car?"

"We dress it up and sell it. That's it. Can I go now?"

"No."

She went to protest, but he tightened his grip on the .357, and she settled down. He felt like a shit for threatening her this way. It wasn't her fault. She was just a cog in the machinery, just like him.

"How did you get mixed up in all this?" Todd asked.

She sagged, seeming to relax, even with the loaded gun pointed at her. "My father. He's a good man, but he's not without his faults."

"What are his faults?"

"There's only one, really. He's a gambler. He'll bet on anything—horses, football, baseball. You name it, he'll put money on it."

"Obviously, he's not a successful gambler."

She snorted derisively. "No. For every dollar he wins, he loses a hundred."

Todd saw where this sob story was heading. "Losses like that mount up."

"Is two hundred and fifty grand a big enough mound?"

Todd said nothing.

She went on to describe how her father's addiction had almost cost them everything. Creditors clued her in to the problem first. They claimed delinquency on bills she swore were paid. When she looked into the accounts, it was all too obvious that her father had been siphoning the sales from the dealership to feed the track and bookies. Before she had a chance to confront him, the money problems went away and a new one started. She received her first phone call telling her to expect an out-of-state delivery. Her father explained these were the terms of the loan he had with his new lender.

"How long has this been going on?" Todd asked.

"Over two years."

"How often do the calls come?"

"Once a month. Sometimes twice. Last November, it was every week."

"Always drugs?"

She sighed. "I try not to look, but yes. Cocaine."

"All part of a flexible payment scheme. How long before your father's debt is paid off?"

"Will there ever be a final payment?" she asked bitterly.

That was the great thing about loan sharks. With interest rates in the stratosphere, there was never any prospect of paying off the principle. The small man had a nice little thing working for him.

"Where's your father now?"

"Retired." The word twisted her features like it had left a sour taste on her tongue. "When the call came to me and not him, he went to pieces. He was no good on the lot. It was for the best."

"Does he still gamble?"

"No. He doesn't go out much, and the bookies know not to take his calls." She straightened, regaining her composure after this confessional. "How do you fit into all this?"

"Similar story to you."

Charlie didn't look content to leave it there—gun or no gun—so Todd told her the whole sorry tale. He shouldn't have told her. In a clinch, she could use it against him, but what harm could it do him? None of this was news to the small man. Deep down, he wanted to tell someone. This wasn't something he could share with his closest friend, but he could share it with someone who'd been down the same road. He felt liberated after he told her, but it didn't last long.

"I don't know who your small man is, but my orders don't come from the Bay Area."

"What?"

"My calls come from Seattle."

Todd drove Charlie back to the dealership in silence. They both had plenty on their minds. At the car lot, he got out and handed her the keys.

"I suppose you're not really buying the car," she said.

"Sorry. No."

She shrugged. "It's not the end of the world. I'll tell them you had a change of heart."

"I'd prefer if you didn't."

"And why would I want to do that?"

"Call it a favor."

"A favor for a man who pulls a gun on me? You're asking a lot."

"I know." From the corner of his eye, Todd noticed Charlie's salesmen watching them. "Tell them I'm moving into town, and I'll be back in a few days to collect the car." He nodded in the direction of the gawking salesmen.

"And is there a reason for all this?"

"How would you like to pay off your father's debt once and for all?"

Todd was risking a lot by trusting Charlie Ruskin, but she was in a bind, just like he was. She had to know that the people pulling her strings didn't care about her. If the drug running ever came crashing down on her head, the puppet masters would find themselves another puppet. It was in her best interests to work with him. He'd outlined a plan to her that could set her free. It wasn't without risk, but it could work. Still, she could sell him out. It might buy her a few brownie points with the people in Seattle. That was why he spent the next couple of hours watching Charlie from across the street. She didn't jump on her cell phone the moment he stepped off the lot, and no one unusual visited her. She looked to be playing it his way.

He returned to his Toyota and went in search of a motel. He found a place that wouldn't keep his details on file and didn't object to cash. He looked forward to the day he didn't have to hide out in crappy accommodations to avoid someone tracking him down and putting a bullet in him.

He changed out of his formal clothes into jeans and a T-shirt. Thoughts of Seattle crept to the forefront of his mind. If the scheme to use stolen cars to traffic drugs originated in Seattle, then what was the small man's part in it? Was this a side business or his role in someone else's empire? Todd liked to think it was the latter. If the small man was a small fish, then he had to report to someone bigger. The bigger boss would have the power to squash him. But if he was the head honcho, then there was no hope of toppling him.

Too nervous to eat, Todd drove back to Ruskin's dealership. By the time he reached the car lot, everyone had left for the day, except Charlie. He parked on a side street. He didn't want the Toyota to tip anyone off. He walked into Charlie's office just as the sun deserted Texas in favor of California.

"Still want to do this?" Todd asked. She looked how he felt.

"No, but I'm going to."

He smiled. "Join the club."

He coached her on what to say then made her repeat it to him three times. He wanted to go for a fourth but she lost her temper, complaining she wasn't a damn actress. It was a fair point. If she rehearsed too hard, her performance would come over as just that— a performance.

"Okay, then," Todd handed Charlie the phone, "let's get this party started."

Todd sat close so that he could listen in. His cheek brushed against hers. Her skin felt good against his. He smelled her perfume. It had faded during the day, but it accented her natural scent. He smelled alcohol too. He didn't blame her. He could do with a drink himself.

She punched in the number to her local contact, and when he answered, she said, "It's Charlie. We've got a delivery."

"A delivery?" Fox said. "We're not expecting a delivery."

"I know, but he's here."

"I'll check it out and call you back."

"No." Charlie put just the right note of fear in the word. "Come now. Please."

That stopped him in his tracks. "Why? What's wrong?"

"It's the guy. He scares me. He's—" she groped for a word.

"He's what?" Fox encouraged with a note of anger building in his voice. It wasn't directed at Charlie but at the nonexistent courier. It seemed that Fox liked Charlie, which might play to their advantage. "Tell me, Charlie."

"He seems violent. He's not the usual driver we get. There's something wrong about him. He means trouble."

"What car does he have?"

"A black Lexus."

"Keep him there. I'll be down in thirty."

"Hurry," she begged and hung up.

"Wow, you're good," Todd said.

She smiled. "I have my moments." Then the smile fell away. "Usually when I'm scared."

Todd wanted to tell her not to be, but couldn't. He was just as scared. He had no feel for the person on his way over to them. The guy might be a pushover when it came down to it, but that was wishful thinking. It was more than likely this guy was going to be all fireworks.

Charlie led Todd to the service bays where the exchanges took place. Todd wanted everything to go down here. Fox would be edgy because he was expecting a hostile situation with Todd, the little drug mule that could, but he would be comfortable in these surroundings. He'd feel that he knew the location and think he had the upper hand. Well, he wouldn't be expecting the welcome wagon Todd had in store for him.

The service shop was clean and free of oil stains. If it hadn't been for the telltale odor of engine oil and other lubricants, Todd would have believed the place was never used. That was to be expected with a prestige automobile dealership, he supposed. Clients expected clean, modern, and efficient. He was used to jalopy shops where the oil was so saturated into the floors, Exxon could drill to reclaim it.

"Which door will he come to?" he asked.

"That one," Charlie replied and pointed at the main rollup door.

"Good." He rolled a pair of tool chests over to the door and positioned them to the right of the entrance to create a blind spot. He hid behind the chests.

"What should I do?" Charlie asked.

"Do as I told you. I just need you to distract him, and I'll take it from there. Just be ready to react if things get messy."

Messy. Could things go any other way? Probably not. Todd removed the .357 from the back of his waistband and checked that all the rounds were safe and snug in their chambers. The backsides of six cartridges stared back at him, just like they had all the times before. It wasn't like they were going to fall out or mutiny against him, but he still checked and double-checked and triple-checked—and give it a minute, and he'd probably quadruple-check. He took comfort in the OCD tendency he'd developed. It helped pass the time.

"Do you think he'll come alone?" Charlie asked.

Todd never considered the connection arriving with his crew. That changed everything. His plan wouldn't work. He couldn't take on a crew alone. He emerged from behind the tool chests. "I thought he worked alone."

"He does."

"Then what makes you think that he'll bring friends along now?"

"Wouldn't you?"

Given the choice, Todd would. "It's a bit late now. We're gonna have play this as it comes."

"Do you think you can handle this?"

"What choice do I have?" He returned to his hiding place and checked the chambers for shells again.

A fist pounded on the rollup door, and a gruff voice called Charlie's name. Traffic must have been kind. He was five minutes early, according to Todd's watch. The fist pounded on the door a second time. The door shook on its track and sounded like thunder. Todd eased the hammer back on the .357.

Charlie's spiked heels clicked on the concrete floor. He peered through the gap between the tool chests and watched her approach the door. She pressed a button and the door retracted. Before it had a chance to open fully, Fox ducked under it. He was tall, easily six-feet, and in his early forties with an athletic build. None of that bothered Todd. The guy's smell did. Fox reeked of crime. Todd saw it in the way he entered the shop and systematically scanned the room. He moved with a predator's pace. Oh yeah, this guy was obviously a career criminal. He drove the point home with the automatic he held.

"Where is he?" Fox growled.

"He's not here." Charlie pressed the button to close the door.

"You said he was."

Fox stopped in the middle of the shop. He was facing in Todd's direction, cutting off any chance of a surprise attack.

"Turn him around, Charlie," Todd murmured under his breath.

"I know, but after I hung up, he said he wanted something to eat."

Fox cursed. "Where's the Lexus?"

"He drove off in it."

Fox cursed again.

"He should be back in a minute." Charlie circled Fox, which forced him to turn his back toward Todd.

"Good girl," Todd murmured.

"That gives us time to prepare," Fox said.

"Prepare for what?"

"What do you think?" he spat.

Nice. At least I know now, Todd thought. The small man still held his grudge. This wasn't going to end unless he or the small man ended it.

"I can't have you kill him here," Charlie said.

"I don't think you've got a choice, darlin'." Fox tucked the automatic into the back of his jeans.

Todd knew the guy would never be so close to being unarmed again. He charged out from behind the tool chests. "DEA. Hold it right there."

Claiming he was a representative of the DEA was a last second thought. Gun against gun, Todd guessed Fox had more than an edge on him, but that might be canceled out if Fox believed Todd was a government agent. Killing a nobody might not faze him, but killing a federal agent might quell his murderous tendencies.

It didn't.

Fox shot Charlie a venomous look of hatred, then spun around and reached for his weapon. Charlie backed away as Todd closed in on Fox. Every foot closer Todd got to Fox improved his chances of hitting him.

"Don't even think about it," Todd warned.

Fox ignored Todd and jerked out his weapon.

Todd had him. It would have been so easy to shoot, to put a hole in one of the problems and make it go away, but he couldn't. He needed the guy alive. He needed him to talk. As Fox aimed, Todd dropped his aim and his shoulder, and plowed into the man.

Fox read Todd's move all too well. He stepped outside Todd's collision course, caught his charging body, and hurled him across the floor. Knowing he was going down, Todd grabbed Fox's waistband and brought both of them crashing to the ground. Todd cracked his head on the concrete floor and a starburst went off behind his eyes. It dazed him for a second, but only a second. He couldn't afford more than that. Fox was recovering from his fall. Todd tried to tighten his grip on the .357 but found he'd lost the gun in the melee.

"You piece of shit," Fox barked and kicked Todd in the stomach. The kick rolled Todd onto his back. Fox stepped on Todd's neck and lazily aimed his automatic at Todd's face. "DEA, my ass."

Todd tried to speak, but Fox pressed down with his foot, turning Todd's words into a gurgle. Starlight filled his vision. He flailed at Fox's pant leg in an attempt to get the man's foot off his throat.

"DEA or no DEA, you don't leave here tonight." Fox trained his weapon on Todd's face. "Pick an eye. Grunt for left. Gurgle for right." He pointed the gun at Todd's left eye, then his right, then back to his left.

A strangled noise Todd hadn't intended made it past his constricted windpipe.

"Was that a gurgle? Sure sounded like it." Fox grinned. "Right eye it is then."

A gunshot roared in the shop, bouncing off the walls and the parked vehicles. A red blossom opened up on Fox's chest. Confusion and pain stained the man's expression. He staggered back, taking his foot off Todd's throat.

Todd sucked in a much-needed breath. Fox wasn't going down, and Todd wasn't about to give the son of a bitch a second chance. He snapped to his feet and drove an unforgiving punch into Fox's wound. Fox's scream filled Todd with satisfaction, and he followed up his first punch with a right hook to the guy's jaw that sent a crackle of electricity through the bones of his fist and all the way into his shoulder. The legs went out from under Fox, and he collapsed in a heap. Todd tore the automatic from Fox's grasp and aimed it at him.

Charlie's heels beat a tattoo on the concrete. She jammed Todd's .357 in Fox's face and pulled back on the trigger. Todd slapped her arm out of the way as the gun went off. The bullet struck the ground, ricocheting off the concrete to embed itself in a wall.

"I need him alive," Todd shouted. He left out that he didn't want to bury a second body.

Charlie looked at him like he'd slapped her. "He would have killed you."

"It's okay. He can't hurt us now." He reached over and took the .357 from her trembling hands.

"That's what you think," Fox laughed.

"Shut it or else," Todd snarled.

"Or what? You just said you couldn't kill me. You're not very good at this."

"I said I needed you alive. I didn't say anything about being nice about it." Todd ground his heel into Fox's wound. Fox squirmed and did his best to keep in a yell that burst out of him in a rush. Todd took some small pleasure from inflicting this pain but not much. He had to put up a front though. This guy had to believe that he was capable of anything. "Charlie, find something to tie this bastard up with."

Charlie returned with a lifting sling. Todd jerked Fox's arms behind him and looped it around his wrists to produce makeshift handcuffs. He hooked the slack on the hook of an overhead winch and hoisted Fox's wrists up behind his back and jerked him forward, but kept it just low enough to keep Fox's feet on the ground. It looked damned uncomfortable, which was just the effect Todd was hoping to achieve. The answers should come quick.

"See that?" Todd spun Fox to face the untidy puddle of blood spoiling the otherwise spotless floor. "You're bleeding bad."

"You ain't no DEA," he said scornfully.

"I don't think it matters what you think." Todd pressed his thumb into Fox's bullet wound. His thumb touched something hard that wasn't bone. His stomach lurched. This was a road he didn't want to venture down, but he had no choice. This was the only language Fox understood. He'd respond to it. Todd had to believe that.

Fox screamed out, and Charlie winced and looked away.

"All you need to know is that you're in a no win situation," Todd said.

"And how do you figure that, tough guy?"

"Do I need to hold up a mirror, moron?"

"This is nothing. They'll give me a pat on the back for this."

"They'll put a bullet in the back of your fucking head when they see you."

Fox snorted derisively.

"They won't let you keep on breathing after you compromised their operation."

"Oh yeah?"

Todd reached inside Fox's back pocket, jerked out his wallet, and pulled out his driver's license. "Yes, Wade Mears of Plano. They can't afford errors, and you can't stop making them."

"That's not me."

"I think it is. It took you less than thirty minutes to get here. How far is Plano from here, Charlie?"

"Less than thirty minutes away."

"Christ, don't you have any brains? You don't bring ID with you."

Mears cursed under his breath.

"Did you let anyone know you were coming here tonight?"

"Worried about the cavalry?"

Todd slammed a fist in Mears's wound. "Did you talk to anyone?"

Mears breathed hard from the punch. "No."

That was good. It meant no loose ends. This could be explained away if no one beyond the three of them knew about it.

The color was draining from Mears's face. Todd guessed it had less to do with his shock and more to do with his blood loss. Mears wasn't losing a lethal amount, but he had to be going lightheaded. Todd had to hurry this up.

"I can crucify you, Wade, but I can save you too."

"Blow me."

Todd thumbed Mears's bullet again with the desired effect. "I demand a little respect, Wade. Especially considering the position you're in right now."

"And what position is that?"

"Fucked." Todd paused to let the enormity sink in. "You're shot, and unless you're a premed student, I don't see how you can avoid a hospital and a hospital means cops. I'm sure you have friends, but that means word getting back and that means questions. Questions you'll have a hard time answering. Questions that lead to answers that are punctuated with a bullet." Todd showed Mears his own gun. "I can compound those problems by putting a kilo of uncut coke in your lovely home detailed on this driver's license. No matter how you slice it, someone will come gunning for you."

"You two will have to explain this mess."

Todd turned to Charlie. "Not really. I could be a bastard and say it's not my problem. This isn't my dealership."

Charlie frowned. Todd smiled.

"But it's not even an issue. Who's going to believe that Charlie runs a drug mule business out of here, Wade?"

Mears didn't answer.

"Yeah, I didn't think so," Todd remarked. "So, Wade, what's it to be—the cops, them, or me?"

Mears pondered his options. "What do you want?"

"You mentioned they. Who are they?"

"You think I'm going to tell you that?"

"Don't make me state the obvious again," Todd said impatiently.

"What do I get out of this?"

"Tell me something useful, and I might just tell you."

"I work for the Carlsons."

"And where would I find the Carlsons?"

Todd prayed for the answer to be in California, but it wasn't to be. Just like Charlie, Mears's orders came from Seattle. Questions about the small man's role in this scheme filled Todd's head again, but he had no answers to make them go away.

"How about San Francisco—deal with anyone there?"

"No."

"Sure? This is important, Wade."

"Yes."

Todd pressured Mears for more. He pressed at the bullet wound a couple of times just to make sure Mears wasn't holding out, but he knew nothing about the small man. He knew the Carlsons, and that was it. He spilled contact numbers, meeting places, and names. It surprised Todd that Mears knew that much. At the end of the day, he was a satellite on the outskirts of the organization, just a drone doing their bidding.

When he'd given up all he was going to give, Mears asked, "Can I get some water?"

"Sure," Todd said. "You've earned it."

Charlie filled a paper cup from the cooler and held it to Mears's mouth for him to drink.

"I think he's had enough. Lower him," Charlie said.

She fixed Todd with a disgusted look. Todd nodded and lowered the hoist until Mears rested on his knees. Mears let out a groan of relief.

Before Todd unhooked Mears and cleaned him up, he bound his wrists and ankles with duct tape. Mears seemed docile enough, but Todd wasn't taking any chances. He wouldn't put it past him to fight back. Todd sure as hell would, if he were in his bloodied shoes.

After they'd patched Mears as best as they could, Todd washed the blood off him in the restroom. Charlie followed him in. She looked haggard. Her hair hung limp around her face, and her sun-kissed complexion had bled away to a ghostly white. Todd imagined this whole business had aged her. She would have grown up a lot more than she liked when Daddy's gambling problems brought mobsters to her door.

"What are you going to do with him?" she asked.

"Let him run."

"Can we trust him?"

Todd exhaled. "We don't have much of a choice, but I think so. He's got just as much to lose as we have. I'll reinforce the fact when I cut him loose."

Fear filled her expression. He'd seen it several times while he questioned—no, interrogated—Mears. It wasn't time to get squeamish over what he'd done.

"You scared me out there," she said.

Truth be known, he'd scared himself. He was changing. Some of it for the better and some of it not. "You know the position I'm in. Yours isn't a lot different. Tonight was never about negotiation. I had to get what I wanted without it coming back to bite me."

"And did you get what you wanted?"

"Some. Not enough, but enough to be getting on with."

"Hey," Mears bellowed. "Cut me loose."

Charlie shook her head slowly.

"Sounds like our guest is getting restless," Todd said.

They returned to their noisy captive, Todd drying his hands on a long ream of paper towel.

"Here come the executioners," Mears taunted. He wriggled slug-like across the floor, and just like a slug, his bloody shoulder left a trail behind him. Todd knocked him onto to his back with his foot, ending his escape.

"So you think we're going to kill you?" Charlie asked in a neutral tone.

"Let's not play games. We all know the rules. You're gonna tell me I'm free to go, then you're going to put a bullet in the back of my head."

"Wade, I don't have to get my hands dirty with you." Todd dropped to one knee. "When word gets out—and it will, I'll make sure of it—the Carlsons will do the job for me. But I realize you're just a foot soldier doing your job, so I'm going to cut you some slack. You split. Tonight. I'll promise to forget all about you."

"It's the best offer life is ever going to throw you," Charlie added.

Mears looked from Todd to Charlie and back. Skepticism claimed his expression.

"Got any cash?" Todd asked.

"About a grand."

It was more than Todd had on him when he'd skipped out on the small man. "That should get you a long way, if you spend it wisely."

Something melted in Mears's expression. "You're serious, aren't you?"

"Do I have to poke you in the shoulder to prove it?" Todd asked.

Mears cracked a smile. "You ain't no DEA agent."

"Does it matter?"

"No."

"We got a deal then?"

"If you cut me loose, we can shake on it."

The fable of the scorpion and the toad flashed through Todd's head. "I'll take your word on it. Got a car?"

"Green Caddy parked on the street. Keys are in my pants."

Todd fished for the keys and tossed them to Charlie. She backed the Cadillac into the garage and helped Todd load Mears into the trunk. They struggled against his buckling and bitching.

"I should have known you'd fucking lie."

Todd pinned Mears's head to the trunk's carpeted interior and looked him directly in the eyes. "Wade, I'm not lying. I'm not going to kill you, but I'm also not just going to let you walk out of here. I'm taking you to neutral ground. Okay?"

"You'd better be."

"Or what, Wade?"

Todd slammed the trunk lid down before Mears could bitch further.

"What do we do now?" Charlie asked.

"Know anywhere remote?"

"You're not going to kill him, are you?"

Todd shook his head. "No, I just want to get him out of the way for a while."

She nodded. "I know somewhere."

Charlie led the convoy in her Audi. Todd followed in Mears's Cadillac. They drove out to Bynum. It was quiet, remote, and a good hour from the city. They freed Mears from the trunk and perched him on the rear bumper. He looked ghastly. The blood loss was taking its toll.

"Know someone who can take care of the bullet?" Todd asked.

Mears nodded.

"Are they connected to the Carlsons?"

He shook his head.

"Good."

Todd went through the Caddy. He wanted to make damn sure the son of a bitch didn't have a spare weapon or anything that he could use on them. The car was clean.

Todd handed Mears's automatic to Charlie. "Keep that on him."

She did exactly as she was told.

Todd pulled out a boxcutter he'd snagged from the workshop and cut the tape around Mears's ankles. "Remember who is giving you this wonderful opportunity to live."

"Some opportunity," Mears grumbled. When he realized that Todd wasn't going to cut the rest of the tape until he got a satisfactory response, he said, "I'll remember you until my dying day. Good enough?"

Todd sliced open the remaining tape. "Move over there."

Mears stood, but tottered. He stopped when he was about twenty feet away from the Cadillac. He wavered for a moment before falling to the ground in a heap.

"Are we all square?" Mears asked.

Todd jammed the box cutter into a tire. "Now we are."

"You shit."

"Have a good life, Wade. Play it smart, and it'll be a long one."

Todd and Charlie returned to her Audi and raced off before Mears got to his feet.

Charlie's speeding Audi crossed Dallas city limits, and she asked, "Is that story about you and the small man true?"

"Yes."

She pondered Todd's one word answer for far too long.

"Why do you ask?" he asked.

"The way you handled yourself tonight. It didn't seem like the first time you had to get information out of a person."

She was right. Even Todd struggled with it. The Todd he knew couldn't bullshit someone like Mears, let alone torture him. Again, the small man's words rang inside his head.

"I don't know what to tell you, Charlie. We're capable of anything when we're backed up into a small enough corner. Who would have thought you'd be part of a drug distribution ring?"

It was a cruel thing to say, but it had to be said. Charlie was in no place to play the morality card, and more importantly, he didn't want her to view him as a bad guy. Charlie absorbed the barb with good grace and nodded.

They drove in silence for the rest of the journey. She parked her Audi inside the workshop. The place had taken on a different appearance. Even ignoring the blood, it didn't look as clean.

Todd found a mop to clean up the blood, but Charlie stopped him.

"I'll clean up. You need to go."

She was right. Even in his current condition, Mears should have changed the tire by now. Todd's window of escape was shrinking.

Charlie offered him Mears's automatic.

"No, you keep it," he said.

"As a memento?" she joked.

He smiled. "No. For protection. There's going to be some fallout when the Carlsons realize their handler has skipped town."

"Or he tells about tonight," she said.

Todd shook his head. "He knows his days are numbered unless he disappears."

"What do I do when the next car arrives?"

"Hopefully it won't."

"But if it does."

"Play dumb. Tell them that you tried to contact Wade, but he doesn't answer. They'll search for him and probably assign someone else to collect the drugs."

"So nothing's changed."

"It will. Give me time."

Charlie viewed the weapon and her smile evaporated.

"I wish I could stick around to help," he said.

"No. You need to go. Besides, I don't think I could survive another day with you around."

He flushed.

"So, I guess you're off to Seattle to see the Carlsons and get the small man off your back."

"Yes."

"Do you think you'll succeed?"

He shrugged. "You never can tell. I might even get them to consider your loan paid up."

Her smile came back. "That would be nice."

"It would be, wouldn't it?"

She was still smiling when he walked out the door.

Part 4: He Said, She Said

Todd reached Seattle by Wednesday morning. If he'd pushed it, he could have made it the day before, but he saw no reason to rush. For once, he left a city without a tidal wave of trouble looming over him. He could afford to take things at his own pace. The small man wasn't going anywhere any time soon and neither were the Carlsons. At last, the tail wasn't wagging the dog.

He rewarded his Toyota with a trip to an oil changers after its two thousand mile drive. Leaving the car in their capable hands, he went in search of a payphone. He called the number Mears had given him.

"Hello," the woman's voice said with exaggerated cool.

"Yeah, my name's Todd, and I'm looking for work."

"I'm sorry this isn't an employment agency. You have the wrong number."

"I was told the Carlsons always had work," Todd blurted before she hung up.

"Who told you that?" She had an edge to her voice.

Todd reeled off the story Mears had told him to use. He'd been practicing it on the long drive up from Texas, and it sounded convincing, even to his ears. The key that opened the doors to the kingdom of crime involved a guy called Munson. Munson had worked for the Carlsons at one time until a botched larceny got him busted. He'd held his tongue and did the time without ever mentioning the Carlsons. The Carlsons rewarded him with a retirement home and an allowance in Florida. Now, if he came across a guy he liked, he sent him to Seattle. The beauty of this was that the Carlsons couldn't check with Munson. The cops had never believed he worked alone, and they hadn't taken the tail off him. The upshot of this was that the Carlsons never made contact with the man again. The whole thing relied on faith. He hoped Mears hadn't lied about all this. He doubted it. The story was too intricate and too involved for Mears to invent while being tortured.

"So how is Munson?" the woman asked, at last showing signs of warmth.

"Shitty. His busted knee doesn't do well even in Hobe Sound."

Apparently, this detail unlocked the door. He was in. The woman reeled off an address.

"Know where that is?" she asked.

"I'll find it."

Todd bought a mocha and Danish at a Tully's and consumed them on the way back to the oil changers. The manager dealt the bad news that his Toyota wasn't long for this world if he didn't have a whole host of parts replaced. Todd told the manager that the Toyota had been through a lot, and it wasn't fair to keep putting it through more. Sometimes you just had to leave things in the hands of God. The manager didn't appreciate the humor and failed to smile when Todd took the keys from him.

Todd bought a map at a local gift shop and drove to the address the woman had given him. The address turned out to be a mixed-use building a couple of blocks from Pioneer Square. Although within spitting distance of the tourist spot, the revitalization failed to stretch this far. The buildings on either side were rundown. The commercial space below the residential was boarded over. He climbed the short flight of steps leading to the door of the residential part of the building and pressed the button to 2A. There was no name attached.

"Yes?" a woman answered.

"It's Todd. We spoke on the phone."

She didn't answer, but the buzzer screeched at him, and the door unlocked.

The hallway was cold and uninviting. He climbed the stairway to the second floor and found 2A. The door was ajar. He let himself in.

2A was nothing like the rest of the building. Where everything else was rundown, 2A was plush. Expensive furniture was nestled knee deep in thick carpeting. The lighting was subdued. The temperature was kept at a toasty optimum. Todd felt at home.

Click!

That at home feeling scurried off just as quickly as it had arrived. Someone had pressed a gun to the back of Todd's head. He raised his hands.

"Take it easy," he said.

"Don't tell me what to do," the woman said. "I knew it would come to this."

"Come to what?"

"Don't play dumb."

It was the only thing he could play. Then he cursed himself in his thoughts. Mears had screwed him. The Munson story was just that— a story. Bastard.

She patted him down and found the .357 in the back of his pants. She jerked it out and pressed it against his spine.

"I suppose you carry that for protection, huh?" she asked.

There was no right answer to a question like that, so he kept his mouth shut.

She swiped the .357 across the back of his head. A blinding white light filled his vision, and he dropped to his knees. He put his hands to the point of impact.

"I asked you a question." She planted a kick to his liver that sent him onto his face.

Two hits and he was down. Yeah, he was a real tough guy. When would anything go his way?

"I thought the question was rhetorical," he squeezed out before she assaulted him further.

She laughed. "Rhetorical? An educated idiot. That's a first."

"No, not educated." He rolled over onto his back. "Just a plain idiot."

She laughed again. She might have been laughing, but it was laughing without humor. Her eye was still on the game. Still on him.

"My question." She pointed a small stainless steel automatic at his face.

"Sometimes I carry the gun for protection."

"And other times?"

"To shoot people."

"At last, an honest answer. Do you want to follow it up with another one?"

"I'll try."

"He sent you, didn't he?"

"Munson? Yes."

She pulled the trigger. The bullet winged past Todd's head and punched a hole in the couch behind him.

"I have a hard time believing Munson sent you when he was killed in a hit and run last month."

Oh Christ, Todd thought. Mears's information wasn't CNN fresh. He was so screwed.

"Do you want to try that Munson story again?" She trained the automatic at his face again.

"Not really."

"Smart man. Why don't you give the truth a little airing this time?"

The truth wasn't an option, and Todd hadn't planned on using a backup story, but staring down the barrel of the woman's gun inspired invention. He sold her a story about meeting some drunk in a bar in Missouri who'd told him about the Carlsons. She quizzed him on a description for the drunk. He fed her a nondescript rundown that matched most of the population.

"Sounds like Tucker," she concluded and lowered the automatic.

Todd released a thick breath that hurt his chest and throat on the way out.

"You have no idea who I am, do you?" She sank onto the couch opposite Todd, keeping the gun trained loosely on him.

Todd shook his head, his gaze on her gun hand.

"I'm Jessica Carlson."

Todd felt slapped, and he didn't mind its sting. Talk about falling on his feet. He expected he'd have to use some fancy moves to get to the Carlsons. He never thought Mears's information was going to take him right to their door.

"You have no idea how close you came to getting yourself killed," she said.

Todd had a funny feeling he did.

"Did my husband send you?" She snapped her gun arm in his direction. "This time I have no intention of giving you a warning shot. Did he send you?"

"No. I have no idea who he is. Honest. I just came for a job."

"Convince me."

"Look, I don't know what to tell you. I don't know him, and I don't know you. I came for a job, not a bullet in the face. Okay?"

She lowered the gun again. What was this? Good Jessica-bad Jessica? Whatever she called this act, it worked. If she didn't let up with this shit, Todd was going to spill the truth.

"You want a job?"

Against his better judgment, he answered that he did.

"When you called me, was I the first person you called about work?"

"Yes."

"You didn't call my husband?"

"No."

"And nobody knows you're in this city?"

"No."

"Then I think I've got a job for you." She stood, gestured to him to follow, and led the way to an office area with a desk, a computer, and filing cabinets. She reached inside a desk drawer and pulled out a ten thousand dollar bundle of hundreds. She counted out ten bills. "Here's a thousand dollars. Find yourself a room. Somewhere quiet that doesn't ask too many questions. Get bathed. You smell like a goat."

Todd let that one go. There was no arguing the point.

"Then come back, and I'll give you another thousand as a down payment."

"For what?"

"For killing my husband."

The next morning, Todd sat in the passenger seat of his Toyota parked opposite an office building in the financial district. People would pay less attention to him if he were sitting in the passenger seat. If anyone asked what he was doing, he was waiting for a friend. As deceptions went, it was a simple yet effective.

Jeff Carlson sat somewhere on the eighth floor of the building. This was the professional face of his business dealings. Unlike the semiderelict building where Todd had encountered Jessica, the office building was modern. This was the headquarters for Carlson Realty and Carlson Shipping. The building's directory listed software companies, accountancy and law firms, and regional headquarters for a number of Fortune 500 companies. Respectable rubbed shoulders with criminal. Not surprisingly, it was a front. The realty firm helped launder dirty money that the shipping firm generated in the shape of unsavory goods and services. If Jeff's neighbors only knew the truth.

It was a typical Seattle day. Gray with the threat of rain. The weather matched his mood. No wonder so many people committed suicide every year in this place. Guilt seeped into him like the dank humidity in the air. He'd agreed to kill this guy. He'd taken Jessica's money, done all the things she'd told him to do, and now he was doing the groundwork before pulling the trigger. He thought he'd reached his limit when he'd tortured Mears, but he was wrong. He was way off plan here. Of all the new skills he was learning, killer wasn't one he'd expected to add to his résumé. The only way he could justify the killing to himself was the condition he'd applied to Jessica's terms.

"And what's that?" she'd asked.

"I need some information on someone."

"Who?"

"Someone you have business dealings with in San Francisco."

A flicker of recognition shone in her eyes. "When you've completed the job."

It was a fair enough trade, at the time. Now he wished he'd pushed a little harder.

An ex-marine pushed his way out of the building. Todd didn't know for sure if this guy was an ex-marine or not, but he carried himself with that ramrod straightness and a precision that he associated with the military. The ex-marine represented half of the double act that lagged behind Jeff Carlson. Todd had to give props to Carlson for that. He wasn't the stereotypical mobster. He didn't draw attention to himself by surrounding himself with thugs. He drove himself while the jarhead twins followed at a respective distance. Todd took this hands-off approach as a sign of confidence. Jeff Carlson wasn't under the threat of attack. He sat very comfortably in his world. He was his own lord and master. Todd guessed this also was a sign he could handle himself in a clinch. Just his luck.

The ex-marine crossed the street toward the deli on the corner. He placed an order and returned with a large paper sack. *Lunch for the boys*, Todd thought.

Todd's driver's door flew open, and a man slid into the seat.

"Hey, what the hell do you think you're doing?" Todd barked.

"Shut the fuck up, before I shoot you." The man, in his forties and blond, jabbed a pocket-sized gun in Todd's ribs.

Todd started to raise his hands, until the blond man told Todd to put them down, remarking, "We're all friends here."

"Friends don't point guns at each other."

"I didn't say we were good friends. Hands in pockets, please." When Todd had stuffed his hands in his pockets, he lifted the .357 from Todd's waistband. "Must be uncomfortable sitting on that."

"You get used to it."

"Jessica hired you, didn't she?"

"Who?"

The blond slammed the butt of his gun down on Todd's thigh, striking a nerve connected to his groin. Todd doubled over and fought the nausea clawing up his throat.

"Don't play games. I might stop liking you if you do. Jessica hired you, didn't she?"

"Yes." Todd's reply came out strangled.

"She wants you to kill Jeff, right?"

"If you know all this, why are you asking?" Todd wondered where he'd gone wrong. Probably from the beginning. He hadn't been looking for anyone because he didn't know he needed to. Another lesson learnt. Always assume someone is following.

"You don't look like a hitter," the blond said, ignoring Todd's point.

"How do you know? Not all hitters look the same or everyone would spot them."

"How much has she agreed to pay you?"

"Fifteen grand."

The blond laughed. "Yeah, you're no hitter. If you were, you wouldn't touch the job without a zero on the end."

Todd was tired of this twenty questions crap. "Who are you? Bodyguard? Cop?"

"Referee. Guardian angel. A mix of both."

"Thanks for clearing things up for me."

"Hey, enough of the smart mouth." The blond raised his gun up for another hammer blow.

That was enough for Todd to cease and desist.

"You don't know anything about the Carlsons, do you?"

Todd said nothing.

"The Carlsons represent an impressive trading bloc in the Pacific Northwest for all things criminal. And when I say the Carlsons, I mean Jeff and Jessica in equal parts. Jessica is no trophy wife. Their marriage is one of sound business. Two factions ran Seattle. Jeff ran one. Jessica the other. They married for purely financial reasons. Now, Jessica wants to liquidate that arrangement, but she doesn't want to split assets. That's why anyone with an ounce of sense won't touch her hit, and why she has to lowball it out to guys like you. No offense."

"And where do you fit into all this as referee and guardian angel?"

"I'm trying to keep them from killing each other."

"Why?"

"Selfish reasons. Seattle is a stable city. Things are under control. If Jessica kills Jeff and assumes control, it will lead to destabilization. Some upstart will think they are entitled and will try to take it from her. I don't want that to happen."

Even organized crime had politicians. *How disappointing*, Todd thought.

"What's your name?" the blond asked.

"Todd Collins."

"I'm Martin Fisk. How would you like to meet Jeff?"

"Who's this?" Jeff Carlson asked.

"One of Jessica's Lost Boys," Fisk answered.

Carlson stiffened in his seat. He looked more annoyed than

frightened. He tossed a glance the ex-marines' way, and they marched out of the office.

Fisk settled into one of the visitor chairs opposite Carlson. Todd did likewise.

As corner offices went, Carlson had a nice one, consisting of the usual modern conveniences required by today's corporate execs. That included the secretary that Todd guessed saw no evil, spoke no evil, and heard no evil. She never looked up from her computer monitor to acknowledge their arrival. The same applied to the dozen or so people working away at their desks. Everyone seemed to be white-collar professionals doing white-collar work. It made for a nice cover. Todd wondered if these people believed they truly worked for a realty and shipping company. It was a reasonable hypothesis, if it weren't for the ex-marines. Their presence spoiled the front. They were a pair of square pegs who did nothing but hang out in an office adjacent to Carlson's.

"My wife hired you to kill me?"

"Yes."

"My wife and I have a complex marriage, Mr . . . "

"Todd Collins."

"My wife and I have a complex marriage, Mr. Collins. One that most people wouldn't understand."

"There's no need to explain. It's none of my business."

"Thank you. Correct me if I'm wrong, but you didn't come to Seattle with the sole desire to kill me."

"No. I came looking for work."

"What kind of work?"

Fisk removed Todd's .357 and placed it on the desk. Carlson studied the weapon and nodded like its presence explained everything.

"I'm guessing you aren't a nine-to-five sort of guy?"

"Not anymore."

"Well, I think we can put you to work."

"What do I do about Mrs. Carlson?"

"Tell her she'll have to find someone else," Carlson said matter-of-factly.

Todd thought about her accuracy with a gun and willingness to use one. "And she'll just accept that, will she?"

"Probably not."

"You'll have to do a good job convincing her," Fisk added.

Carlson and Fisk pumped Todd for information. He gave up as much as he could without giving it all up. He was wedged between a pair of hard places after all. They seemed satisfied with his answers. Carlson said Fisk would put him to work starting tomorrow. Fisk handed Todd some walking-around money and Carlson handed Todd back his gun. Todd wasn't sure if this was a test of trust or a suicidal bent on Carlson's part. He thought about the four rounds left in the .357's cylinder. Enough for Carlson, Fisk, and the ex-marines, but not enough for the witnesses. He slipped the revolver into his waistband.

Back on the street, Todd asked Fisk, "Now what?"

"I've got a lunch date, and you've got a parking ticket."

Flapping from the windshield was a newly applied ticket.

"I would pay that. Those things stack up, if you don't."

"Thanks."

Fisk produced a cell phone and punched in a number. He told the person answering that he'd be a few minutes late, then hung up.

"Todd, play it square with Jessica. She'll write you off as a pussy that bitched out on her. She'll complain, but she'll move on and find someone else to do the deed."

"What happens then?"

"That's not your problem." Fisk tap-danced down the concrete stairs from the building. "Meet me at Pike Place Market at nine tomorrow. Don't be late."

Todd watched Fisk hail a cab before crossing the street back to his Toyota. He peeled off the parking ticket, screwed it into a ball, and tossed it on the backseat. He had no intention of staying in Washington long enough for it to matter.

He returned to the phone booth he'd called Jessica from the day before and called her. "We need to talk," he said.

"I'm busy. Be here at seven, tonight."

He didn't mind the brush off. It gave him time to rehearse his speech.

He returned to the Travelodge where he was staying. It might not be situated in the prettiest part of the city, but it was quiet, clean, and a block away from a strip club that boasted hundreds of sexy girls and three ugly ones. It was nice to be among honest folks for a while.

He inched by the cramped reception area to get to his room. He made the mistake that women are warned against in parking lots late at night. He didn't have his key handy. He didn't bother to get out his cardkey until he reached his room, and that was when they pounced. He didn't even sense them until they drove him face first into the door. The inside of his skull rang with the same off-key tone as the hollow core door when his head bounced off it. Too dazed to fight back, the cardkey was out of his hand and into somebody else's. The door flew open, and two sets of hands thrust him into his room then slammed him down onto the carpet. He tried to scream for help, but he only assisted them in inserting a gag into his mouth. Seven seconds later, zip ties bound his hands and ankles behind him, and another zip tie bound the ties together to complete the hog tying demonstration. The hands hoisted him up and tossed him onto the bed. Carlson's ex-marines looked down at him, pleased with their work.

Carlson walked into the room and closed the door. He sat on the bed opposite Todd and nodded to one of his thugs. The one Todd had witnessed going out for lunch tugged the gag out of his mouth.

"So my wife hired you to kill me."

"I don't think she's going to take no for an answer."

Carlson laughed. "That sounds like Jessica. Bet you wished you'd been more persuasive."

"Under the circumstances, yes."

"Well, I want to help you out of your difficult situation."

Todd didn't like the sound of that. Handling Jessica was going to be a problem, but not that much of a problem. After Fisk left him, he'd considered getting in his car and just driving off. Sure, he needed information about the small man, but he could find it elsewhere. The Carlsons weren't worth this much crap. But the time to run looked to have just run out.

"How can you help me?" Todd asked, losing sensation in his hands and feet.

"You're going to kill Jessica for me."

"I thought you said—"

"Forget what I said. That was for Fisk's benefit. He's got a thing for Jessica. He thinks he can save her from herself and me. He's wrong. He can't. How does twenty-five grand sound?"

Not that great. Money was being thrust at him from all directions and the numbers kept getting higher every time, but none of it was reaching the echelons Fisk had mentioned.

"Seeing as I know a bit more about the job and the ramifications associated with it, I was thinking of a number in the six-figure range."

Carlson and the ex-marines found that hilarious.

"If you were worth six-figures, I'd pay it," Carlson said, "but you're not. You'll take the twenty-five, which is damn generous for a guy who was planning to put a bullet in me. If you don't, I'll put a bullet in you. Now, what do you think?"

"Twenty-five sounds great."

"Good man." Carlson jerked a nod in the direction of the ex-marines.

One of the jarheads flipped out a switchblade and sliced open the zip ties. The rush of blood back to Todd's extremities forced a sigh of pleasure from him.

Carlson rose to his feet and headed toward the door with his ex-marines in tow. "As far as Fisk knows, this didn't happen," Carlson called out. "Okay?"

Todd didn't move until Carlson was long gone. He rolled onto his back and massaged the red rings around his ankles and wrists. He glanced over at the clock on the nightstand. It wasn't quite two o'clock.

"It's me" was the magic phrase to open the doors to Jessica's building. She greeted Todd without a gun or a pat down. Music spilled from an unseen sound system. It was low and soothing, but did nothing to take the tension out of the air.

"He's not dead, is he?" she demanded.

"No," Todd replied. "Do you know you're being watched?"

Todd had to keep things tight from now on. He couldn't afford to say too much and risk Jessica's hair-trigger temper. Also, he wanted her opinion of Fisk. Was Fisk the lynchpin in the Carlsons' affairs he believed himself to be?

"Fisk, you mean?"

"Blond guy, mid-forties, stands around five ten."

"That's him."

"Yeah, well, it made it real hard to follow your husband with him tagging along behind me. Who is he?"

Jessica guided Todd to the sofa, sliding in next to him. She laid out a story, which pretty much tallied with Jeff's. Fisk had worked for Jeff since the beginning. She'd noticed him tailing her. At first, she'd suspected Jeff just wanted to keep tabs on her, but over time she realized that Fisk had a thing for her.

"That's precious, but that pretty much screws up my chances of killing your husband."

"You've grown some balls since yesterday." She patted his cheek.

Condescension shone in her eyes.

"No, I have a sense of urgency. You asked me to kill your husband, and that's fine. I can do it—not my thing—but I'll do it. But that's real hard when I've got a witness hanging over my shoulder." Todd's words tumbled out in an avalanche of inspired neurosis. It was a convincing act, because he believed every word. The Carlsons and Fisk were crowding him, cutting off his air. One of them had to give him room.

"Steady there. Don't you worry about Fisk. I'll keep him occupied. Is that all you wanted from me tonight?"

"No. This Fisk knows me. I can't afford to hang around town and to follow your husband until a gap opens up. Your husband is never alone thanks to the two military types that follow behind him at a safe distance."

Jessica smiled. "You've impressed me. I didn't think you'd pick up on them so quickly."

Todd didn't like that remark. What was she expecting? For him to just walk up to him on the steps of his building and cap him there in the street with his bodyguards twenty yards behind? Suddenly, Todd felt the sticky wet stamp of expendable on his back. It made sense from Jessica's point of view. He caps Carlson, and the ex-marines cap him. The circle of silence is kept sacred. The money she'd promised him seemed to have shifted from her desk drawer to another hemisphere. Jessica wasn't the one to give him the space he needed.

"So how do you want to play this thing?" she asked.

"I need him alone. I need his entourage to be occupied elsewhere when I do this."

"I think that can be arranged," she said with a cat that's just got the cream look. "Lie low for a couple of days while I sort some things out."

Todd got up to leave.

"I do have one request."

"What's that?"

"I want to be there when you do it."

Fisk was already waiting at the coffee shop opposite Pike Place Market's north arcade when Todd arrived. Fisk indicated to a waitress for another menu. Todd glanced over the menu, but his stomach churned at the thought of food. Nerves were setting in. This was taking too long and getting too messy. He couldn't see himself getting out of this without something sticking to him. The waitress waited for him to order and he disappointed her by just ordering coffee.

"Not hungry?" Fisk asked when the waitress walked off.

"Not much of a breakfast guy."

"You should try. You'll feel better."

Todd sipped his coffee. "Maybe tomorrow."

Fisk's breakfast arrived, and Todd's stomach churned at the smell of eggs and sausage. Todd brought his coffee to his mouth so he could distract his nausea with the aroma. Fisk missed the charade.

"What do we do today?" Todd asked.

"We've got a little business over here."

"Doing what?"

"You'll see."

Fisk paid the check and walked Todd to 1st Avenue. He stopped at an Asian-owned knick-knack store at the edge of the market district. It sold the usual touristy crap you found in every big city. A couple of Asian teenagers straightened stock on the shelves. The place smelled freshly decorated. The woman behind the register recognized Fisk immediately and broke into a wail of happy shrieks, not all of it in English. She came out from behind the register to pump Fisk's hand with a two-fisted shake and did the same with Todd. Fisk greeted her in what Todd took to be Chinese. It came out smooth yet practiced.

"Friend?" the woman asked, looking at Todd.

"A colleague, Mrs. Ho. I'm showing him the ropes."

"Good. Good."

Mrs. Ho called over the teenagers and introduced them as her children. She gushed about their potential for greatness. The teenagers did their best to ignore the display. Nobody liked to see their parents act beneath themselves.

Feeling awkward under her intense gaze, Todd smiled.

The store's only customer left with no purchases in hand.

"Is Mr. Ho here?" Fisk asked.

"Yes. Out back."

Fisk strode to the rear of the store like he knew the layout well and opened the door marked private. The Ho teenagers kept their gazes downcast as if eye contact would turn them to stone.

Fisk waited for the door to close before shouting out, "Mr. Ho." He walked through the stock room, examining open boxes containing the unsold items resting in popcorn chips, and calling out Ho's name.

"What are we doing here?" Todd asked.

"Our job. Mr. Ho."

Mr. Ho emerged from a poorly framed box that pretended to be an office. He was small and frail. His clothes hung off him, making him look older than he was. Todd guessed he was in his late forties carrying a ten-year penalty. Unlike Mrs. Ho, Mr. Ho exhibited no joviality.

"Mr. Fisk," he said, his accent distorting the words. "Good to see you."

"Good to see you again, Mr. Ho. I thought you'd been avoiding me. This is my colleague, Mr. Collins."

Todd didn't like how his name was being bandied about. Fisk was tossing his out, too, so Todd guessed no one would be telling tales. This was going to be a town Todd could never return to, that was for sure.

"We've come about——"

"I know," Mr. Ho interrupted. "I'm sorry." He dropped his head.

"You see, Todd, this is the harsh reality of the true American dream." Fisk backed the man into his office. "Mr. Ho here came to this great nation to start a business, to prosper, and he needed money for that. Money that he didn't have. He needed a loan. But as an immigrant, he had no credit record in the U.S. and conventional lines of credit weren't available. That's where Carlson Realty stepped up to the plate. They provided these wonderful premises and a generous loan. But Mr. Ho hasn't been paying back what he owes, have you. Mr. Ho?" Fisk picked up an illustrated jewelry box where the illustration had been an adhesive transfer that had been lacquered over. "And I can see why when you try to sell crap like this. No wonder you have more staff than customers in the store."

Fisk hurled the jewelry box at the ground. It bounced off the concrete floor and broke apart. Mr. Ho flinched at the sight of his merchandise's destruction. Todd felt nauseous all over again.

"I'm expecting a payment of at least three thousand dollars, Mr. Ho. Please tell me you have it, because that interest is killing you."

"Mr. Fisk, if I could hold off paying you for a month, I would be in your debt."

Fisk choked out his derision in the form of a laugh.

"It would give the store a chance to bring in customers."

"I don't think so. I think, Mr. Ho, you have to be taught a lesson about the rules of a free market economy. Todd, don't mark his face. Keep it to the body. I don't want anyone getting curious."

"What?" Todd said. Everything snapped into place. This was racketeering 101.

Fisk turned his attention away from Mr. Ho to Todd. "I want you to hurt him."

"I think he's got the message."

"Just do as I tell you."

Mr. Ho backed away from the men into the confines of his office.

Todd crossed a line he never thought he'd cross and followed Mr. Ho.

The Chinese man, realizing he'd backed himself into a corner, panicked. He searched for a route of escape that would take him past Fisk and Todd. There was none, and it only served to fuel his panic. He flailed at the weak walls in hope of bursting through. The walls weren't to code but strong enough to withstand Mr. Ho. Todd closed in on him.

"Body blows only, Todd," Fisk advised.

Mr. Ho whirled around to face Todd. He dropped his arms down as not to provoke a fight. In his native tongue, he pleaded to Todd.

Todd grabbed Mr. Ho by the throat and pinned him to his desk. The man begged for time and consideration. Todd locked gazes with him and saw into him. He felt the man's struggle to attain his dreams and felt them being shattered all at once. Todd raised his fist to strike. Hitting a defenseless man should have been easy, yet it was anything but. What possible satisfaction could anyone feel from beating this man? It was no different from pulling the wings from a bug. He couldn't do it and dropped his fist.

"Get out of my way."

Fisk jerked Todd aside. The flicker of relief that appeared on Mr. Ho's face died when Fisk drove a fist into his gut. The blow sounded like a two-by-four striking a side of beef. It cut Mr. Ho's strings, and he crumpled. Only Fisk's steadying hand kept him from crashing to the floor.

Fisk delivered blow after blow, until the man's flesh and spirit surrendered. Todd never challenged Fisk. He didn't fear his own beating, but his interference would have made Mr. Ho's worse. Fisk would have done it out of spite, just to teach Todd a lesson. After Fisk delivered his last punch, he released Mr. Ho, and he slid to the floor.

Fisk dropped to one knee and loomed over the Chinese man. "This is your first and last warning. I won't ever hurt you like this again.

You have two lovely kids out there. You won't if you disappoint me next time. Have my money for me next week."

Mr. Ho wept in reply.

"Both of you have ruined my morning."

Fisk grabbed Todd by the shirt and thrust him out of the store the way they'd come. Mrs. Ho looked confused and asked if something was wrong. Store patronage had swollen to three and they looked just as confused. The kids understood and immediately rushed in the direction of their father.

"A small misunderstanding, Mrs. Ho," Fisk said. "Nothing to worry about." And he shoved Todd out onto the street.

By the time he'd gotten Todd to his car, he'd cooled down. He let go of Todd's shirt, unlocked the doors to his Saab convertible, and told him to get in. He drove to the outskirts of the town to a dingy bar that overlooked the city. The bar wasn't open, but Fisk had keys and let them in. He poured two heavy measures of bourbon, never bothering to ask Todd if he drank, let alone liked, bourbon. He set the glasses down on the bar with the freshly opened bottle.

"I don't know whether to be disappointed or not," Fisk said after knocking back his bourbon.

Todd dodged a response and gulped down half the liquor. He let it burn his insides. He needed to be sanitized.

"You came to kill Carlson, but you couldn't drop a punch on a poor, dumb immigrant."

"You should have warned me."

"It was a test."

"You get to study for a test."

Fisk refreshed their glasses. "Not all tests."

"I failed, I suppose."

"I haven't made up my mind. Pass or fail depends on your perspective. To the Carlsons, you failed. You're no good to them. To your pastor, you passed. You're a good Christian."

"I don't have a pastor."

"You're not the only one." Fisk made short work of his second bourbon. He poured again and capped the bottle and returned it to its shelf. "What did you really come to Seattle for? You said work, but I don't think so."

"The name of a man in San Francisco. I believe the Carlsons deal with him."

"Deal with him—how?"

"I don't know the details, but he's part of a drug distribution scam. Stolen luxury cars get driven across country carrying shipments of cocaine in the interior."

Fisk made no attempt to deny or confirm the operation. He sipped his bourbon this time.

"What do you want with this person—a job?"

"I've already worked for him. I just want to give notice."

"And you don't know this person's name?"

Todd shook his head.

"You do suck at this game."

"But I'm learning fast."

"I'll take your word for it. Describe your employer."

Todd outlined the small man's description. "Know him?"

Fisk shrugged. "Let me look into it. I'll see what I can dig up."

Todd drank. This time, he let the liquor warm him and not burn him.

"What about Jeff Carlson?" Todd asked.

"What about him?"

"What are you going to tell him about me?"

"Haven't decided, so don't press me. Okay?"

They sat in silence for a while. Each of them lost in their own thoughts. The silence never became awkward or ugly. Todd broke it when his glass was empty.

"How did you get into this?"

"In a lot of ways it just happened, but I owe my career to one man."

"Jeff Carlson?"

"Hell, no. I owe everything to someone I truly respected. You would have liked him."

"What's his name?"

"Munson. He's dead now."

Todd made it back to his motel by late afternoon. Fisk had left him to his own devices when the manager came to open the bar. Away from anyone that had anything to do with the Carlsons, he'd wandered around the town. He ended up at Gas Works Park, sitting opposite the water, watching the boats and rowers wander up and down the Sound. As the sun set, the strip club's boast of hundreds of sexy girls and three ugly ones lured him. He wanted to see just how ugly the ugly ones were. It was the best way to end the day.

But it wasn't to be. The ex-marines were waiting for him in the motel's parking lot. This time, they kept their hands and zip ties to themselves. The ground rules had been set.

Todd didn't ask what they wanted and got into the car with them.

They drove him back to Carlson's office. It was after five, and the building had been evacuated, except for the guards on the security desk. People had better things to do. The ex-marines left him at the doors, and he checked in with the guards. The guards okayed his arrival and sent him up. Carlson met him at the elevator.

"You had a good first day, Fisk tells me."

So the man had covered for him. Todd didn't know why he should have. Maybe Fisk realized the hole he was in and was giving him a way out. It could have been out of kindness, but Todd guessed it was for more business reasons. He could make a real mess of things if he botched something. Even if Carlson learned the truth about Todd and gave him a bullet severance package, that would still bring Carlson attention he didn't need. Fisk was a guardian angel after all—and not just for the Carlsons.

Carlson led Todd to his office. "Fisk had some ideas on where you can fit in this organization, and I'm happy to let that happen."

"Thank you." Todd wasn't really sure what else to say. There was a but coming, and he braced himself for it.

Carlson breezed by the unoccupied desks. Even organized crime kept corporate hours these days. He sat down at his desk with the city he ran behind him. Todd sat in the same seat he'd sat in this morning.

"Obviously, your part in this organization is dependent on you passing your probation."

"Jessica?"

Carlson smiled. "Got it in one. Dispose of her, and you've got a job for life."

"Like Munson?"

Carlson maintained the smile, but it looked brittle.

"Like Munson," he conceded. "I'm in his debt." The smile fractured and fell away. "And I'll be in yours, if you can get the job done."

"Mr. Carlson, it will be done. By this time next week, Jessica will no longer be a thorn in your side."

And Todd meant it.

Two days later, Jessica called. In those two days, Todd had done nothing. Fisk covered for him. The word back to Carlson was that he was doing good work. Todd turned tourist and discovered the strip club underestimated the number of ugly girls at their club. He couldn't fault the management for trying. Their marketing ploy had worked. God bless the free market economy.

"Todd, I have something."

Jessica reeled off an address on the waterfront, and he met her there. He'd expected a pretty marina setting, but this was where fisherman worked. She waited for him at a quay in front of a corroded fishing boat.

"What's the plan?" Todd asked.

"A burial at sea."

"I'm going to have a hard time getting him on this boat with you and a gun. I don't know anything about boats. I'm going to need someone to captain this thing, and I'm not too keen on witnesses."

"Jeff will drive you out, and I'll drive you back."

"Again, there's the problem of keeping you hidden."

"Don't worry. I won't be here. I'll be there." She pointed to a barge floating out in the distance.

Jessica piloted the trawler out to the barge. She explained that the place acted as a nice drop off for their incoming cargo. Not all of it reached the port.

"A floating smuggler's cove," Todd said.

"And a quiet place for a murder."

"It's done," Todd said.

"What?" Carlson spoke with sleep in his throat.

He'd called Carlson's private phone number. He'd given it to Todd at his office. Apparently the phone was a cell of the pay as you go variety. It would be going in the trash after tonight.

"What you asked, it's done."

"Is it now?" A grin made it down the line. "Come to the office in the morning."

"Do you want to see the body before disposal?"

Carlson pondered that one. Todd knew he couldn't resist. There was too much pent up hate for him not to want to see.

"Sure. Where are you?"

"The barge. Come alone."

"Alone?"

"I don't want people knowing what I did for you. You bring someone, they are going to tell someone. Eventually, it's going to get back to Fisk or someone else with alliances belonging to Jessica. When that happens, it's over for me."

"Okay. Alone it is."

Todd almost felt sorry for the guy.

Todd waited for two hours in the cold on the barge. The wind and spray cut through his clothes. What was taking so long? He hoped Carlson wasn't shafting him. He couldn't rely on anyone for this to go as planned. Carlson could take this opportunity to take care of him. It was just as easy to dispose of two bodies as it was one. All he could do was hope.

The trawler's engine won the battle with the wind. Todd went to the side of the barge, and the boat's spotlight picked him out. He waved back to the boat, his hand tight on the .357.

Carlson brought the boat alongside the barge with practiced ease. He climbed up the rope ladder just as easy.

"How the hell did you get her here?"

Todd used the truth, so he wouldn't screw up the details. The story came out smooth without sounding false. Every convincing lie needed to sit on a solid foundation of truth to work. "This is where we planned to kill you."

Carlson belted out a laugh. "That's brilliant. I bet she never saw it coming."

"And neither did you," Jessica said back. She emerged from the shadows pointing her automatic. "See what he brought to the party."

Todd jerked out the .357. He approached Carlson with caution. The man bristled with rage.

"Hands up," Todd ordered.

"You sided with her after all I did for you?"

Todd shrugged. "You didn't offer that much, and she did ask first. I've got to show some loyalty. Without loyalty, you aren't anything."

"You piece of shit."

Todd relieved Carlson of a Glock. Oddly, it was the only weapon he found on him. Somehow, Todd expected to find a backup.

Todd went behind Carlson and stamped down on the back of his knee. Carlson folded and sprawled face first on the wet, checkerplate decking. Todd stepped on the man's back to keep him from moving. He aimed both guns at Carlson.

"Do it," she said.

Todd didn't look up. He didn't want her seeing the fear.

Carlson's head twisted to see Todd and spew expletives. He looked up with contempt and hate, but Todd saw Mr. Ho's frightened face. When did it become so simple to extinguish a life? What had to be wrong or missing in someone that they could cross the line between person and killer? All Todd knew was that he didn't have it. He aimed his .357 at Jessica. Hers had been on Carlson, and she jerked her gun at Todd.

"This is one marital dispute you'll have to sort out between the two of you."

"You gutless bastard," she hissed.

"Yeah, well, at least I know what I am."

"Jessica, you were always a bad judge of character," Carlson berated.

"You don't put a bullet in him," Jessica warned. "I'll put one in you."

"That might be a bit difficult." Todd dropped the Glock on the ground. It landed just out of Carlson's reach. "I'm going to take the boat now. You do whatever you need to do."

"You said you didn't know how to pilot one," Jessica said.

"I'll learn."

"Don't think this lets you off the hook with me," Carlson warned

Todd.

"I don't, but it depends who's the quicker on the draw."

Todd eased the pressure on Carlson's back. He squirmed for the Glock. His fingers snagged on the trigger guard. Jessica shifted her aim to Carlson.

"Leave it where it is, Jeff," she warned.

"Good luck," Todd said and bolted for the rope ladder. The quick succession of shots and the order stopped him.

"Put the gun down and turn around."

Todd put his .357 down and turned around. Jessica lay on her back with half her face lost under a mask of blood. Carlson lay face down with the Glock wrapped in his fist and his brains deposited on his back, the shot having gone through the top and out the back of his skull. Fisk stood between the two, casting a glance over his handiwork.

He kicked the gun out of Jessica's dead grasp while keeping his aim on Todd. "I'm glad you didn't go through with it. I didn't want to have to kill you too."

"How do you know we'd be here?"

"Who did you think gave her the idea?" Fisk yanked the Glock from Carlson's grasp and hurled it into the water.

"You and she were in it together, but you killed her?"

"There was a time when I would have killed Jeff for her, but those days are long since gone. I was just playing the game. These two were so focused on getting rid of each other that they never looked outside the goldfish bowl. Help me roll these two into the water."

"Are we cool?" Todd asked.

"Yeah, we're going to be after all this is out of the way. Now pick up your gun, take the bullets out, and put them in a pocket, then put the gun away."

Todd did so and helped Fisk weight the Carlsons down and roll them into Puget Sound. Fisk claimed Jessica's automatic and tossed that in after her.

"I'll give you a ride back," Fisk said.

"Why?" Todd asked back aboard the trawler.

Fisk was at the controls. His gun was holstered and no longer a barrier to questions.

"Munson."

"The guy in Florida?"

"He wasn't just run down crossing the street. Jessica and Jeff ordered that. The cops were closing in on him. The Carlsons couldn't take a chance, but Munson wouldn't have talked. It wasn't his way. It was a shitty decision for a guy that everyone owed." Fisk went quiet after that.

"You used me." Todd put no malice on the statement.

"Yeah. Word got back to me that Munson's accident was no accident, and I knew then I would take care of Jessica and Jeff. I was looking for a way and when you fell into my lap, you were too good a tool not to use."

"But not a tool you want to keep around."

"No." Fisk smiled. "You've got things to do, and I can't use a guy like you."

"Fair enough."

They moored the boat up, and Fisk walked Todd to his Toyota.

"The name you wanted," Fisk said. "You want it?"

It was a good question. This was all getting to be a little much just to get back at the small man. It was stretching him directions he wasn't used to or wanted to get used to. But the small man wasn't going to go away until Todd stopped him or died trying. Dying. He hadn't thought this would cost him his life, but it was the small man's end game, and Todd would have to keep playing until someone won.

"Yeah."

"Leo Cochrane. That's your small man."

Leo Cochrane. Todd ran his mind over the name. He didn't know what to feel at this point. He felt only as if he had learned a fact like any other fact. Nothing would feel good until he had disposed of the small man.

"I'll throw in a bonus name too. Jeremiah Black."

"Who's that?"

"Leo's competition. You might find him a useful wedge."

"How will I get to them?"

"That's for you to work out."

Fisk put out a hand. Todd took it and shook. There was strength and friendship in Fisk's tight grip, and Todd returned it.

"Don't ever think about returning to Washington. You're a loose end, and you can dangle anywhere but here. Got me?"

Todd nodded. "I'll leave tonight."

"Good. Now piss off."

Fisk went to leave, but Todd stopped him.

"One more favor?"

"You're pushing your luck."

"I know, but I'm repaying a favor to someone."

"Okay."

"There's a dealership in Dallas where you send stolen cars with coke in them. The dealership is called Ruskin's."

"What of it?"

"Forget that it exists."

"Consider it forgotten."

"Thanks."

Fisk pulled out a cell phone and made a call for a pickup. Todd guessed it would be a busy night. Everyone had to be prepped on the new power structure before the start of the next business day.

Todd gunned the Toyota's engine. It struggled in the Seattle cold. He let the car warm up. Fisk came around to the window.

"Where to now?" he asked.

"Home."

Part 5: The Small Man

The Bay Area felt different to Todd. Colors were vibrant. Even the air smelled different. Someone had played with the controls while he'd been away. Had the Bay Area changed or was it him who'd changed? Regardless, Todd felt good to be home.

He didn't hide. Cochrane wouldn't be expecting him to return, and Todd had no allies in the Bay Area that he would know. He liked the idea of hiding in plain sight. It was a small victory he could celebrate.

He drove by his old apartment in El Cerrito to find the place had been cleaned out. He'd expected as much. He wasn't back to rake over old coals. This was fresh start time—as soon as Cochrane was taken care of. And there was no better time to start.

He parked his road-weary Toyota at El Cerrito Plaza. It reminded him of the faithful horses of the Pony Express that had galloped their guts out until they dropped and the rider simply switched to a fresh horse. Sadly for the Toyota, that day was close. The detour back to Texas had sealed the car's fate. Todd had stopped to pick up the cocaine in the bus station locker. The coke would be a useful bargaining chip for Todd. He could trade it, sell it, or plant it to bring Cochrane down. How sweet would it be to skewer him with his own junk?

Getting to Cochrane was the problem, though. It had occurred to him on his drive from Texas to the Bay Area how unfamiliar he was with Cochrane. Other than the chop shop, he knew nothing about him or his operations. He needed someone who could inject him into Cochrane's world, and that person was John "Felix" Katts. He parked and called Katts on his cell.

"Yeah." Katts seemed to have put all his worldly energy into that one word and still came up short. It was the response Todd expected for a Saturday afternoon.

"Felix, it's me."

"Jesus, is that you, Todd?" Katts was wide awake now. "Fuck, we all thought you were dead."

"And I'd like to keep it that way."

"Does this have anything with the two apes that came sniffing around the factory?"

"What apes?"

"They weren't cops, that's for sure." Katts described Cochrane's gorillas, Dalton and Vasquez. "They swung by twice to see if anyone had talked with you, and they weren't too frightened about leaning on anyone who didn't talk up."

"They been by lately?"

"Nah. Your job's toast, by the way. I went by your place too. The manager cleaned it out, the bastard. Ebayed your good shit and Goodwilled the rest."

"No great loss," Todd said and meant it. There was a time when his crappy jobs and apartment defined him, but not anymore. If he had Cochrane to thank for anything, it was that. He'd shown him a future where possibilities could exist. He had no idea what he was going to do once he'd dealt with Cochrane, but he wouldn't be punching a clock. "Like I said, I want everyone to think I'm dead."

"Are you in deep shit?"

"Yeah, but I'm climbing out. Can I come by? I need your help."

Understandably, Katts hemmed and hawed, but agreed after a little pressure from Todd. Todd drove out to the duplex Katts rented in Rockridge. Although he lived a block from the rejuvenated

Oakland suburb with its fancy restaurants and pretty boutiques, the duplex was an earth tremor away from demolition.

"What do you need, man?" Katts asked, after checking the street to make sure no one was scoping out the place and closing the drapes.

"It's cool, Felix," Todd said. "I'm not being tailed."

"Yeah, yeah, right. Come in."

Todd followed Katts into the living room. Katts lived how Todd expected. He forwent furniture and all modern conveniences so that he could support his extra curricular activity of trying every drug known to illegal medical science. General consensus was that Katts would smoke kitty litter if he believed he'd get a hit off it. Todd sank into a disheveled futon across from Katts's beloved La-Z-Boy.

"Do you need something?" Katts asked. "I've got a couple of cold ones in the fridge."

"No, I'm good."

Katts tossed out more hospitality until Todd stopped him. It was a delaying tactic. Todd felt Katts's apprehension. He wasn't the sharpest tool, but he'd guessed Todd wanted something less than kosher from him.

"So what do you need?"

"Answers to some questions, Felix."

Katts shrugged. "If I can."

"Do you know a guy called Leo Cochrane?"

"No."

"Jeremiah Black?"

"No times two."

This wasn't going the way Todd had hoped, but it was expected. Katts bought drugs and occasionally sold part of his stash to friends when his funds ran short. He didn't run with San Francisco's drug elite.

"Is that it?" Katts asked.

"Pretty much."

"I hate to ask, but who are they?"

"Heavyweight drug dealers."

That lit Katts up. He leapt to his feet, pouring out a string of curses. He leaned over Todd pinning him to his spot on the futon. Todd put his hands up in defense.

"Okay. I like weed and pills, and I've freebased once, but I'm not an addict. Look, do you see tracks?" Katts offered his unmarked arms for inspection. "Do you see?"

"Yeah, I see, Felix. You're clean."

"Damn straight, Todd." Too angry to speak, Katts turned away from Todd and fell into his La-Z-Boy. This simple act took the sting out of him. "I know what everyone thinks and says about me. I know I'm a joke to most people, but I don't find it funny."

"Sorry, Felix."

"Yeah, well, it doesn't fucking matter, does it?"

Todd hadn't expected this reaction and felt bad. It was true what he said though. He was the butt of the jokes everyone told in the lunchroom.

"I didn't mean it to sound the way it did," Todd said. "I came to you because you know people, not because you're a junkie."

Katts failed to look impressed and sulked.

"The reason the apes came looking for me is that I've pissed off Leo Cochrane, and I'm trying to square things. Jeremiah Black is someone who might be able to help. I'm wondering if any of the people you know might be able to hook me up with Black or give me some info on Cochrane."

Katts ran a hand over his shaven head. "I might be able to help. I deal with a guy for X. He's no bottom feeder. He knows people. I'm guessing these guys you want are hardcore. My guy won't be on their level, but he might get you to the next. Sound good?"

"More than good."

"Come back tonight, late. I'll take you to him."

The house party in the Oakland hills was jumping. At least a hundred people packed a vast, two-story house in a new development not far from the Claremont Hotel. It looked to be a house warming for a young couple. Katts cut a swath through the people, and Todd followed in his wake.

Katts stopped a guy dancing with a hot Hispanic girl who was in a low cut top that drew the eye. Over the sound system, Todd couldn't hear what was being said. Katts thanked the guy who was only too glad to get back to his girl.

"He's upstairs," Katts said to Todd.

They found Katts's dealer in a guest bathroom. He sat on the toilet with his wares spread out on his lap. Three eager guys and a girl, who had yet to graduate, stood with money in their fists. He played to his audience with a nice line of patter, but he cut the patter short when he saw Katts. He took their money and handed out prepackaged pills in tiny plastic bags.

"Tell your friends about Mickey," he said as the foursome filed out.

One of the guys flashed Todd and Katts a baleful look that Todd guessed was the guy's tough guy look. A month ago it would have mattered to Todd. Now, who cared?

"Hey, Felix, how's it going?" Mickey said. "Is this your friend?"

"I'm good, Mickey. Yeah, this is Todd."

Todd and Mickey exchanged nods. Mickey seemed to appraise Todd with his. Todd felt as though he'd just been X-rayed.

"Let's take this outside," Mickey said.

Mickey was mid- to late-twenties, tall and skinny. He talked tough, but one good punch would fell him like a tree. The glasses, with their cool looking frames, and the Xbox geek face helped his image. If Mickey worked crowds like this one, he was the perfect person to service them. He kept people in their comfort zones.

They retreated to the backyard. The fall chill kept people in the house, although a couple were fooling around somewhere in the darkness, judging by the grunting sounds. Mickey found a spot he liked where the patio lights failed to reach. They were silhouettes in the night, voices in the dark. If no one saw them or heard them, then it never happened.

"You want to know about Jeremiah Black?" Mickey asked.

"And Leo Cochrane," Todd said.

"I don't know him."

"But you know Jeremiah?"

"Look, I'm a foot soldier. I receive orders, and I follow them. The Jeremiah Blacks of this world don't come down to my level. I know his rep, and you'd be better off not pushing this any further."

It was impossible to ignore the note of panic building in Mickey's voice. Black sounded mean. That was good. If Todd was going to topple Cochrane then he needed someone like Jeremiah Black doing some of the pushing for him.

"I don't have a choice," Todd said. "I need to meet Black."

Mickey shifted his weight from one foot to the other. His nervousness spread to Katts.

"Maybe you should listen to him, Todd, man," Katts said.

"I wish I could. If you can't help, Mickey, that's cool. No harm, no foul, but I have to get to Black one way or another."

Mickey shook his head and sighed. "I can help. I'm not saying I can't. I just want you to know the risks."

"Duly noted. I'll make it worth Black's while."

"How?" Mickey asked.

"That's for Black to know, but you can pass it on to him that I can help his empire flourish more than it already does."

Mickey cast another appraising gaze over Todd. "Serious?"

"Serious."

"Okay. I know someone who's close to Black. I'll see if I can get you a meet."

"Thanks," Todd said. "I appreciate it."

"You should. This is going to cost me a lot of favors. I'm only doing this because Felix is a friend and a good customer."

Mickey came through on the following Monday. Todd got a call from Katts in the morning saying to be at Scala's Bistro in San Francisco at seven. A reservation would be in Todd's name. The news made Todd feel sick to his stomach, but he thanked Katts for his help.

"Todd, don't take this the wrong way, but I'd like it if you forgot all about me."

"Sure, Felix."

Katts ended the call.

Todd was on his own again. It was probably for the best. Things were bound to get messy from now on. It wasn't fair to drag people like Katts and Mickey into it any more than necessary.

The Scala's Bistro thing worried him. It was an odd place to meet. It was visible, for one. They'd be seen. It was safe though. It wasn't like Black could shoot him in a public place and not have some of the drama splash back on him. Of course, they'd done that in a hundred gangster movies. This wasn't the movies, but it wasn't far off. There was nothing he could do but play by Black's rules.

Todd had checked into a rundown motel in San Pablo. The place was relatively clean and their weekly rates were low, but their main selling point was they took anonymous cash. He hung out there until it was time for his appointment with Black. Scala's was attached to the Sir Francis Drake Hotel. A pair of beefeaters guarded the hotel's main entrance and carried in arriving and departing guests' bags. He arrived early. They couldn't seat him yet, so he sat at the bar. He was on his second beer when the hostess fetched him and led him to his table at the rear of the restaurant. A waiter arrived within the mandated ninety seconds of seating and fussed, but Todd sent him packing with a curt remark.

Seven p.m. came and went without Black's arrival. Todd caved to the waiter's repeated visits and ordered an appetizer he didn't want.

Todd knew what was going on. Black was testing him. He didn't know who Todd was, and he probably used all day to check him out. Having found nothing that made the radar, they'd force him to wait it out. He was probably being watched at this moment. He scanned the diners and the wait staff for someone paying too much attention to his table. Black's people were good. He didn't spot anyone. Still, he didn't feel he was in safe hands, and his anxiety grew with every passing minute.

At seven fifty, the hostess approached with a young African American man dressed in a tailored business suit that made him look like a newscaster. The man smiled when he reached the table. He put out a hand and said, "Mr. Collins, it's good to see you again."

"Likewise, Mr. Black." Todd rose and shook hands. Black's hand was cool and dry.

When the hostess left and they'd given their order to the irritating waiter, Black said, "Not what you were expecting, am I?"

"To be honest, I don't know what to expect these days. Life's been like that lately. But to answer your question, no."

"Regardless of my product, I'm a businessman. I want to sell to as many consumers as possible. That means I have to deal with people from the cream to the dregs and that requires me to be a chameleon. I have a degree in business from a well-respected UC college, and I speak fluent Ebonics. I can be anything I need to be. I thought you might like this environment."

"Not really my thing."

"So I understand. I thought it would make a nice change for you." Black snapped open his napkin and rested it across his lap. "You need to leave, now."

"What?"

"Room two-ten. Now. I need to see if you're fucking me or not."

They were waiting for him, three of them. Whereas Black claimed to be a chameleon, these guys couldn't boast the same. They were predators. One of them introduced himself as Kenneth, and he ordered the other two to strip Todd and look for a wire. Todd was glad he'd left the .357 in the Toyota. One of them barked at him to put his clothes back on.

"Can I go?"

"Mr. Black told us to give you this," Kenneth said and slammed a fist into Todd's gut.

Todd deflated, collapsing to his knees. He held his stomach, half expecting to find a hole there.

"He says, keep things on the level," Kenneth said.

Todd nodded. It was about the only thing he could do.

Black's men saw themselves out.

It was another ten minutes before Todd rejoined Black in the restaurant.

"I told them to keep your salad in the kitchen," Black remarked like nothing had happened.

Todd said nothing.

"Hey, don't take it so personally. You know I had to check."

The waiter deposited Todd's salad before him and departed.

"So what is it you want, Todd?"

"Do you know Leo Cochrane?"

Black speared an heirloom tomato and nodded.

"Leo doesn't like me breathing. I want to change that."

"Leo wants you dead. So what?"

"The guy tried to set me up, and I got wise to it. I'd like to return the favor."

"Again, so what?"

"I thought you'd be interested in helping me. It would be in your interest. With Leo out of the way, his clients become your clients. You said you're a businessman. Doesn't a hostile takeover sound good to a businessman?"

Black put his fork down and pushed his plate away from him. "You want me to become your triggerman? I ice Leo for you and all your problems disappear." He paused for Todd to comment. Todd didn't. "Do I look fucking stupid? If I kill Leo, that brings a bunch of unwanted heat down on me. There's nothing there for me. Leo kills you. Who cares? Leo will carry on. I will carry on. The world will carry on. There's no incentive for me. Although, I could buy myself a few points with Leo by selling you out to him."

Todd swallowed. He'd made a mistake. Black was going to hang him out to dry.

"But that can change," Black said.

"How?"

"What have you got to offer me?"

"Six kilos of cocaine. Leo was using it to set me up. I kept it."

"That's a lot of blow. Got any of it with you?"

"In my car."

"I think we should take a look at it."

They finished their meal. Black handed Todd the check. Well, it was Todd's date after all.

He walked Black to his Toyota at a nearby parking garage. Black's backup followed in a Dodge Magnum. They parked behind Todd's Toyota, boxing him in and giving the transaction some privacy. Todd popped the trunk and unzipped the backpack letting Black see one of the six kilo packets.

"I thought you said you had six kilos."

"I do," Todd said, "but I saw no reason why I should bring them all."

Black stepped back and snapped his fingers at Kenneth. He took the packet from Todd, slit it open with a switchblade and brought out a sample of the cocaine on the tip of the blade. He tasted some and rubbed some between his fingers before nodding at Black.

"Looks as if you've got something."

"So are you in?" Todd asked. "Will you help?"

Black pondered. Todd felt he'd already made up his mind and this was a performance for his crew.

"No."

Todd felt slapped. "What?"

"Six kilos of free blow is nice but not nice enough. You're on your own."

Todd went to say, "you can't." But Black could. This wasn't his fight, so why get involved? Todd decided Black was a good businessman.

"I think I'll keep this." Black took the coke from Kenneth. "Call it dessert. That okay with you?"

Kenneth eased back his leather jacket to let Todd see his Tec-9 machine pistol.

"It's the least I can do."

Black smiled and got into the back of the Dodge. His crew fell in behind him. Black powered down the window. "Good luck, brother, because you're going to need it."

Todd shrugged.

"If you can bring me something better than another five of these," Black held up the coke, "I'm willing to listen. Seriously. Okay?"

Todd nodded and watched the Dodge drive off. He supposed he should have felt pissed, but he didn't. He didn't want the drugs around him in the first place. Besides, this was the price of doing business. He still had more than enough coke left to use against Cochrane.

He left the parking garage and threaded his way back to the Bay Bridge. With the never-ending bridge construction, getting to the bridge these days was an epic quest that sent the driver twice around the city before access could be granted to an on ramp. Todd was turning right onto Harrison when a Malibu rear-ended him. The impact jolted Todd's Toyota into traffic.

"Son of a bitch," Todd groaned.

He waited for the light to change, then made his right and pulled into a parking lot with signs proclaiming For Authorized Personnel Only.

The driver of the Malibu followed into the parking lot. He popped out of the car and put his hands to his face when he saw the damage to Todd's car.

"I'm sorry, man," he said. "I totally misjudged my braking."

"Yeah, well," Todd said. He was more pissed at the inconvenience than the damage. Besides, he'd never invested in any insurance for the Toyota. The damage to his car was pretty bad. The bumper dangled, and the impact had caved in the back to the extent that it popped the trunk lid.

"Look, I was about to scrap this car." Todd attempted to reattach the plastic bumper. "I don't want go through insurance."

"And I don't want to shoot you." The driver had come in close, jammed a gun in Todd's ribs, and forced him against the trunk.

"Just take my wallet. Take the car if you want."

The driver ground the gun hard against Todd's ribs to shut him up. Todd complied.

"What were you doing with Jeremiah Black?"

Oh God, Todd thought. *Who the hell have I upset this time and more importantly, which side does he play for?*

"Nothing."

The driver bounced Todd's head off the Toyota's trunk. "Try again."

"What makes you think I'm going to tell you?" Having his head bounced off the trunk pissed him off. He wasn't about to be taken for a ride twice in one night, and he wasn't about to sell Black out to just anyone. He wanted some answers first.

The driver reached inside his pocket and filled Todd's vision with a San Francisco Police Department's detective shield.

"Oh, shit," Todd murmured.

"And you expect me to believe that pile of horseshit?" Redfern asked.

But he did. Todd watched the gears working in the detective's head as he spoke. A plan was forming in Redfern's brain. Todd wouldn't be going to jail tonight. If he worked this right, he might have just found the backup he needed to go after Cochrane.

They were sitting in Redfern's car a few blocks from the parking lot Todd had stopped in. Todd's battle-bruised Toyota still sat in the parking lot with the doors unlocked, the key in the ignition, and the .357 sitting in the glove box.

"I know it seems crazy," Todd said.

"That's a word for it."

"But it's all true." Admittedly, Todd had kept a number of the details from Redfern. He'd muted his encounters with Moran, Charlie, and the Carlsons. It would only create clutter.

"So what are you expecting to get out of this?" Redfern asked.

"Freedom. Cochrane has already shown me that his reach exceeds mine. Unless I do something to put him down, I'll always be looking over my shoulder."

"Put him down? Are you thinking of killing him?"

Todd wasn't sure how he should answer. Redfern was a cop after all, but Todd saw the hunger in his eyes. He wanted a big score, and Cochrane might just fit the bill.

"I don't know what I'm thinking," Todd said. "It might come down to that."

"Is that why you met with Jeremiah Black? You thought you'd use his muscle to get the job done, is that it?"

"Something like that," Todd conceded.

"You know how to pick your friends, don't you?" Redfern shook his head. "And what was that he took from your trunk?"

Todd said nothing.

"Have it your way. You told me Cochrane planted six kilos of coke on you. If you don't turn six kilos over to my custody, I'll know where to find the rest."

"So where does this leave us?" Todd asked.

"I don't know. You present a number of interesting possibilities, but it's just as easy to turn you in for a quick bust."

Redfern was trying to scare Todd, but he wasn't buying it. That look of hunger on his face was still there. Redfern needed Todd.

"Help me bring down Leo Cochrane," Todd said.

A police unit blew by with its lights and sirens going. Redfern watched its passing with professional interest. He was bulldog of a man, but a tired one at that. Muscle had given way to fat, but Todd had no fears that if Redfern wanted to knock him down, he wouldn't get up in a hurry. If it weren't for the badge, Todd wouldn't have believed Redfern was a cop. The hunger he'd seen in Redfern was a product of desperation. He looked like a gambler on a long losing streak. The man was a burnout. Given the choice, Todd would have preferred a different partner.

Redfern gunned the Malibu's engine. "I'm going to check you out. Where are you staying?"

Todd told him. "Aren't you frightened I'm going to run?"

"Where are you going to run? You told me Cochrane would find you wherever you go. You need me."

"And if I check out, then what?"

"Then you're bait."

Redfern left Todd on the street. It was a cheap play. No doubt a demonstration to show who was in charge. Todd let him play his games. He found his car just as he'd left it, .357 and all. He thanked whoever was watching over him and drove back to his motel. He found Redfern waiting for him in the parking lot in front of his room.

So leaving Todd on the street wasn't such a cheap play after all. Redfern just wanted a head start.

"It didn't take you long to make up your mind," Todd said, unlocking the door to his room.

"I'm a fast thinker," Redfern remarked.

Todd flicked on the lights and the TV. The walls were thin and he didn't want to be overheard.

"Can I see the coke?"

"It's not here. It's in a luggage locker in the city," Todd said. It wasn't. The coke was under the bed, but it wouldn't be by morning. It would be in a luggage locker. The stuff was drawing too many flies.

"What if I were to check the contents of the toilet tank?" Redfern asked with a smirk.

"Be my guest, but you'd only find water."

Redfern checked the tank and a couple of other places, but gave up before he looked under the bed. "I want to see it tomorrow."

Todd sat on the end of the bed. "Okay."

"Got anything to drink around here?" Redfern asked, looking about the room.

Todd's stomach clenched. Did Redfern have a problem? He hadn't smelled booze on his breath in the car or the telltale cover-up smell of Altoids. He hoped to Christ Redfern wasn't a drunk. Chances of success just took a nosedive if he was. "There's the water in the toilet tank."

"Ha, ha, very funny."

"So what's the plan?"

Redfern sat in a threadbare chair that represented the only other place to sit. It sagged under his weight. "Cochrane doesn't know you're here?"

"No."

"You're going tell him that you are. You're going to tell him that you've got his coke, and you'd like to give it back. In return, you want to be off his shit list."

"Sounds tricky," Todd said. It sounded more than that. It sounded lethal. But it also sounded like the only way.

"You'll be wired for sound and videotaped."

"And where will SFPD be when this exchange happens?"

"I won't be far away. You'll be totally safe."

"Only if you can travel faster than a speeding bullet, because if Cochrane pulls a gun, I'm screwed."

"For this to work, you have to be seen giving the drugs back, and Cochrane needs to acknowledge that they were his in the first place. You'll be in good hands. It's not like we're breaking new ground here. There have been plenty of operations like this."

"Sounds like a cakewalk."

"Hey, watch the mouth."

Todd brushed the warning aside. "Don't you think Cochrane will check me for a wire, weapons, and undercover cops?"

"That's why we'll test the waters tomorrow." Redfern pushed himself free of the chair. "Meet me outside the Metreon tomorrow, the 4th Street side, at eleven. You're going to give Leo a call."

Todd found Redfern standing under the vertical neon sign for the Metreon. He'd stashed the remaining five kilos of Cochrane's cocaine in a locker, and it felt good not to have it in his possession.

"You're late," Redfern said.

"I slept in."

Redfern took him inside the complex and bought coffees. They sat at a table in an unoccupied area of the dining section. The lunchtime crowd had yet to arrive.

"I've been doing some checking up," Redfern said.

"And?"

"Paul Helfers, the drug dealer you had that fender bender with, hasn't been seen since the traffic stop."

"That's because he's in a hole in ground a thousand miles from here. So you believe me now?"

"Let's say your story has some credibility. What makes me like it more is that when we bust Cochrane for the drugs, we can tack on a murder rap."

"Well, I do know where the body is buried."

Redfern fished in his pocket and handed Todd a scrap of paper with a number on it.

"What's this?"

"Leo Cochrane's private cell phone number."

"How'd you get that?"

"Police work. Now listen."

Redfern walked Todd through the call to Cochrane. He provided Todd with a cover story for how he got the number and the line he was going to feed Cochrane. Redfern made him rehearse. There was no judging what Cochrane would say exactly but there were likely outcomes. Redfern changed the script every time to counter for the possible scenarios. They role-played for an hour until Redfern was satisfied Todd sounded genuine enough to make the call.

"Ready?" the detective asked.

"About as ready as I'm ever going to get."

They left the Metreon and searched for a phone booth, which proved harder than it should. With so many cell phones out in the public domain, phone booths were a dying breed. They found one in the lobby of the Moscone Center, and Redfern handed Todd a phone card.

"I don't want you running out of quarters."

Todd took out Cochrane's number from his pocket and the nerves hit. Until now, he'd been feeling cool and calm about the call. Cochrane couldn't harm him while they talked on the phone. He was untouchable. But now his stomach clenched and he had an overwhelming desire to take a leak. Cochrane was connected. He could get to anyone. He was the bogeyman. Todd was screwed.

"What are you waiting for?" Redfern demanded.

"Nothing," Todd said and punched in the number.

The phone rang for a long time. Todd thought it was going to switch to voice mail when it was answered.

"Yes."

It was Cochrane. Todd's legs went weak, but as the adrenaline flowed, his fear evaporated.

"Remember me, Leo?"

There was silence, but it wasn't from confusion. Cochrane had recognized Todd's voice. Todd felt his surprise coming down the line.

"That sounds like my friend Todd."

"I didn't know we were friends. Especially after the wild goose chase you sent me on."

"You know what they say, you only hurt the ones you love. How'd you get this number?"

"Know a guy called Ruiz?"

"That piece of shit. Remind me to squash that bug."

"I'll do that."

"You sound edgy, Todd."

"Understandable, don't you think?"

Redfern, eager for feedback, motioned to Todd. Todd gave him the thumbs up.

"Are you close?" Cochrane asked.

"I'm in the city."

"We should meet."

"Under the circumstances, you'll understand if I'm not too eager."

"Fair enough. Why don't you tell me what you want?"

"I want to be off your shit list."

"What makes you think you're on it?"

"Don't piss about. I've been reading up. I know how important Paul Helfers was to you, and you iced him and stuffed him in the back of a Lexus. That was my fault. You aren't going to forget it in a hurry."

"If I remember, when we last spoke, you weren't too kind to me."

"Yeah, well, I'm sorry. I didn't really know how big a hole I was in and at the time, I was angry. I thought I was working off my debt, but you were setting me up."

"I was angry too. Maybe I was overzealous. I certainly underestimated you."

"Likewise."

Todd took a second to assess his performance. Cochrane sounded like he was taking the bait, so far. Todd didn't put it down to his acting or Redfern's coaching abilities. The script had gone out the window. There were no lies or deceptions at work. He was speaking from the heart.

"Look," Todd said, "I know how much I cost you."

"You have no idea how much you cost me."

"I think I do—a dead body, a gun, and six kilos of coke. The body and the gun told me enough and throwing in a little coke was overkill, but six kilos—that's a vendetta."

"Like I said, I was overzealous. Heat of the moment stuff. But I'm listening now. How are you proposing to heal the rift?"

"The blow. I should have thrown it out, but I kept it. I don't know its street value, but it can't be cheap. You can't afford to be throwing away that kind of money. I'll return it, and then we're quits. Agreed?"

Cochrane paused for effect. It was to make Todd sweat. Todd knew this because it was working.

"You've thought this out." The suspicious note in Cochrane's voice was difficult to ignore.

"I've had plenty of time to do it. Living the underground life teaches you what's important."

Cochrane laughed. "Been having a hard time of it, Todd? Well, it's not a lifestyle that suits everyone. Okay, Todd, I like you. Give me back my coke, and you're a free man. Remember the shop in Oakland where you picked up the Lexus? Come there in an hour."

Redfern flashed him a hand signal to wind things up.

"I don't think so."

"You don't trust me?"

"I like the idea of neutral ground, with plenty of witnesses."

"You have come a long way. Have it your way, Todd. When and where?"

"I'll call with instructions," Todd said and hung up. He sagged and leaned against the lobby wall before his legs gave out.

Redfern grinned. The grin took years off him. "Very nice. I couldn't have done better myself."

"I have a real incentive to make this work."

"C'mon, let's get out of here. I doubt Cochrane was linked up to anything to trace the number, but I don't want to take any chances."

The phone on the wall rang. Todd and Redfern froze.

"Him?" Todd asked.

"Just trying his luck." Redfern picked up the phone and dropped it back down on the cradle. "C'mon."

Outside the Moscone Center, Redfern talked Todd through the arrangements for tomorrow's sting. It sounded straightforward enough. Well, as straightforward as anything that had happened to Todd in the last month.

"I'll see you tonight," Redfern said.

"Where are you going?"

"Where do you think? These operations don't just appear. There's a lot of preparation." He fished in his pocket and handed Todd a key and another scrap of paper with an address on it.

"What's this?"

"Keys to a safe house. Not exactly a safe house. There're keys to my place. I want you there. Now that I've got you, I don't want anything happening to you. Check out of that motel and hole up at my place. I don't want you out there advertising you're back in town."

Now the machine was in motion. It would be all over by tomorrow.

Redfern called an apartment at a four-unit, three-story townhouse on the edge of Noe Valley home. Individual garages occupied the first floor and the apartments the second and third. The exterior paintjob, the color of boiled-cabbage, sapped the building of its art deco charm. Todd parked the Toyota on the street and went inside.

The interior was exactly what Todd expected. It resembled Redfern's appearance—shabby and neglected. Takeout containers filled the trash and towered on the kitchen dish drainer. The bed in the apartment's only bedroom looked as if someone had danced on it in their boots. The neglect carried over to the other rooms as well. The absence of a woman's touch was obvious, but a photo above the fireplace of a woman with two teenage boys painted the picture of a broken marriage.

Poor bastard, Todd thought. *Never thought I'd find someone worse off than me.*

He dumped his meager possessions on the floor next to the pullout sofa, but kept the .357 on him. He took out the trash and tried tidying up, but it was a job for a professional. He couldn't bum around all day in this place waiting for Redfern to return, especially when there was nothing to eat or drink. He locked up and went in search of groceries.

On 24th Street, he found an overpriced specialty market, but for once, it didn't hurt his bankroll. He still had plenty of cash left over from his various jobs he'd picked up. He and Redfern wouldn't eat like kings tonight, but they would eat food that didn't feature delivery.

On the walk back to Redfern's apartment, Todd played the next twenty-four hours through his head. There was little for him to do now. He would simply hand over the coke and Redfern, and the SFPD would do the rest. Obviously, Cochrane could ice him on the spot, but if he got him to say the magic words right off the bat, there wouldn't be time. Still, he wished the cops weren't involved. Redfern had yet to tell him where he stood in all this. He'd disposed of a body. That made him an accessory after the fact or something.

And that seemed to be the least of his crimes. No matter how he sliced it, there were going to be charges of some sort.

"Hey, Todd."

Reflexively and stupidly, Todd turned toward the voice behind him. Before he could utter a word, a fist drove into his solar plexus. He dropped to his knees, the grocery sacks spilling from his grasp. All attempts to cry out for help ended in a strangled squeak. Thoughts of reaching for his gun never even materialized.

The owner of the fist dropped to one knee, as if to help. He snatched a fistful of Todd's T-shirt and jerked him up to his ear. "It's your unlucky day, dickhead," he rasped and jammed a 9mm automatic in Todd's gut.

He guided Todd to his feet and spun him around. He felt for a weapon and found the .357 in the back of Todd's pants.

"I'll take that. Not like it was yours in the first place."

Todd recognized his captor. It was Dalton, the black linebacker Cochrane had brought with him to Todd's apartment. His sidekick, Vasquez, sat at the wheel of a Lincoln across the street. The linebacker bundled him into the back of the car. He slammed Todd twice with the butt of the .357 and that was it. Todd was out cold.

Todd came to while they were on the road. His wrists were cuffed behind him. He lay face down in the foot well for the rear passengers. Dalton's feet pressed down on Todd's back, pinning him in place.

"He's awake," Dalton said. "Enjoy these minutes, Todd. They are your last."

The comedians laughed.

Todd didn't bother asking where he was going. He didn't want to know.

The Lincoln came to a halt inside a building. Todd listened to the clatter of a garage door closing. He knew they'd taken him back to the chop shop at Jack London Square. The linebackers yanked him from the back of the car. This time, the place had been cleaned out of vehicles and equipment. In the middle of the shop sat Cochrane on an uncomfortable looking tubular steel and wood chair with a fixed back. Next to him laid a body bag. And next to that sat a bucket. He rested a silenced pistol lazily on his lap. These simple props and the stark surroundings struck fear into Todd. No explanation was necessary. All that was needed was a meager imagination to construct a scenario. This was where he was going to die. There was just time enough to lament how close he'd come to winning this one.

Cochrane stood and pointed to the chair. The strength went out of Todd's legs and the linebackers had to drag him over to it. They planted him in the seat. His head sagged under its own weight. Cochrane lifted it with the pistol.

"I never thought you were stupid enough to come back, Todd. Honestly, I didn't," Cochrane said. "After I sent you on your way to Dallas and you didn't end up in custody, I put the word out on you. I expected to receive a call from some corner of this country to tell me you'd ridden into town and they'd taken care of business. I thought the coke would bring you down. I was sure you'd try to hustle it. Do you really have it?"

Todd swallowed. His Adam's apple nudged the end of the silencer. "Yes."

Cochrane forced the pistol hard against Todd's throat. "Honestly?"

All saliva escaped down Todd's throat, and it burned when he answered, "Honestly."

"You wouldn't be lying?" Todd went to answer, but Cochrane shushed him. "I wouldn't blame you if you were. Stronger men than you have when faced with this predicament."

"No."

"I think I believe you. The question is, is it worth the bother of getting it back?"

Dalton had wandered around behind Todd positioning himself in Todd's blind spot. Cochrane nodded to him. He upended the chair, pitching Todd onto his knees then his face. Cochrane jerked Todd back and shoved the bucket under his face. Vasquez held his face over the bucket, and Cochrane pressed the pistol against the back of his head.

"I don't know anyone who does this. I fill the bucket halfway with water. When I shoot you, the bucket will catch the spattered remains of your face and the water will stop the bullet from ricocheting off the walls. You wouldn't believe how much this saves on cleanup."

Todd stared at his reflection. This was the last thing he'd see: his terrified expression before Cochrane's bullet ripped it to pieces. He tried to close his eyes, but fear kept them wide open.

"Where's my coke? And please don't waste my time."

Todd answered before he even comprehended what he'd said. His survival instinct had reacted on pure reflex and answered for him. It had bought him time. Even a second chance.

"Show me," Cochrane said.

Todd traveled with Cochrane and his two linebackers in the Lincoln. This time, they let him sit up. Still cuffed, he sat on the backseat with Dalton and his angry looking hand cannon. Vasquez pulled up across the street from Redfern's Noe Valley apartment.

Todd searched the street for his lucky talisman, and he found it. Redfern's battered Malibu was parked on the street. Redfern was home and that was good. The trick was warning him that he was bringing company for dinner.

"I'm at this place over here," Todd said.

"Better than your old place," Cochrane remarked.

"I wasn't planning on staying long."

"Make him presentable."

Dalton turned Todd around and uncuffed him. The respite from the cuffs' bite was temporary. Dalton re-cuffed Todd's hands in front of him and covered them up with a jacket. Suitably camouflaged to the world, they led him over to the apartment.

"Keys," Cochrane said at the top of the apartment's marble stairs.

C'mon, Redfern, please be watching the windows. Please be primed and ready. Todd wished he and Redfern had agreed on some secret entry code. Three knocks and all is well. No knocks and all guns blazing. He dug in his jeans for the solitary key Redfern had given him.

Cochrane snatched the key out of Todd's grasp and stuck it in the lock.

Todd couldn't see around this one. It was a lose-lose situation. If he screamed out a warning to Redfern, his brains would be all over the wall before he got the first word out. If he stayed quiet, they'd have the drop on Redfern.

Then Todd saw the edge he needed. Cochrane and his linebackers weren't expecting anyone to be at home. Their artillery stayed firmly rested in holsters. Nobody had the drop on anyone. It was a fifty-fifty game. Not the greatest odds, but better than he was accustomed to sporting. Cochrane twisted the key and opened the door.

He went through the door first. The linebackers shoved Todd ahead of them.

"Collins, where the fuck have you been?" Redfern shouted from inside the apartment.

The four of them froze in the foyer to the apartment. This was a barrel shoot for Redfern. The foyer was at the bottom of a long, narrow flight of stairs that led into the apartment. Redfern might be one gun against three, but his vantage point gave him the better odds.

Redfern's feet pounded on the hardwood floor. "What did I say about flying under the under radar, dickhead?"

Cochrane fixed Todd with a look of pure hatred as he and his linebackers reached for their guns. Dalton released his hold on Todd and reached for his shoulder rig. Cochrane had his silenced pistol out. Redfern didn't stand a chance.

"We've got company," Todd shouted then dropped his shoulder and charged Cochrane. He slammed him into the wall, and they both fell onto the stairs. The pistol bounced from Cochrane's grasp.

Redfern appeared at the top of the stairs with his gun drawn. He had a clear shot of the linebackers, and they had a clear shot of him. Vasquez made the mistake of reaching for Todd to tear him off Cochrane. Redfern showed no mercy and drilled him with two rounds. The first caught Vasquez in the meat of his shoulder, but the second was a headshot that dropped him on the spot. He fell against the back of Todd's legs, and Todd's grip on Cochrane slipped. Cochrane wriggled himself free from Todd and reached for his pistol.

Dalton got off a shot, but missed. Redfern ducked out of sight, then reappeared. He fired two rounds at the linebacker again. Redfern's bullets couldn't miss that big target and both rounds hit home in his chest. Dalton staggered back, hit the wall behind him, and slid down. The linebacker got off three shots as he went down. One glanced off Redfern's head, and he fell out of sight.

Now it was just Todd and Cochrane. Todd shrugged Vasquez off his feet and lunged for the recovering small man. Cochrane swung his gun toward Todd. In the close quarters, Todd moved inside Cochrane's reach and batted his arm out of the way. Cochrane put too much effort in keeping a hold on his gun, and Todd looped his handcuffed wrists over his neck. He jerked the short length of chain links into Cochrane's throat.

"Die, you bastard," Todd screamed.

"After you," Cochrane choked out. He reached his gun arm behind him to point the weapon straight at Todd's stomach.

Todd turned sideways to avoid the two shots. He twisted his wrists to tighten the garrote around Cochrane's throat and before

Cochrane could fire again, he threw his weight against Cochrane, driving him forward into the stairs. Cochrane's gun went off as his head bounced off the sharp edge of the stair. None of this deterred Cochrane. He bucked and jerked under Todd, fighting for any opportunity to get the better hand.

"Hold it right there."

Both of them froze.

Redfern stood at the top of the stairs, his gun pointed their way. Blood masked half his face where the bullet had creased the side of his head. He descended the top stair with the dexterity of a toddler's first steps and used the wall for support, but he never lost his aim.

"Is that you, Redfern?" Cochrane croaked. "I thought I'd crushed you a long time ago."

"Get him up, Todd."

Todd hoisted Cochrane to his feet with the handcuff noose as his helping hand. Cochrane choked out a gurgle.

"Drop the gun, Cochrane," Redfern ordered.

Cochrane hesitated.

"Do it."

Todd tightened his chokehold just to underline Redfern's request.

Cochrane dropped the gun. To Todd, it made the sweetest sound as it struck the stair.

"Where are the keys to the cuffs?" Redfern asked.

"My pocket," Cochrane said and indicated to his pants pocket.

Todd retrieved the keys and uncuffed himself.

Redfern took another unsteady step. "I'm going to enjoy saying this. You're under arrest."

"Boss," a voice from behind Todd murmured.

The voice weakened Todd's grasp.

Either reacting to the voice or Todd's weakening hold, Cochrane fired an elbow into Todd's gut. The blow connected with the bruises put there by Kenneth, and Todd folded up. This unbalanced Cochrane, and he pushed back on his heels to topple himself and

Todd. Todd tried to stay upright but couldn't, and he went down with Cochrane on top of him.

"Todd," Redfern shrieked, but the shots cut his cry short.

Dalton, with a clear target, hit Redfern twice in the chest. It was the last thing he did before he died.

Redfern's legs buckled. He crashed down on his back and slid down three stairs before he came to a halt.

Now on top of Todd, Cochrane jerked his head back and head-butted Todd in the face. Pain lit up like a flare in Todd's head when Cochrane connected with his nose. Blood poured immediately. Todd's cries spurred Cochrane on, and he head-butted Todd twice more. Todd's grip around Cochrane's throat loosened, and he threw Todd's arms over his head. He scrambled for his gun, grabbed it, and swung it around at Todd. Todd lashed out with his only ready weapon, his feet. He smashed Cochrane in the chest, launching him backwards and tripping over the bottom stairs. Todd rolled backwards out the front door and fell down the marble steps. His bones impacted every sharp edge the hard stone had to offer. Cochrane fired twice. The bullets bit chunks out of the marble, the crack of the splitting stone louder than the silenced weapon.

Sirens wailed in the near distance.

Todd ran for his Toyota still parked where he left it. He expected bullets to punch holes in his back, but the bullets never came. Cochrane had his own problems to worry about. Todd reached his Toyota in time to see Cochrane racing over to the Lincoln.

Everyone had to cut and run sometime.

Traffic stopped Todd's escape from being a speedy one. He managed only half a dozen blocks before police units sped by him. None gave him a second look, and he slowed. He didn't need to make his erratic driving memorable to all and sundry.

Without the fear of arrest occupying his thoughts, his predicament rushed in to fill the void. Redfern was dead. The last person who could help him out of this was dead. What did he do now? He could run back to Charlie Ruskin but why screw up her life just as it was on the level again? There was Fisk, but he'd made it very obvious that his return to the Emerald City wouldn't be appreciated. He had to face it; there wasn't a way out, not this time.

An additional weight pressed down on Todd. He had finally done it. He'd gotten someone killed. And a cop at that. The SFPD had just turned into a lynch mob, and they wouldn't care how many they had to string up to settle accounts.

The only thing going for him was that Cochrane was in the same position. Worse, even. It would take time before someone worked out Todd's identity from Redfern's files, but it wouldn't be necessary to look up Cochrane's info, not with the two linebackers dead on Redfern's doorstep. Cochrane would have to run now. He couldn't waste his time on settling a score with Todd, regardless how large it had swelled with this latest development. Todd might not have to run if Cochrane ran first. The next few hours would determine everything. Todd could afford to weigh his options. For now, he'd be okay if he kept circulating. He'd become a shark. As long as he kept moving, he'd stay alive.

The plan worked for a while. He threaded his way through the city's streets, shifting from one neighborhood to another. He listened to the radio for news. The stations reported a fatal shooting in Noe Valley, but released no details thanks to the police not providing any. That made sense. They didn't need the public's involvement. They already knew the identities of all the players.

Todd thought the cover of night would give him anonymity, but that went out the window when he spotted a Dodge Magnum turning onto the street behind him. It could have been any Dodge Magnum, but he knew, just knew, it was the one belonging to Jeremiah Black's crew. Panic broke out in icy trails originating from the coldness in the pit of his stomach, but he kept his head. He could be wrong about the Dodge. It could be one of a hundred Magnums in the city. There was one way to find out.

He was on California. He took the first right. The Dodge did likewise. His fingertips began to sweat and turned the wheel slick in his grasp. He made another right and another and another until he was back where he started. Still the Dodge filled his rearview mirror.

So there it was. If the cops or Cochrane didn't get him, then Jeremiah Black would. Well, not if Todd could help it.

Todd stamped on the gas. The Toyota gathered speed. So did the Dodge.

He cut between cars and buses. Drivers honked at both him and the Dodge. He hoped one of the moving obstacles would do him a favor and collide with the Magnum, but none did.

The chase ended in Presidio Heights. Todd lunged across oncoming traffic to make an unexpected left. Black's crew didn't react in time and didn't make the turn. He expected them to appear a couple of blocks later, but they didn't. Had he done it? It looked that way after five minutes, and he eased off the gas.

The Toyota's brakes felt spongy underfoot, and he had to press harder than he should. He wanted to pull over, but the water temperature gauge was in the red so he drove around until the needle dropped back into the green. He pulled over and gave the Toyota a rest.

He'd no sooner switched the engine off when a blue Econoline van pulled up alongside him. Before the passenger finished winding down the van's window, Todd gunned the engine, but an Escalade pulled across the front to block his path, and the Magnum stopped behind to box him in.

The person in the Econoline's passenger seat held Todd in place by poking a shotgun out the open window. Todd raised his hands.

Four black guys poured from the Escalade and pulled him out of the car.

Kenneth emerged from the back of the Dodge Magnum.

"Don't think about yelling," he said. "It wouldn't help."

Todd glanced up at the townhouses with their lights on and drapes drawn. *So close yet so far*, he thought.

Kenneth ordered his guys to put Todd in the Dodge and told one of them to take care of Todd's Toyota. By the time Kenneth had slid next to Todd on the Dodge's backseat, the Econoline, the Escalade, and Todd's Toyota were gone.

"Let's go," Kenneth said to the driver.

"Where?" Todd asked.

"I'm going to let that be a surprise, white boy."

Kenneth struck with cobra's speed and tenacity. His hands snapped out, grabbed Todd, and pulled him in close. He tied his arms in a knot around Todd's neck. Todd thrashed to stop Kenneth from breaking his neck. The other guy sandwiching Todd in the back seat smothered Todd's legs to prevent him from breaking loose.

"Don't fight it, Todd," Kenneth said.

But he had to fight. He didn't want to die. Not like this. It wasn't right, and it wasn't fair. But when was anything fair? He clawed at the arm across the front of his throat. He wasn't going to let Kenneth break his neck.

But his neck didn't break. Instead, he slipped into darkness as consciousness let him fall.

A slap jerked Todd from the realms of unconsciousness. He found himself in the half-completed carcass of a building project. A couple of work lights lit the area. The framing and a little sheetrock was in place and made the large expanse of unoccupied space seem cramped. He sat with his legs splayed out in front of him with his back to one of the studs and his arms pinned behind him and cuffed around it. He was high up with a view of the Bay Bridge and the drone of the traffic rushing across it. He knew where he was. This was the Bay Towers, an exclusive SOMA condo development that came with a price tag that made most weep. *At last, I'm moving up in the world, just as I'm checking out of it*, he thought. He smiled at his own joke. He was too punchy to cry.

Cochrane had provided the slap. So Black had followed through on his promise and given him up for the points it would earn him. He tried to be angry, but couldn't. It was all way beyond petty squabbles now.

Cochrane looked a mess. He still wore the same ripped clothes as he'd worn earlier. Bruises had blossomed from their tussle on the stairs. Todd tried not to take pleasure from the purple necklace in the pattern of a handcuff chain across Cochrane's throat.

Cochrane jammed his pistol under Todd's chin. "I should fucking kill you and be done with it, but I can't let you off that easy."

Cochrane's cool was gone and along with it, his power of menace. Todd no longer found him frightening. He was nothing more than a barking dog staked to a spot in a backyard. True, the gun could end his life at the squeeze of a trigger, but that was inevitable, and he couldn't be frightened of an inevitability. He wouldn't die in fear of Leo Cochrane and without that hanging over his head, things didn't seem so bad.

"I thought about turning you into a human torch. I even brought the gas along." He pointed at a plastic gas can behind him. "But I thought of something better." A sadistic leer spread across his face. "Where's my coke?"

"In a luggage locker at the Caltrain station on 4th Street."

"Where's the key?"

"In my pocket."

Cochrane rooted around in Todd's pockets. "You know what I'm going to do with the coke?"

Todd shook his head.

Cochrane jerked out the locker key. He held it up close to Todd's face like it was the Holy Grail. "I'm going to feed it to you. I'm going to watch you choke, spasm, convulse, and die eating my coke."

"No, you're not."

The voice startled both Todd and Cochrane. Cochrane jerked his gun up in the direction of the voice.

"Put it down, Leo," the voice ordered. "It's over."

"Redfern," Todd said unconsciously.

Cochrane picked up on what Todd had said, and the tension went out of his body. "Is that you, Redfern?"

Redfern emerged from the shadows with his gun aimed at Cochrane. A bandage replaced the blood Todd had last seen masking half his face.

"I thought you were dead."

"Kevlar, Leo. You've gotta love it."

"Wearing it now?"

"That would be telling."

"I can make a headshot."

Elation rushed Todd by surprise. It was over. Whatever Cochrane tried, it was over. SFPD and SWAT had it covered. Yet something was missing.

"Where's the backup, Redfern?" Todd asked.

Cochrane laughed. "What did he tell you? That he's one of San Francisco's finest? Have you been fibbing to our friend here, Redfern?"

Redfern said nothing. He grimaced like he had the onset of a migraine and maintained his aim on Cochrane.

"Redfern, here, hasn't been a cop in five years."

How have I been so stupid? Todd thought. He'd never seen any ID, just the shield. And how hard was it to get one of those? He wanted to be sick.

"Rumors of taking bribes, wasn't it? Bribes paid by me to you, wasn't that it, Redfern?"

"You framed me."

"And you think this is going to win you back your career. Is that it? This isn't a movie. Hell, not even a TV movie."

"Just put the gun down, and give yourself up. That's all I want."

"You make it sound so easy, but I'm sorry. No Hollywood endings this time around."

Todd saw Cochrane's trigger finger tighten. Cochrane was still crouched over him, still within reach. Todd snapped out a leg a second before Cochrane fired. His foot smashed into Cochrane's hip, knocking him on his side and sending the bullet wild.

Cochrane swung the gun around on Todd. Hatred burned up his features a moment before a bullet from Redfern's gun tore it away. The impact jerked his head around before he collapsed on his back.

Redfern rushed in and kicked the pistol from Cochrane's hand. He fired a glance Todd's way. "You okay?"

"As soon as the cops get here."

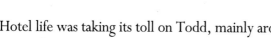

Hotel life was taking its toll on Todd, mainly around the waistline. Normality would résumé in the coming days. The San Francisco Police Department's investigation was drawing to a close and ending his free stay at the Holiday Inn Fisherman's Wharf. When he wasn't giving statements, he was exploring the city, for once as a tourist. When he lived there, he never got to this stuff, but with the speed of a major criminal investigation, there was plenty of free time.

After returning from a tour of Alcatraz, he was walking back to his room when a midnight blue Bentley Continental GT pulled up next to him. The window glided down into the recesses of the passenger door, and Jeremiah Black leaned over from the driver's side.

"Get in." When Todd didn't move, he said, "Look, you're cool. I'm alone. My boys aren't around. They're plenty busy, thanks to you. I just want to talk. Get in. Please."

Todd eyed the street for the Dodge Magnum or any other

suspicious vehicles in the vicinity. He saw none and got into the car. Black pulled away, and Todd watched his hotel get small in the distance.

Today, Black had left the sharp suit at home and had gone with an urban look. The contrast went well with the best-that-money-could-buy automobile.

"Nice ride," Todd said.

"Nice? Are you tripping? This is a premium ride."

"My mistake. What do you want?"

"You're a suspicious son of a bitch, aren't you? Can't a man say thank you?"

"Not when you served me up to Leo Cochrane."

"That? You're going to let something as small as that come between you and me?" He sucked air through his teeth and shook his head in mock disgust.

Todd decided he was trying a little too hard with all this. It was time to keep it real.

"You masterminded all this, didn't you?"

Black attempted a poker face, but the gleam in his eyes gave him away.

"I've had plenty of time to think all this through. Redfern, Cochrane, they didn't fall on me just because I gave off some scent. They were pointed at me, and you did the pointing."

"So you found me out."

Black steered the Bentley onto the Embarcadero and drove slow. The car caught every pedestrian's eye. Todd guessed half of them thought they'd caught a glimpse of some celebrity.

"I knew Leo and Redfern had clashed in the past at Redfern's expense. He's a private citizen, and I had someone whisper in his ear that it might be worth his while to follow you because you might just lead him to Leo and a crock of drugs. I spiced it up with the idea he might win his job back—and he has, so I hear."

Pending an internal investigation, Redfern would wear his shield again, but not in his old capacity. What capacity it would be, only politics would decide. That had been Redfern's opinion when Todd had spoken to him last.

"I had to tell Leo so that he and Redfern could collide."

"You used me as bait."

"I object to that. Bait is expendable. You were never in any danger. My boys had your back. They would have swooped in if you'd needed saving." Black laughed. "I gotta say you shaved a few years off their lives with all the fireworks at Redfern's crib."

"With Leo out of the way, I just made you king."

He smiled. "And your monarch thanks you."

"I thought you weren't interested in rocking the boat. You were happy with your turf."

"Did you think I was going to tell you anything? Besides, I told you that I wasn't going to be your trigger man."

"Instead, I became yours."

"I think it's time you chilled out. I came here to say thanks."

"For what?"

"For being a good soldier."

Todd saw where this was going. "Hey, I don't work for you."

"But you can."

"No thanks."

"Can't work for a brother. Is that it?"

"No. I've been in the firing line one too many times of late, and I'm looking for a different career. I don't need thanking. Leo Cochrane is off my back, and everything is right with the world."

"Then what am I going to do with what's under your seat?"

Todd pulled out a nylon bag. The material was so flimsy it was easy to tell what it contained. He unzipped it for confirmation and came face to face with a brick of hundred dollar bills six inches thick.

"I shouldn't take this."

"Why?"

"Because you'll have something on me. It'll keep me quiet about your involvement."

"But you're going to take it."

Todd smiled. "Oh, yeah."

Black stopped the car in the shadow of SBC Park. "Just tell me you won't piss it away, and you'll do something good with it."

"I will."

They shook hands, and Todd got out of the car. Black roared away.

Todd glanced back up the Embarcadero. He had a long walk back to his hotel ahead of him. He could catch a cab. He could afford it, but he doubted that a taxi driver could break a couple of hundred thousand. He liked the idea of a walk.

He pulled out his cell phone and punched in Charlie Ruskin's number. They'd been in touch constantly since Redfern had killed Cochrane. A bond had grown between them, and he liked that. She answered on the second ring.

"How'd it go today?" she asked.

He filled her in on the finer and duller details of the investigation. He didn't want to talk about it and switched subjects.

"How's business?" he asked.

"Fine. Inventory is turning over."

"What are your prospects?"

"Good. This is Texas. Everyone has to own at least one car. Why all the questions?"

Todd cast an eye down at his money in its nylon bag. "I was wondering if you'd be interested in taking on a partner."

"What makes you think you can sell cars?"

"You wouldn't believe the skills I have."

Simon Wood is a California transplant from England. He shares his world with his American wife, Julie. Their life is dominated by Royston, a longhaired dachshund, and two cats, Bug and Tegan. In the last five years, he's had over one hundred stories and articles published. A number of his stories have appeared in "Best of" anthologies and his nonfiction has appeared in *Writer's Digest*. He's the author of *Accidents Waiting To Happen* and *Dragged Into Darkness*. Readers are encouraged to visit his Web site: www.simonwood.net.